FALLEN CHILD

KATHLEEN MORRIS

CONTENTS

Books by Kathleen Morris

The Lily of the West

Fiona Rising

The Transformation of Chastity James

Risk

Fallen Child

Golddigger

Copyright 2022

ALL RIGHTS RESERVED

This novel is a work of fiction. Names, characters, places and incidents are either the product of the author's imagination, or if real, used fictitiously.

No part of this work covered by the copyright herein may be reproduced or distributed in any form or by any means, except as permitted by U.S. copyright law, without the prior written permission of the copyright owner.

Ebook Edition ISBN 978-17379866-2-1

Paperback Edition ISBN 978-1-737866-3-8

Hardcover Edition 978-1-7379866-4-5

Dunraven Press, January 2022

Cover Art and Design by Tabulanis

For Andrew, my candle in the dark.

Vengeance and retribution require a long time; it is the rule. – *Charles Dickens*

Sometimes you have to change the rules. – *Josephina Fallon*

I tried to make a difference for those who couldn't fight back and it's landed me in this cell on what is likely to be my last night on earth. I'm not sure I'd change a thing, but I'd sure like a chance to get out of here before it's on the wings of angels. That never seemed to me the best way out of a situation. I'd prefer one that had me on my feet or in the saddle of a fast horse right here on earth.

I ran my palms down my dirty pants and sniffed, recoiling at my own smell. I'd been stuck in here for three weeks without a bath and I was no cleaner than the soles of my boots.

"Hey honey," the deputy on guard tonight called. "You want a little lovin'? Gonna be your last chance before the hangman and I'm just the man to give it to you."

I sure wished I still had my .44. I'm just the woman to give him a bullet between his eyes.

When you hear stories about me, or many more about him, remember that stories are just that. Truth, on the other hand, lives in unknown, twisting and sometimes very dark places and only those that have followed those paths truly know what it was like to walk them.

CHAPTER 1

"You can't go," I said, my arms around Isabella's thin frame, my tears damping her dark curls. "I can't stay here without you."

"Ssshh, Josie." She hugged me back tightly. "You'll have to. I can't stop them, you know that well as I do."

Despair filled me because I knew her words were true but they only made me cling tighter. I had no more words, only my tears and the nearness of her. She put her hands on my shoulders and stared into my eyes.

"Listen to me," she said. "You're smart, Josie. Much more than me so you know what I'm saying is right. You wait for your chance, because there'll be one. I don't know where I'm going, but I'm afraid you were right and it ain't likely where they say. If I was smart like you, I'd have run away before but now I got no choice."

I felt her sigh against me. "Maybe it's not what we think. Silver City's not that far, least I don't think it is. You can come find me some day and we'll make our way like we always talked about."

"I will," I sobbed. "You know I will, Isabella."

The door opened and the sharp voice of Mrs. Higgins sliced

into the small room. "Come, Isabella, there's no time for silliness. You've said your goodbyes so let's be on with it." She stood there, her face in its usual stern lines, dressed in black like the witch I suspected she was. "Josie will learn to be independent, much as you have."

"Wait," I said. "Let me go in her place. I can do anything Isabella can do and I'm a hard worker. You know that, Mrs. Higgins. You always say I'm nothing but trouble so this will work out fine for everyone."

Higgins looked at me and smirked. "I don't think so, Josie. Besides, Mr. Avery would be most upset at the loss of your company. You will be with us for some time. You still have a lot to learn."

She pulled on Isabella's arm, not gently, and my friend followed her from the room, glancing back at me, her eyes bleak as Mrs. Higgins slammed the door shut. I heard the key turn in the lock but I hadn't expected anything else. I walked over to the window and peered out. The wagon had pulled up in front of the house, and I saw four other girls with their small canvas bags of belongings already sitting in the back. Bob Maloney, surly as always, sat in the wooden seat, smoking a cheroot and flinging the reins impatiently at the flies that sought the mules's ears. Isabella scrambled aboard, sat down on the bare wooden boards and glanced up at the window.

She gave a small smile and I smiled back as best I could, placing my hand on the window, palm out and fingers spread. The wagon rolled away down the dusty road.

That was the first time I ever thought about killing someone. It wasn't the last.

I ARRIVED AT THE ORPHANAGE NAMED ANGEL'S REFUGE WHEN I was five. The big clapboard house loomed up out of the desert like a mirage amid the cactus and sagebrush and it frightened me, then as much as now. My parents and my little brother had been killed by Apaches when we were on our way to our new ranch in the southern Arizona territory. Soldiers found me hiding under the wagon seat and I ended up at the orphanage. I don't remember much about my first year or so there, because maybe I was too young, too traumatized by their deaths and what I'd seen from where my mother had hidden me under old blankets in the wagon. Or perhaps it was because the people who were supposed to provide gentle care and loving guidance at Angel's Refuge were not quite what the good citizens of Arizona thought they were. Maybe it was both.

Jesus, threats and beatings aside, I was never an obedient child, and certainly not one that met the strict standards of Angel's Refuge. None of their rules seemed to stick with me and my defiance only angered them more. I was called the spawn of Satan more times than I can remember, and the whippings were so commonplace I learned early on to cry to Mother Mary and Jesus to make me a good girl, which sometimes led them to stop, depending upon who was doing the beating. The couple that ran Angel's Refuge contrarily seemed to have it in for children, especially ones that talked back, but they sure loved Jesus. They hadn't known him as a child, apparently.

By the time I was ten, I nearly forgot what color my hair was, as it got shaved off with dull knives now and then. They said it was to keep me safe from lice, but I knew better. It was just because they liked to do it. It wasn't just me, it was quite a few of the girls, except for the ones that smiled and prayed a lot, like Isabella although she didn't mean it. She called me smart, but I think she was the smart one, at least back then. Isabella was like an older sister to me, giving me good advice which I usually didn't take. She was pretty, and her long dark curls stayed on her head. In the end, it didn't do her much good. Looking like a sheared sheep with gouges in my skull had so far served me well on that score. That and the fact that I was ugly.

I knew that because Mrs. Higgins said so and whenever I

passed the only mirror in the house, a huge dusty old thing that hung in the entry hall, I thought she had it right. I had big lips and big green eyes, both too large for my face with its high cheekbones and pointed chin, and the sparse diet at Angel's Refuge didn't do much to fill me out, face or body. Mrs. Higgins would always point to me when disciplining the younger girls.

"See what unclean thoughts and lack of discipline can lead to?" she'd say, pointing to me. "You could look like Josephina Fallon there. Only God can help her, as much as she resists his call. Don't be like Josephina. She may come to a bad end, dragged to hell for her faults."

We children worked hard at Angel's Refuge. We cleaned the kitchens daily, scrubbed the floors, washed windows, tended the gardens and took care of the chickens, six horses and two mules in the stables. For our reward, we had oatmeal for breakfast and sometimes a spoonful or two of scrambled eggs, a thin vegetable soup at noon and usually a stew of some sort for supper. If you wanted to keep your appetite, you didn't look too closely at what was in it. Sometimes it was identifiable as one of the old chickens because of the bones but other times I figured it was jackrabbit, rattlesnake or lizard. We couldn't afford not to eat it, so we learned. Besides, we were so hungry all the time, it didn't matter. I had a vague memory of juicy fried chicken and fluffy biscuits with honey but I tried to not think of it.

Our clothes were all the same rough cloth, pants for boys and skirts for girls with the same shapeless shirts. We each had a pair of rough leather boots and Mrs. Higgins and her counterpart, Mr. Avery, were reluctant to replace them when our feet grew too long, but finally would, when it became evident that someone couldn't walk, but generally with an old pair of someone else's in a bigger size. While I didn't remember well what sort of clothes I'd worn before, I did remember my mother's blue woolen shawl that felt so soft and comforting to my hands. I had a vague memory of wearing a pink dress with a ruffle, so I knew there were other choices besides scratchy muslin or the stiff black serge favored by Mrs. Higgins.

Once the cold weather hit in November, we wore jackets, all the same, cut from a heavier cloth, but until spring came we were always cold. Sometimes I didn't even mind being called into Mrs. Higgins's office, cozy and warm with a woodstove even though I didn't like what came next. The minutes of warmth nearly made up for it.

There were thirty of us, a mix fifteen boys and fifteen girls, most of the time. As new kids would come in, the older ones would leave, and sometimes kids would get adopted or just disappear. Every once in a while people would arrive in a carriage or a wagon and a child would leave, usually a young one and usually pretty. Sometimes the balance would be off for a time, and then new kids would show up, standing in the hall, their eyes wide with apprehension. We didn't really feel too sorry for them because it wouldn't do them any good. You had to learn to be tough at Angel's Refuge.

It was about six months ago when Isabella and I overheard a conversation about where children went when they left the orphanage, usually when they were fifteen or so. We'd always been told that if you didn't get adopted by good Christian families perhaps whose own children had died like some of the luckier ones, then when you were old enough you'd go on to learn trades, like apprentices to blacksmiths, farriers or work on ranches and farms, and that most of the girls were sent to learn dress or hat making skills, and even in work in general stores, restaurants or schools. A rosy future was painted by our overseers and that when our turns came, we too would be fortunate to learn new things and become independent citizens of a community. We all looked forward to leaving Angel's Refuge even if hard work was required, because we were used to that. It was the independent part that really resonated with all of us, after the drudgery of our existence in this place. But it seemed none of that, or at least very little of it, was true.

"How many does Nesbitt need at the mines this year?" Mrs. Higgins's voice was clearly audible from where we stood silently in the hallway outside the office door. We'd been working in the stable but it was cold and we came back in to get our jackets. So far no one had seen us return. Isabella looked at me and pressed her finger to her lips, clutching my arm. We pressed our backs against the wall as though somehow that would make us invisible.

"Many as we can give him," Mr. Avery said. "I told him seven, including that damn Eggers kid. He's only thirteen but he's big for his age and I'll be glad to see the last of his ass. He's another troublemaker."

"Good," she responded, and we could hear pages turning. "Did you hear from Molly?"

"Not yet," Mr. Avery said. "But between Benson, Tombstone and all the rest, we're always low on supply. She needs all the girls she can get. Whores have a short run and some of these places use them up pretty fast. Maybe we should take in more kids. Between that and the mines, they can use every kid we supply, you know that, Joanie. More kids, more money. Besides, we sold three of the little ones just in the last six months, so we're going to need more anyway. That's been pretty lucrative. That damn orphan train those Bible-thumpers run has been a gold mine."

Mrs. Higgins laugh was harsh. "I'll say. Good thing perverts have lots of money to spend. Even so, my skin crawls at some of them. You know I don't get attached but every once and while I think that's something I may regret when the final count comes down."

"Don't get soft on me now," Avery said. "It was MacNeil's idea in the first place and we keep most of the money, especially when he doesn't know about it."

We heard the squeak of the wooden chair as he sat down and for a few moments there was silence from behind the door. Mrs. Higgins's heavy sigh was audible and we heard the ledger book slam shut.

"Jim, we've been over this so many times. We're making good money here, but we're losing sight of the end game. We hadn't planned on running this place even for this long. Taking in more kids would put us at risk. Don't forget there's only the four of us to keep control around here: you, me, Bob and Stony, and he's gone half the time. Some of these older kids, especially the boys, ever turn on us, we could be in real trouble. In fact, I've been thinking."

We heard her push back her desk chair, the wheels rolling on the bare wooden floor and Isabella gave a tiny gasp, ready to bolt. I grabbed her hand.

"Not yet," I hissed. "I want to hear the rest."

Mrs. Higgins's voice was louder and her footsteps resounded, which led to Isabella dropping my hand and bolting soundlessly down the hall. I was scared too but I stayed where I was.

"Listen to me, Jim. We got into this to make money to start over in San Francisco and get out of this godforsaken shithole. We've got enough now so there's no point in getting greedy. Sometimes I think we should just get rid of the whole lot or leave them to fend for themselves. I'm tired of this, and a week or two now and then in a hotel in Tucson or Tombstone isn't enough when we have to come back to this place. McNeil sits on his fat ass in Prescott and it's only you and me that have to do the hard work. The cut we're getting just isn't enough, no matter how much I lie about the costs and cut the food rations."

I heard his boots hit the floor. "Well, hell, Joanie, we got to make the best of it for now. Let's do something a little more pleasant now that business is settled."

There was a rustling of skirts and murmurs of what evidently passed for endearments between these two and no more discussion. I crept silently down the hall, my mind whirling. If I'd thought they were monsters before, I had no doubt now. There was another monster, too, whoever McNeil was. He'd never shown up here. It was just those two, and Bob and Stony. I discounted the cook and the maids, because they weren't treated much better than we orphans were, except in the kitchen they could get extra food.

Since then, we'd kept the knowledge to ourselves, I'm not sure why, likely fear of someone telling on us and the punishment for that I didn't even want to think about. We'd talked of running away but nothing had come of it. We were far out in the desert, with no idea where to go and while Isabella was my friend, she was a timid sort who convinced herself that what we'd overheard couldn't be true, at least not for her. She'd followed all the rules and was destined for something finer than some saloon. Somehow she just couldn't accept it and life as we knew it went on, until the day when Mrs. Higgins announced Isabella was going to Silver City to learn to be a dressmaker. I knew it for a lie and so did Isabella, but it was too late.

I'd be damned if was going to be too late for me.

CHAPTER 2

Chickens. I'd come to love them. We had two dozen or so, and they were good layers, especially in the spring and fall. Occasionally the old ones would end up in the stewpot and Stony would bring new chicks from town. That was my favorite part, cuddling those little balls of fluff to my cheek and watching them quickly grow. I named them and treated them like pets, but I never let anyone know, except for Isabella. I liked gathering the warm eggs from their nests, brown, blue and pale green and I was very careful never to break one before I got them to the kitchen, having learned the hard way.

"Look at you, Mabel," I said to the white and brown speckled hen, carefully plucking two blue eggs from their nest. "What a good girl you are." I ran my hand down her back and she preened. Chickens could be good friends, especially when you didn't have any. Sometimes I wondered what it would be like to have a chicken army, one that could fly on command at Mrs. Higgins and peck out her eyes.

I picked up the full basket and headed for the house. My routine didn't vary much. I gazed around. The big weathered wooden house where we lived, ate, slept and had lessons, the outbuildings of the stables and an old bunkhouse where Bob and

Stony lived, and the adobe houses of the cooks and housekeepers. I'd heard the place was once a ranch, built by some Easterner who went broke and left for a better life. I could certainly imagine that. I had to imagine everything outside of this place, since I'd never stepped foot off the grounds. They talked of "town" or bigger places like Tucson and Silver City but I didn't even know in what direction those places were. I dreamed they were full of buildings and people, people who might be kind and helpful but knowing the adults I'd lived with here, that might not be. Still, I hoped it was.

I missed Isabella. She'd been gone for almost two years now. The days had passed by with little difference and the routine dulled all of us down to the simple existence of our lives in this place, even as we grew taller and learned more at our lessons. Six or seven new girls came in, along with more or less the same number of boys each year, while others left, never to be heard from again. Since Isabella, I'd never grown close to any of the other girls. Most of them were ninnies and some downright mean. To trust them was impossible for me.

Although I'd expected they might leave as they'd talked about, Mrs. Higgins and Mr. Avery were still here so I guess they were still gathering more money before they abandoned us for San Francisco. I was too scared to say a word about the conversation we'd overheard that day and no one seemed the wiser, especially the rest of the orphans, not suspecting anything bad could ever happen to them, at least nothing worse than living here.

They were wrong but here was different for some of us. Jim Avery still accosted me every chance he had, unceremoniously dragging me into an empty room whenever he found me alone or the opportunity arose, throwing up my skirts and burrowing his hand inside me, his face getting red and his breathing heavy.

The week after Isabella left he began visiting my room now and then at night, since I was alone before new girls came. He said if I told, no one would believe me because I was the skinny ugly one and besides, he'd kill me and no one would care. I believed him but I knew in my heart that Joanie Higgins was fully aware of what he did.

The days dragged on monotonously, work and lessons, but at least we were getting some sort of an education, learning basic arithmetic, reading and writing. They needed to stick to the idea that we were being properly raised to go to better places and it was easier to teach us and keep up pretenses than not, I suspected. That, and Higgins loved discipline and its enforcement. I'd found some old books, one by someone called Shakespeare and another of fairy tales buried in dust at the back of the cabinet in the schoolroom and hid them under my mattress. I didn't understand most of the Shakespeare but I kept reading it because I liked the sound of the words and it got some easier. But the fairy tales were simple. I knew likely none of the tales could be true even in some olden time and place, but the wonders they told of were like a salve to the bleakness of my life in this place. Could there be princesses or dragons? I knew well there could be wicked witches and ogres that looked like everyday humans so maybe the other things might be true as well. The Bible was certainly full of strange things. Some nights I dreamed of a sword and a fast horse. Other nights I dreamed I was Lady MacBeth or Rosalind, lost in the woods of Arden.

Other than that, nothing had changed, except I suppose, for me. I was sixteen and I had "developed", according to Mrs. Higgins's appraising look at my small breasts and fuller hips on bath nights, along with the monthly bleeding which was an unpleasant surprise. I learned to keep my mouth shut most of the time and my hair had finally grown down to my shoulders, a wavy cornsilk blonde that surprised even me. Most of the time I jammed it under an old straw hat I'd found in the barn and paid no attention to it. But the older boys did and I kept away from them as much as I could whenever we worked together in the stables or the gardens. I could feel their eyes on me in the same way that Avery looked at me and overheard their occasional sniggers or whispered words which made me uncomfortable. Except for one.

Colin Donnelly was different. He always had been, arriving at Angel's Refuge when he was eight, the same age as I was at the time, a skinny pale red-haired Irish boy with a pronounced limp, fresh from one of the orphan trains, making its last stop in Arizona with the children that hadn't been chosen from the other stops along the way. Mr. Avery had plucked him up and brought him to the orphanage, like he occasionally did, always on the lookout for boys and girls to fill the contingent at Angel's Refuge. I guess we really were the last stop. Colin was from New York, and he had rather the same experience I had when it came to discipline at the hands of our caretakers. His head was shaved as often as mine, the nicks on his scalp showing his lack of reverence, but by the time he was sixteen, years of work had turned his fair skin tan and created sinewy muscle on his lanky six foot frame. He'd learned, as I had, the virtue of silence when it came to his opinions and his red hair was a tangle of sunbleached waves.

We began to talk on days when we worked on the gardens together, alone under the hot sun and over the years we came to trust each other. He was kind, this boy whose life hadn't been kind at all, and gentle even when pulling weeds. He had a way about him, smiling at my mistakes and helping me even when it meant giving me credit for his own work. His life hadn't been easy even before he came to be here, but I loved to listen to his stories about faraway places I could hope one day I'd see, too.

"Josie, you can't begin to imagine what New York is like. It's both terrible and wonderful, depending on where and who you are. It's got buildings so tall you nearly crack your neck trying to see all the way to the tops of them. It's full of rich people driving carriages and eating wonderful food. We used to watch them through the windows from outside on the streets. We lived in a tenement with a lot of other people and it wasn't so nice. I hardly remember my Da and Ma died when I was five so my brothers and I were left on our own. We slept on the streets and sometimes in shacks, stealing food and charcoal to build fires in the winter. I broke my leg running from the Mott street greengrocer's dog after stealing some apples and they put me in the charity ward for a month while it healed, but I couldn't stay another night there and I got out."

He slapped his hand on his right thigh and grinned ruefully. "Should've given it a little more time 'cause it's never healed right. Then my brother Declan got pinched for pickpocketing when he was ten and sent to the workhouse and it was just Daniel and me. The train people picked us up one morning and before we knew it, we were headed west with new clothes and proper food for the first time since I can remember. We discovered by the time we got to Pennsylvania that Declan was on the train too."

He looked down and I said nothing when I saw a tear fall into the lettuce we were picking. He looked at me briefly before returning his gaze to the plants.

"Daniel and Declan got chosen in St. Louis but they didn't want me. I stood on that stage by the rail depot and those people came and prodded us like we were animals, checking our teeth and arms to see if we were fit. I was small for my age then and I didn't pass their inspections, and of course, there was the leg."

I knew Colin didn't want my pity and he wasn't likely to get it anyway. The only way to stay strong here was to give no sympathy but just stand up for those you cared about, if you could and he knew that as well as I did.

"You move fine, Colin. You can outpick me any day of the week and run circles around this lot," I said, gesturing towards the other boys in the garden. It was true, too, and he could, limp or no. "Besides, it's your head, not the rest of you, that makes the difference, and you know that well as I do."

He laughed softly and threw a weed at me. "Josie, you always cheer me up. I just hope some day when we're out of here I can find Daniel and Declan and we can be a family again."

I respected that, unlikely as it was. I didn't know exactly where St. Louis was but I knew it was a long way from Arizona. Still, it was good to have dreams. I only had one: getting away from Angel's Refuge. I'd figure out the rest after that. That said, in nearly two years, I hadn't gotten very far towards my goal.

Most nights I was just too tired to think further than my bed and the days went by, even though I knew like no one else did, that the eventual outcome would be dire. I felt sometimes like my feet were rooted in the earth of this place while my mind flew about like birds on a wing, soaring towards an unknown but endless blue sky. There was always this ominous black cloud hovering in that sky, waiting to swoop down and cover me up, blotting out the blue skies forever. Sometimes I dreamed about that, and no matter what else was in the dream, that cloud was always there. When I woke in the morning, at first I'd think, Josie, you have to mind that and make a plan but within minutes it would fade away and another day at Angel's Refuge would begin. Oatmeal, chickens, gardens and stables took away the urgency of anything but what I had to do right that minute to save myself and the dread cloud was gone. Until it came again.

FEBRUARY ARRIVED. IT WAS USUALLY IN THE EARLY SPRING AND fall that the wagons were loaded with girls or boys and driven away. This year, we had a lot of older boys but when the first four were packed up and on their way with hardly a wave of the hand, it was a shock and much earlier than usual. They never announced these things, just told us those orphans were on their path to a glorious future and soon it would be the rest of us who would be lucky enough to be on a wagon just like them.

I had a hard time swallowing my oatmeal that morning. I'd never told anyone what Isabella and I had overheard that day, because I'd never trusted anyone enough to tell it to, even Colin. I knew those boys were being sold to the mines or worse and I'd let that happen, time after time, just like with the girls. There were many nights I couldn't sleep, trying to convince myself that if even one other person knew what I knew, we could do something to help ourselves but I was too frightened to try. This time I couldn't do it anymore. I gazed around the tables, looking at my fellow orphans, knowing I couldn't keep quiet any longer, but still not seeing a single face that I trusted enough to believe me. Many times, especially before we fell asleep at night, I'd almost confided in one of the other girls but I'd held back. If they went to Mrs. Higgins, the consequences could be horrifying, and in fact I had no doubt these people would do anything to protect themselves, their money and their dirty secrets. I might not even be lucky enough to land in a brothel, but more likely in a shallow grave somewhere in the desert.

My eyes landed on Colin Donnelly, who for some reason, was staring back at me. He seemed to be having a difficult time with his oatmeal, too. We were working in the garden this morning. I made a decision.

Even by ten o'clock, the sun was warm and I was grateful for my straw hat. We knelt in the dirt, Colin and I, pulling weeds and thinning the shoots, our knees in the still cold ground. A gentle breeze smelling of mesquite and sage wafted across the field and I welcomed the clean sharp scent. Perhaps an hour passed without either of us saying a word but I could tell his thoughts were as dismal as mine, although perhaps for different reasons. When our hands met inside the poke bag unloading a fistful of weeds, he grabbed my fingers.

"I'm going to be on the next wagonload out of here," he said. "They haven't said anything, but I know."

I squeezed his fingers. "Colin, I think so, too." I swallowed hard. "Listen. I have to tell you something. I been keeping this secret too long and it's about to choke me."

He dropped my hand and stared at me, his green eyes intent.

Even though it wasn't that warm, I could feel the sweat running down my ribs. I just blurted it out. "A while back, I overheard Mr. Avery and Higgins. We aren't going to farms or stores or anything like that. It's all lies. The boys are sold to the mines and the girls to whorehouses. That's what they do."

Colin sat back on his heels. For a minute or so, he didn't move, his arms hanging over his knees, staring at the dirt. My heart was thumping in my chest. Had I made the mistake I'd worried about for two years? Finally he raised his head and gazed at me. "Why didn't you tell me before?"

"I wanted to, please believe me." I grabbed his arm, fingers tight and I could feel his muscles tensing. "I've been too scared. You're the only person I've come to trust enough to say anything. I think they'd kill me if they thought I knew."

His eyes softened and he put his hand over mine. "Yeah, I think they would. It's all right, Josie. I believe you. I've been thinking something of the sort for a while now. These people don't really give a damn about us, but that's been something I knew since the day I got here. We'll figure something out."

He ducked his head back to the row of plants and began industriously pulling weeds, moving quickly down the row on his knees. I did the same, in the opposite direction. I didn't have to look up to know that Mrs. Higgins was watching from the kitchen window as she often did. We'd have to find another time to talk or plan anything but I had a bad feeling that time was running out for both of us.

That evening we had bible study after dinner, as usual. Mrs. Higgins and Mr. Avery took turns doling out readings and parables and then asking us how we would react to a situation they'd concoct based upon what Jesus or his disciples would do. Inevitably, some eager newcomer would blurt out something stupid and they'd pounce like hawks, demeaning the poor soul and then waiting for their acolytes, anxious to please, to come up with something better. It was the standard fare for these farces and I'd learned years before to keep my mouth shut and hair intact. My fairy tale book had better morals and consequences, if you asked me, and nobody got shamed. Turned into a rosebush or a frog, maybe, but that seemed to me to be a happenstance that could be changed with magic. There was no magic at Angel's Refuge and that fact had been cemented in my brain.

On the walk down the hallway to our separate dormitories, Colin nudged my shoulder and whispered in my ear. "Talk tomorrow. I'm in the stables all day."

I nodded and followed the rest of the girls to our rooms.

I could hardly sleep that night, thinking up plans, none of which sounded very good but finally dozing off before dawn, and sleepily waking only when one of the other girls shook my shoulder when it was time to get up.

More oatmeal and I was with my chickens, watching as Colin and two other boys headed for the stables. Maybe we'd get a chance to talk but someone was always watching when you least expected so we'd have to be careful.

"Miss Sweetie," I said to the brown chicken that always nudged her head into my palm. "You're such a good girl." She was, too and I gathered three blue eggs from her nest and placed them carefully in my basket. By midmorning, I was done gathering eggs, feeding and cleaning out the chicken house when Colin gestured from the stable door. I saw no one watching from the kitchen window, so I ran over to the stable and slipped inside.

Colin stood just behind the door and grabbed my arm. "Josie. I stole some supplies from the kitchen last night and hid them behind Charlie's stall," he said, and I glanced up at Charlie, a placid but sturdy gelding where he stood munching his hay.

"I want to get a little more, it may take me a day or two, and then I'm thinking we load up and you and I get on Charlie and get the hell out of here. We may not have much time left, either one of us."

My heart soared. This had been my dream for the last three years but I'd been too afraid to do it on my own. With Colin, it was a different story. To have someone that believed me and to depend upon made all the difference. I hated myself for being cowardly for so long. This is what we had to do. I threw my arms around him and pulled him close.

"Thank you, thank you," I stammered, muffled against his chest. "Yes, yes. I don't know what else to say."

He hugged me back. "You don't have to say anything, Josie. We're not going to end up like the rest of them. We're in this together."

We held each other for a long minute before breaking away, eyes averted and cheeks flushed. I scurried back to the chicken coop and gathered up my basket. I thought I was going to explode with joy. At last, I had someone to share this burden with, and I'd been waiting a long time with the hope that some day Angel's Refuge would just be a bad memory.

CHAPTER 3

"Josie, get dressed and gather your things. No dawdling."

It was instantly chilly as the bedcovers were thrown back and there was no mistaking Mrs. Higgins's stern voice in the grey pre-dawn light even if her form was indistinct, standing beside my bed. She turned to the other three girls in the room and woke them as well, with the same instructions.

"I'll expect you in the front hall in ten minutes, girls. This is a special day for you." Her skirts rustled as she briskly left the room, leaving us all in surprise, blinking the sleep from our eyes but with me it wasn't just surprise, it was despair. I knew where we were going while the rest of them did not. We'd been so close, only one more day. How stupid we'd been to think we had time that we did not.

While we got dressed and stuffed our meager belongings in the burlap sacks Mrs. Higgins had provided, my mind was racing. How could I let Colin know what was happening, when everyone was likely still asleep? The boys' rooms were on the other side of the house and maybe they'd never hear a thing, not even the wagon pulling out of the yard. Somehow I had to slow this down, make some racket, do something. I finished with my clothes and threw in the two books hidden under my mattress. I saw April, the girl who slept next to me, eye them suspiciously.

"Where'd you get those, Josie?" she hissed. "We're not supposed to have our own books, you know that."

There was good reason I'd never confided in any of these girls. Trusting sheep, the lot of them, unlike Isabella. I glared at her.

"You say one word and I'll tell Mrs. Higgins I got them from you," I whispered. "Then maybe you'll never get to go on this special trip to a new life. Think about that."

She pressed her lips into a thin line but I saw the fear in her eyes as she turned her back and marched to the door. She was eager, that one and she wasn't going to take a chance she'd be left behind. The other two girls, Maryann and Amy, followed and I brought up the rear as we walked down the long hallway to the stairs. As we passed the door to the boys' rooms, I pretended to stumble and slammed my bag with the two heavy books into the door with a resounding thump. It might rouse somebody and it was all I could think to do as we began to descend the steep narrow staircase. Halfway down, I came up with a better idea and shoved Maryann into Amy, who careened into April, all four of us landing in a screaming heap at the bottom of the steps.

Mrs. Higgins came out of her office, descending upon us like a flying black crow. "What in God's name is going on out here?"

"I tripped," I said, producing tears born of desperation but not remorse in my eyes, "I'm so sorry, Mrs. Higgins. It's just so early and I'm not hardly awake yet and the stairs were so dark and . . ." She put up a hand and I knew well when to stop talking. Mrs. Higgins pulled us to our feet, tsk-tsking away, and shushing April and Maryann, who were complaining loudly.

No serious damage had been done except for a few bumps and bruises. What I did accomplish was waking up the rest of the household. One of the Mexican cooks peered out from the kitchen and quickly withdrew. The thud of feet and opening of doors came from above us and I hoped with all my heart that

Colin was one of those so rudely awakened. Mrs. Higgins quickly ushered us out the front door into the yard where Bob Maloney had pulled up the wagon, the mules' breath steaming in the chilly dawn air. With little choice and no kind goodbyes, we clambered into the wagon bed and we were off into the desert, following the road to a somewhere none of us had ever seen.

I looked back at the big clapboard house that had been my home and prison for eleven years and felt a sense of loss, as ridiculous as that seemed. Then I saw Colin's face staring at me in the window, still trapped within and I knew the true loss was that of the second honest human connection I'd made in all that time.

You're on your own, Josie, and it's time you figured it out before someone else does it for you, I thought. *Look how it turned out the first time.*

THE SUN ROSE HIGHER AND HIGHER IN THE BLUE SKY AS WE plodded along the dirt road and before long all of us girls were covered in gritty reddish dust from the mules' hooves. Bob Maloney was too, but he'd covered his mouth and nose with a bandanna and Bob always looked like he was a stranger to soap and water anyway. For a while, the other girls, nestled together against the seat, chattered about their imagined futures but I sat near the back and kept silent, scanning the desert for some sign of life or a place to shelter if I somehow managed to slip away. There was a covered pail of water in the wagon, but no provisions and the prospect of finding any in the bleak desert landscape didn't look promising. I knew people ate lizards and desert hares out here to survive but I didn't even have a knife to kill one with and little desire to do so, at least not yet.

Bob Maloney had a gun in the holster around his paunchy middle and I jealously eyed the bone-handled knife that hung from a sheath on his belt but there was little chance I was going to get my hands on it unless Bob went blind or fell off the wagon, neither of which seemed likely. *If wishes were horses, beggars would ride,* I thought. I glanced over at the others and they were drowsing, their heads nodding and April leaning on Maryann's shoulder, while Amy sat in the other corner. I was tempted myself but knowing the danger we were in, my mind was racing too fast to allow that, even if I had been able to come up with any sort of a plan. I didn't particularly like these girls, but I didn't want any of them to end up in a whorehouse any more than I wanted that fate for myself. Maybe there was nothing to do but wait until we got somewhere that had some resources to escape, since walking in the desert and dying of thirst seemed a bad option.

When I first saw the cloud of dust far behind us, I thought it was just the usual desert dustdevil but it kept getting steadily closer as I stared back down the trail. I glanced at Bob, but he hadn't turned around since we left Angel's Refuge, and the girls were asleep. As I watched, it resolved itself into a horse and rider, pulling a second horse beside him. My heart leaped in my chest. My fingers gripped the edge of the buckboard and I raised up on my knees to get a better look.

It was Colin, his red hair blowing in the wind, a grin on his face. I waved and ducked back down as Bob Maloney turned around, alerted by the hoofbeats behind him. Bob halted the mules and Colin pulled up alongside, his face solemn now.

"What the hell, kid?"

Colin stayed in the saddle. "It's Mrs. Higgins. She sent me to bring Josie back," he nodded towards the second horse. "I've had to ride hell for leather to catch up to you."

Bob eyed him suspiciously. "What for? What's so special about her?"

Colin shrugged. "She didn't say, just something about a mistake is all."

Bob didn't seem convinced.

I stood up in the wagon. "But I don't want to go back. I'm on my way to a new life like everyone else here, she said so. I don't want to just be an orphan anymore." I tried a little sniffle but it came out more like a snort. Still, Bob seemed to think it over for a minute or two. Then he came to a decision.

"Kid, you're full of shit up to the roots of that red hair." He looked back at me and then at Colin. "You think I haven't seen the two of you sidlin' up to each other out there in that garden? Little slut's probly not even a virgin anymore. You're here to rescue your lady love and I ain't buyin' it."

"Sir, I swear, that's not true," Colin protested, holding up one hand. "Mrs. Higgins sent me and I'm just doing what she said."

"Bullshit," Bob said. "Tie them horses up to the wagon and get in back with the girls. We'll deal with you when we get back to Angel's. Right now we're going on to Tucson."

Colin stared at him and then shook his head. "No sir, can't do that."

Bob drew his gun and pointed at Colin's head. "The hell you can't. I'm counting to three and you better get your ass off that horse before I get to three. One."

The girls were transfixed at the drama playing out in front of them and Bob was concentrating on Colin. I felt like I was in a bad dream, standing there like a statue that nobody was listening to, waiting for direction that nobody was going to give.

"Two."

I took two quick steps and grabbed the knife out of Bob's belt. It was a very large knife and I stuck the end of it into Bob's back, just far enough that he'd notice. He noticed right fast.

"Put the gun down, Bob," I said in his ear, but loud enough for everyone to hear. "Don't make me do this."

For the longest minute of my life, no one moved or said a word. I could almost see Bob's brain weighing the outcomes and the odds that I'd really have the strength to stab him. I guess he'd seen me wielding a hoe often enough that he slowly lowered the gun towards the seat.

"Now let go of it," I said, pushing the knife in a little more. "Put your hands up in the air."

Everything went wrong very fast. Before I could reach down and grab the gun, Bob beat me to it and shot at Colin. Instead he hit the horse Colin was riding, who went down with a high-pitched shriek, taking Colin with him.

"No," I said, putting both hands on the knife and shoving it up to hilt in Bob's back and his scream sounded pretty much the same as the horse's had. Bob pitched forward, ripping the knife out of my hands as he fell between the mules's harness. He landed on the road below us, the reins flying out of his hands. The mules took off, spooked by the gunshot and I fell back into the wagon, amidst three screaming girls who were flailing at me in terror.

I scrambled up onto the seat and saw the reins flying below the mules. There was little choice and I leaped onto the left mule's back and holding onto his harness, grabbed the top of the leather reins flying below and hauled as hard as I could on them. To my immense relief, the mules responded, slowing and stopping. I'd never driven a wagon in my life and wasn't sure what to do next but I knew I had to get back to Colin.

Keeping the reins in my hands, I climbed back up onto the seat and turned to the girls crying behind me.

"Shut up," I said. "This is hard enough without listening to you. You're going to be fine, better than you would have been, so no more."

They looked at me as though I was Mrs. Higgins and miraculously, they silenced, glaring at me but I didn't care. Through trial and error, I turned the wagon around and trotted back the way we'd come.

Bob was lying on the road, motionless in a pool of blood that spread into the dirt and Colin was trapped under the dead horse, struggling to free his left leg. His face was dead white. Not trusting any of the girls, I tied the reins to the seat and jumped down off the wagon.

"Christ Jesus, Josie, get this damn horse off me," he said and promptly passed out.

Well. That was a very big dead horse. I was going to need some help.

"Get off that wagon and help me," I said to the girls, who sat there like three scared rabbits. They stared back at me as though I was speaking a language they didn't understand.

"Now!" I shouted and surprisingly, they did.

Between the four of us we lifted the horse enough to pull Colin's leg out from underneath it. We sat in the dirt, breathing heavily and watched as Colin's eyelids fluttered and then opened, focusing on me. He winced and tried to sit up, propping himself on an elbow. He smiled ruefully.

"That didn't go quite the way I planned it," he said, gazing at the girls sitting in the dirt. "Some rescue, eh?"

Then he saw Bob's body, lying in the road a few feet away. "Oh no." He looked up at me. "What happened to him?"

"I stabbed him," I said. "He would've killed you with the next shot. At least, I think so. He wasn't a very good shot, but you were awfully close. I didn't really have time to think about it."

My words sounded full of bravado but inside I was shaking like a foxbit chicken. I'd just killed another human being, even if it was Bob Maloney, not the best person I'd ever met, but I'd bet there were worse around.

April started crying again and the other two looked on the verge of it. I ignored them and bent over Colin's leg. "Can you move it?"

He winced. "I think so." He wiggled around a little and I pulled up his pant leg. There were no bones sticking out but it was already red and swollen, especially around the knee.

"At least it was the bad one anyway," Colin said. "Help me stand up, will you?"

I stood up and helped pull him up. He groaned in pain but he managed, and we hopped over to the wagon, and between the two of us, got him onto the boards. Even if it wasn't broken, it was going to take some healing and he couldn't ride a horse.

I went to Bob's body. it took both hands to pull out the knife, bracing my foot on his shoulder. It made a little sucking sound and I had to look away and take a deep breath. I wiped it on his shirt and unbuckled his gunbelt, an unpleasant task as well. The gun itself was lying in the dirt and I picked it up and put it in the holster. We'd need both weapons, I was pretty sure. I turned back to the girls, still sitting speechless on the road. I put my hands on my hips and stared down at them.

"Listen to me. I know this is terrible for you and it certainly wasn't how I planned to spend the day," I said and gestured towards the wagon, "nor Colin. But the truth is, you aren't going to some store or schoolhouse. Mrs. Avery sends us girls to be whores and that's how it is. I found out about this some time back and maybe it's not what you want to hear, but it's true. I'm real sorry about Bob there, but things just got out of control. I couldn't let him kill Colin, not when he came to save me from that, and you too, if you want."

Their faces displayed shock and April leapt to her feet, pointing her finger at me. "You're a liar, Josie Fallon, an ugly little liar. You just want to run away with that boy," she shifted her finger to Colin. "And you're a filthy godless murderer." At the end her voice rose into a shriek and she collapsed on the road beside Maryann who started crying again, shaking their heads. Amy stared at me like she was paralyzed, hardly blinking.

Well. I wasn't too surprised to find they didn't believe me. I'm not sure I would have, in their place, especially when I'd just killed somebody, not that I'd wanted to. Mrs. Higgins might be right and I really was going to burn in hell but there was no time to fret over that now. Still, I crouched down beside them.

"I'm telling you true," I said, wiping my damp hands on my skirt. "Now, you have to make a choice. I'm taking the wagon with Colin, since he can't ride the state he's in. You can have the other horse and make your way back to Angel's Refuge best you can. Or, you can come with us and find jobs of your own. Believe me, they'll be better ones than what Bob was taking you to."

None of them would meet my eyes, even April. I sighed and stood up. I went over to the dead horse and took the saddlebags off and threw them in the back of the wagon. Then, I went to the other horse and untied the sacks of provisions and waterskins Colin had brought and did the same.

I checked on Colin, who had passed out again. I put a sack of somebody's clothes under his head and climbed up into the seat on the wagon and took the reins. We didn't have any more time to waste.

"Well? What's it going to be, girls? You coming?"

April and Maryann wouldn't look at me but to my surprise, Amy stood up and climbed up on the seat beside me.

"I am," she said. "I think you are tellin' true, Josie. I know you didn't set out to hurt nobody and I don't believe nothin' those people at Angel's Refuge been tellin' us. I only been there three years but I sure know there's a better way to live and I know liars when I hear 'em."

I blinked. Amy Fisher had never had much to say to anybody, even me. She was a stringy little thing with red-brown hair and light brown eyes, from somewhere in the South. I didn't know much about the South or even exactly where it was, but if the people there were like her, they were survivors, just like me and Colin. I smiled at her.

"All right then, Amy." I looked over my shoulder at the meager supplies in the wagon. "Throw one of those waterskins over to April and Maryann. They'll need it." I didn't need any more people dying because of me. Besides, we still had the other one and the water pail.

She did so and settled back down on the seat.

"Where we goin', Josie?"

"I haven't got the slightest idea, but I know it's as far from here as we can get, at least for today. Down that road, and I hope we can find somebody who can help Colin and direct us towards something. I been stuck at Angel's Refuge most of my life and it's just about all I know so you got any advice, it's welcome."

Amy shrugged. "I know there's a lot out there, Josie, we just got to find it." She grinned at me. "Besides, we're outlaws now."

Good Christ. This girl might be crazy, but she was most likely right. I flicked the reins and the mules plodded off. We were on our way to freedom but I knew it was going to be hard-won, not just from Angel's Refuge but now with Bob dead, the law would be after us too. Even so, a thrill ran down my spine as I looked ahead at the open road. I was in charge of my own future for the first time in my life and I loved it.

CHAPTER 4

Maybe four hours later, covered with dust, the open road wasn't looking quite as good as it had. We'd stopped often, checking on Colin and giving him water. At first there had been no sign of any habitation or even a shady grove of trees that could give us some shelter. The last couple hours, though, the landscape had gradually changed from mesquite-studded sand to gently rolling hills with more vegetation and occasional trees. Amy insisted we were going northeast, but neither of us was sure what was in that direction. The mules didn't seem to care, plodding dutifully along but giving me no hint they were headed for anything, only my hands on the reins guiding them down the road.

"You got any ideas?" I said to Amy.

"Nope. You?"

I shook my head. At least there was no sign of pursuit from Angel's Refuge. I hoped April and Maryann would make it back safe but truth be told, slowly. We didn't need anybody catching up to us before we had somewhere to hide. Stony Logan's face sprang up in my mind's eye and that was not something I wanted to see for real. The road stretched out before us into the desert, broken here and there by cactus and mesquite, but little else on the horizon, and the prospects for concealment were beginning to worry me.

As the sun began to sink, Amy turned to me. "Listen. We need to get off this goddamn road, Josie. If they come after us, we're just goin' along here like sittin' ducks and they'll catch us sure."

I knew it too. "But at least we know the road goes somewhere, Amy. Once we get out there in the open, we could end up anywhere and we don't have much in the way of supplies."

She grinned at me. "You lookin' to shoot somebody else, Josie?"

I snorted. "Not if I can help it."

"Well then."

We plodded along in confused misery for another few miles when we saw a light in the distance. I think we both jumped up in the seat at the same time. I didn't know who or what that could be, but I did know it was better than what we were doing, and I turned the mules off the road southward and headed for it.

It was almost completely dark when we came to a low house whose one window showed some light, maybe two miles or so further. It didn't look like much, a barn and corral off to one side with a couple of horses that whinnied as we pulled up. A big man came out of the house, a shotgun in his hand and I could see that clear enough.

"Hello," I called. "We're friends." I wasn't sure that was true but it seemed a good thing to say when you came to a stranger's place, especially when he was pointing a gun at you. Amy put her hand on my arm and nodded.

He lowered the shotgun, maybe it was because he heard a woman's voice and walked over to the wagon.

"You lost?"

"Well," I said, "sort of. We could use some help. We got an injured man here in the wagon."

He peered over the side at Colin and nodded his head. "Pull them mules over and let's get him inside."

We did just that, no questions asked. Amy and I jumped down just as a woman came through the open door. She was older but very pretty, her long dark hair tied back, wearing an apron over a printed dress.

"Hiram, who's that?"

"Some girls with an injured man, Sally," he said. "Let's get him inside and see what's what."

I jostled Colin awake, and with him groaning in protest, Hiram and I got him onto the porch and inside the house. We laid him down beside the fireplace, as there was nowhere else to put him. The house was small but nicely appointed, a kitchen with an iron woodstove and some cupboards, a table with four chairs and two benches before the fireplace. Towards the back of the room, I glimpsed another room with bed and a chest of some sort, a drawn curtain hung to give some privacy.

The woman approached me and held out her hand. "Sally Young, and that there's my husband Hiram. You girls look done in. Sit and let's have a look at this boy."

She bustled over to Colin and stretched out his leg, ignoring his groans. She pushed his pant leg up and poked and prodded, turning his leg this way and that for a few minutes and stood up.

"Nothing's broke," she pronounced. "But sometimes that's worse. He's got stuff tore up in there."

She turned to me. "What happened?"

"His horse fell on him," I said. "Stepped in a snake hole or something and fell right over on his leg. Broke his own leg and was screaming something awful, ma'am. I had to shoot him."

Sally looked over at her husband. "Hmm. Well, we'll get him to rights. Hiram, get me that horse liniment from the barn and a couple small pieces of kindling. Girl, get me that towel sheet by the stove."

It didn't take long before she had Colin's knee slathered in the worst smelling stuff I'd ever encountered, wrapped tight with half the towel, and then bound rigidly in place with two pieces of wood and the rest of the towel. Colin propped himself up on his elbows to watch her ministrations, his face pale.

"I can't walk with my knee held like that," he said.

"That's the idea, boy," Sally said. "You keep that on for at least a week and then maybe you'll be able to walk, least at well as you did before, which I suspect wasn't perfect to start with."

Colin gave her a small smile. "Well, that's the truth. Thank you, ma'am."

"Yes," I chimed in and Amy nodded. "Thank you so much. We really appreciate it."

Sally grunted and pushed to her feet. Her husband sat on one of the chairs and they shared a look. The warmth from the fire and the air in the small house was filled with the smell of liniment and our desperation.

"So where you all headed?" he said.

There was a small silence and then Colin said "Tombstone" at the same time as I said "Tucson" and Amy just rolled her eyes and sighed.

"Jesus, y'all are the worst liars I ever met." She looked at Hiram and Sally. "We don't know where we're goin', we're just goin'. Can y'all point us in a direction out of here?"

Hiram shook his head. "Not tonight, anyway." He looked at me. "Come on. We'll unharness the mules and get them some food and water. You can get your things out of the wagon and spend the night here."

I went outside with him. There wasn't much else I could do. We got the mules into the corral and I gathered the sacks of clothes and food out of the wagon, stuffing the gunbelt and the knife into mine while he was throwing some hay at the mules and shutting the corral gate. I met up with him on the porch and he looked pointedly at the four small sacks of clothes and the bigger burlap sack of food in my hands.

"That's it, then?"

I shrugged. "Yes."

He shook his head and opened the door. Amy was sitting

at the table, wolfing down a bowl of some kind of stew and Colin was doing the same, propped up on his elbow on the floor. Another bowl sat on the table and Sally Young gestured to me.

"Set them sacks down and eat, girl, before it gets cold."

I didn't waste any time. Whatever it was, it was the best thing I'd eaten in a long time. Sally was a pretty good cook and she set down a plate of warm tortillas that we made short work of as well. I figured if they were going to hurt us they'd have done it before now so there was no point in wasting food or worrying about it.

I couldn't remember being this tired. Driving a wagon and all that gone before that wasn't in my usual daily chore routine. My eyes had grown heavy and I barely registered Amy picking up the plates and helping Sally clean up. I blinked and Hiram Young's face came into focus, sitting across the table from me.

"What's your name?" he said.

"Josie," I replied. "That's Amy there, and Colin on the floor." His gaze flicked towards Colin, asleep under a blanket, snoring softly.

"You're safe here, Josie," he said and for the first time, he smiled and it transformed his face from a man who scared me into one I maybe could trust. "There's blankets by the fire. We'll talk in the morning."

I scarcely remember lying down beside Colin and Amy on the floor, which felt as soft as a bed to my aching body. Some outlaw I was.

❧

A SHAFT OF SUNLIGHT HIT MY FACE AND JUST AS FAST, someone closed the door that had allowed it in. I blinked and rolled over, colliding with Colin's back. Memory returned and I bolted upright, looking around. There was no one in the house except my two companions, both still sound asleep. I folded up the blanket I'd slept under and stepped outside, closing the door softly behind me.

The murmur of voices led me to the barn, where both the Youngs were putting out water and food for the horses. There was more horses than I'd noticed the night before, but no sign of the mules, or the wagon we'd driven in.

"Morning," I said. They both gazed at me and all I wanted at that moment was to be on the road again. I'd been so tired I wasn't even sure where I'd put down my sack with the gun inside and a frisson of panic went down my spine. We didn't know a thing about these people except they had good stew and a nice fire. I remembered that fairy tale about Hansel and Gretel and nearly choked on my own spit. If Sally Young said a word about baking I was ready to run for my life. Instead I smiled and walked towards them.

"We need to talk," Hiram said, glancing at his wife, who nodded. "Sally, would you get us some coffee and we can set on the porch and have a chat with Miss Josie, since I think she's in charge."

He was right about that but I didn't have much choice and soon on the porch we sat, coffee in hand. Amy and Colin hadn't roused, according to Sally, and that was just as well.

"Where'd you come from, Josie?" Hiram said.

"Well, you see, my parents had this ranch west of here and they died, so we set out——"

"The truth, Josie." His brown eyes bored into mine. "Cause that ain't it. There was blood on the wagon seat and your skirt."

My stomach lurched. The truth could damn us for sure but maybe it was the only thing that could save us, too. I took a deep breath.

"We came from Angel's Refuge. They were sending us to be whores and Colin tried to rescue us and I had to stab Bob when he tried to shoot Colin and I wish I hadn't but I'm glad I did and now they're going to be after us and they'll hang me for murder if they catch us and now we got to run." The words came out of my mouth like a torrent and floated there in the morning sun, damning me.

Neither of them seemed surprised. Hiram sipped his coffee and Sally patted me on the shoulder.

"You ain't the only ones to come here, girl. Somebody should've put a stop to this long afore now," Sally said and my stomach slid back to its usual place. "You might be the first one to have killed one of them, though, I'll say that. Not that he didn't deserve it."

Hiram nodded. "They'll be mighty displeased about that. This might be a little different than the last times. You up for defending yourself some more, girl?"

I could hardly think. Not only did they not care about what we'd done, they might even help us.

"How handy are you with that Colt in your bag, Josie?"

"I've never shot a gun in my life," I said.

Hiram gave a small smile. "Well, I think it's time you did. You take it off that man you killed?"

I nodded. "I figured it might come in handy."

Hiram wasn't smiling now. "Oh, sweetheart, I fear it will. You're a forward-thinking young woman, Josie. You up for some gun practice?"

The shots woke Amy and Colin, who came out onto the porch, looking scared despite Sally Young's coffee, staring across the yard at me. So far the bottles Hiram had set up on a board twenty feet away were entirely intact.

"Focus. Now squeeze that trigger like you were just barely touching your face and then, pushing down on your nose like it was too big." The shot rang out and a bottle exploded and Hiram finally smiled at me. "That's the way. Now give me a few more."

I did. My arms were sore from holding the gun but I felt exhilarated. There were no bottles left on the rail on the other side of the corral.

"Kid, you're kind of a natural." Hiram lifted the Colt from my hands and checked to see the chambers were empty. That gun felt good. I felt kind of lost without it. "Don't see that very often. Let's have some breakfast."

We had breakfast, Sally's pancakes and agave syrup, and it was the best breakfast I can remember.

Plates cleared, we sat around the table and Hiram stared at each of us, as though assessing our worth and cleared his throat.

"Thing is, you're not the first to find your way here. We know what Angel's Refuge is, and it's not an orphanage, just a breeding ground for slaves. Sally and I been going to do something about it for a long time, but we got other obligations that keep us busy, so's the most we can do is help out any of you that manage to get out of that place. This's the first time anybody's got killed, so this time it's different." He lit a cheroot and the smoke curled its way over to the fireplace while we sat in silence and Sally took up the talking.

"We got the mules and the wagon out of here last night, to a place we know," she said. "We've been talking about it and come to a decision." She looked over at Hiram who nodded. "We want to help get you out of here in one piece, if you're up for it, and we got a place you can hole up for a while, least until Colin's leg heals some."

First off, though, you need to know something. Hiram used to ride with the Strickland gang."

Colin, Amy and I looked at each other blankly. We knew nothing about outlaw gangs or what they did but we found out a lot in the next few minutes.

The Strickland gang was active in the Southwest, ranging from Colorado to New Mexico and into Arizona. They robbed banks, stagecoaches and everything in between, and more than few people had gotten killed in the course of their work. When Hiram met Sally in Santa Fe, he decided to leave that life and settle down on a ranch, raising horses. That's what they did, but his old companions hadn't left him to his new life for long. Now, Hiram and Sally raised horses but many of their old companions were still part of their lives. The Youngs also provided a safe haven and a ranch that provided horses for Hiram's old friends. It paid well and kept him and Sally out of harm's way for the most part. To their neighbors in the county they were just a harmless couple who bred horses and they'd kept it that way as had the Strickland gang and a few others. Their main operation was a few miles from their homestead here and things had worked out well for everyone, as long as no one asked too many questions or caused any problems.

"I've done some things I regret," Hiram said, "more than a few. Now, I just lend a hand to old friends, people I like and people who need one. You three left on your own are going to get yourselves killed and it ain't gonna take long. Shoulda done something about those shitweasels at that so-called orphanage a long time ago, so I figure I owe you."

I caught Colin's eye and Amy's. They both nodded.

I stared at Hiram and Sally. "I've only known you for less than day, but I know this: if you're what people think of as bad, that's just what I want to be. Thank you, we'd appreciate any help you can give us. We don't even know where we are," I said. "Wandering around the countryside until somebody catches up to us sounds like a pretty bad idea."

"Y'all are damn nice people," Amy said, and threw her arms around Sally Young, while Colin struggled to his feet and shook Hiram's hand.

"Thank you," Colin said. "We haven't known any nice people in a while, damned or otherwise."

Hiram chuckled. "Damned we likely are, son, but we're in good company." He stood up. "Let's get your stuff and get on the road. Colin, we'll have to get you on a horse but it won't be too far this time."

Hiram looked out the window. "Shit. There's dust down the road. Looks like we got company. You all have to hide while I get rid of them.

Before we knew it, Sally hustled us out of the house and into the barn, brushing away hay to open a trapdoor in the floor.

"Stay down there until Hiram or I come to get you," she said. "Don't make a sound."

She shut the door and the three of us sat in the pitch dark, trying not sneeze from the hay dust. I hadn't had much of a chance to see what else was down here, but an occasional rustling sound told me we weren't alone. *Just don't let a rat run across my foot*, I thought, and clutched at Colin's arm. He'd had a hard time getting down the ladder and I knew he was in pain but he hadn't complained at all. Amy's fingers bit into my other arm.

"I hope we ain't down here for long," she whispered, a tremble in her voice. "I don't like closed in places."

Neither did I and all I could hope for was that Hiram and Sally Young really were nice people.

"Hello, the house!"

Even though we were underground, pale light filtered through the hay-covered slats and we could hear just fine. It sounded as though two horses had pulled up outside and the voice sounded familiar.

"Hey cowboy. Ain't seen you in an age," Hiram said. I could picture him with that shotgun or at least I hoped he was carrying it. "It's been since, what, Silver City?"

"Hiram Young, I'll be damned," Stony Logan said and my stomach lurched at the sound of his voice. Stony worked at Angel's Refuge and Hiram knew him. We were in big trouble.

"Yeah, been out of that game for a long time now, just like you," Stony said and his voice held a note of not just recognition, but respect. "This here's Jim Avery from over to Angel's Refuge, the orphanage."

So you got a place out here, then, raising horses just like you always wanted. Didn't have a thought this place could be yours. Funny how things turn out sometimes."

"Funny," Hiram said but he didn't sound amused. "What brings you here? Looking for a horse?"

"No, we're looking for something else. Seen any sign of three kids around the last day or so?"

"Kids? They lost?"

I held my breath and clutched harder on Colin who whispered "It'll be OK, Josie." I wasn't as sure.

"Sorta. More than they know. One of 'em killed Bob Maloney, know him?"

"Never heard of him. They're dangerous, these kids? Old enough to kill a man sounds bad," Hiram said. "Ain't seen anybody like that. They runaways from that orphanage?"

"Yep. Two girls and a boy, maybe sixteen or so. They can't have gotten too far. You sure they haven't been around here?"

"Sally, come on out here," Hiram yelled. A few seconds passed and I could picture Sally Young on the porch, wiping her hands on her apron. "Honey, you seen any kids wandering around here?"

"Hell no. What would some kids be doing out here on their own?" Sally said. "I got bread to make, Hiram, so don't be pestering me with any more silly questions like that. Howdy to you, gentlemen, but if you'll have to excuse me. Y'all need water for your horses, the trough's there in front of the barn."

It was silent for a couple minutes but I thought I could hear low talk from Stony and Avery, although nothing from Hiram.

Then, "We'll be going along, Hiram. Keep on the lookout for them kids and it'd be a kindly gesture to let us know if you should catch sight of them. Nice to see you again."

"I surely will, Stony. They sound like a bad lot. You take care now."

I heard the horses turning and starting off. "Be seeing you," Stony called.

Seconds later, Hiram walked into the barn. "Not if I can help it, you dumb bastard."

Now I could breathe. He flung the trapdoor open. "Best to wait a few minutes to be sure they're well gone and over the ridge before you come out."

We stood in the barn, brushing off hay and dust.

"Stony Logan's a rotten sonofabitch that Strickland kicked out after he murdered a whore in Silver City and that Avery fella looked like a rounder to me," Hiram said. "We need to get you kids out of here right now. Sally, you got the rifle and don't hesitate to use it if they come back. You all right with that?"

She snorted. "I could smell bad on both of them the minute they came up. Don't worry about me."

None of the three of us had said a word since we emerged from the hole. We all knew what these people were risking for us, we'd heard it loud and clear. Angel's Refuge may have met its match here, though.

Hiram saddled up four horses while I watched closely. Colin helped, despite the leg and after saying a heartfelt goodbye to Sally, we took off into the countryside. There was no road but Hiram knew where he was going and I could see the tracks of wagon wheels here and there as we rode by. Hiram pushed us hard and before noon, we came in sight of a large barn and a big corral with at least twenty horses in it. As we rode closer, I saw more buildings, and some men sitting on the porch of the house. We pulled up and they came to greet us.

"*Hola*, Senor Young," said the first man who took the reins from Hiram's hands as he dismounted. "We did not expect you so soon." He glanced over at us. "These are the *ninos* you spoke of, then?"

"*Si*, Mateo," Hiram said. "Everything ready?"

"Of course, *jefe*." The man called Mateo smiled, his teeth very white in his brown face. "We have been looking forward to your arrival." He gestured to two other men who helped Colin down from his horse. Colin's teeth were clenched and his face was so pale his freckles stood out like tiny red suns but he didn't utter a word. I knew this ride hadn't been easy for him but we all knew that our choices now were life and death and I was so proud of him. The men carried Colin into the house.

Amy and I both got off our horses, not exactly gracefully and

I staggered a few steps before Hiram caught me by the elbow. Mateo did the same for Amy. I didn't know about Amy but I'd never ridden a horse before. My butt ached and my legs felt like jelly. We made our way into the house.

Bigger than Hiram and Sally's other place, it was shadowy and cool inside, a pitcher of water and cups on the table, and we drank thirstily. They had placed Colin in a bed in one of the two bedrooms and I took him a cup of water. I sat on the side of the bed and he took my hand.

"How's the leg?"

He grimaced. "Hurts like hell, but it'll get better, 'specially now I'm off that horse."

I nodded. "Looks like we got a safe haven for a while at least. Get some rest." I gazed at him for a second. I'd never felt this way about a boy before and I was anxious and happy at the same time. "Listen, there hasn't been time to really talk to you, but what you did, coming after us, was, well, heroic, Colin. If you hadn't, we'd be in real trouble."

He gave me a twisted smile and his grip on my hand tightened. "You're welcome, Josie. But we're still in real trouble, it's just a different kind. Maybe worse."

He wasn't wrong. I held his hand until his eyes closed.

❦

WE'D BEEN AT THE RANCH FOR NEARLY TWO WEEKS BEFORE Colin was able to get around well on his leg. Between Sally's horse liniment and good food, usually cooked up by Mateo, all three of us were feeling better than we had in a long time. Before he left, Hiram had talked with me.

"Josie, all of you got a lot to learn if you're going to last longer than a week out there. From what I hear, the law's going to be after you, and that's one." He held up a finger. "You're green as new grass and if the law don't get you, plenty of other things will."

I opened my mouth to protest but he held up another finger and I shut it quick.

He held up four fingers now. "These are good men here and they're going to teach you some things. By the time I get back here, I'm hoping all of you will be in shape to deal with what life is going to throw at you. That's the best I can do."

I didn't remember my father but if I'd ever wanted one, Hiram Young would've been my first choice. I couldn't remember when anybody had ever given a damn about me but this man did even if was out of some misplaced guilt and I was grateful. Before he got back on his horse and rode away, I hugged him. I think he was as surprised as I was but he patted me on the back and smiled. If he was what the rest of the world called a bad man or an outlaw, I hoped to be just like him.

Learning how to shoot a gun wasn't something I ever thought I'd do, but I took to it like a chicken to feed, so Amy said. She was no mean hand herself. Colin, on the other hand, looked at those guns like they were devils come to life.

Mateo took us aways out from the buildings and set up bottles and targets. He taught us how to load and fire that Colt .44 I'd taken from Bob Maloney. It held six bullets but Mateo shook his head.

"Only five, unless you want to shoot off your foot with a jump or stumble," he said and showed me just how easy that was to do. "Keep the chamber empty when you carry, at least for now. You're not likely to be in a gunfight around here."

Day after day under that desert sun I shot that Colt until I thought my arms would fall off. They seemed to have an amazing supply of bullets here. Amy was a pretty good shot after the first day, telling us her dead daddy taught her how to shoot snakes when she was six. That left Colin and me, neither of us who knew a pistol from a rifle, but we learned. Colin had a distasteful look on his face every time his hand gripped that gun or even the Winchester rifle which he liked a little more but after a few days, Mateo declared him good enough too and told him to go rest his leg. That left me. I didn't think I'd been all that bad and felt resentful towards Mateo for keeping me. Finally, a day later, he stopped me and took the Colt from my hand.

"Miss Josie. *Lo siento*. I have kept you out here for selfish reasons. I wanted to see how much better you could do because I can hardly believe it. You're better with that Colt that any man on this ranch. For a *pequena*, you surprise even me. Hiram won't believe it when he gets back. All you need is more speed but I am reluctant to tell you to become a *pistolero*. That is not the road I am sure your departed parents would have wanted for you."

Mateo's kindly meant doubts aside, when we walked back into the house that night, I felt like I'd just passed an important test and maybe I had. For the first time ever I felt like I had power over my own life. I put extra holes in the gunbelt and cut off the extra length with Bob's knife so it would fit my hips. The weight of the Colt felt good, a security that I needed and I took to wearing it all the time. Amy smiled when she saw me the first time.

"You some outlaw for sure, Josie," she said. "I need to get me one of them, too."

Colin didn't say anything but he looked at me and smiled. I thought we could probably use a couple more guns. I didn't know where we were going from here, but I knew one thing. Nobody was ever going to control my life except me from now on. It's better to be prepared than to be a victim.

Hiram's hidden ranch was a busy operation. Men came in a few times, sometimes at night and changed out horses, staying for a few hours in the *vaqueros'* big bunkhouse and riding out again. I liked hanging around the corral and the barns, watching them break and train the horses and I loved the colts, their velvety soft noses nudging me as I gave out carrots and pieces of apple. Then came Hiram's second piece of advice and schooling.

If I'd thought my backside was sore on the trip to the ranch, I found out that was nothing compared to my first few days in the saddle under Francisco's teaching. Amy was a natural, much better than I was, having ridden horses since she was little but for me it was a new experience. When we'd ridden out from Sally and Hiram's small place, it had passed in a painful blur but soon I came to love being on horseback. Like the gun, it gave me control and that was worth every twinge. It wasn't just the riding but the horses. My favorite was a mare named Lucia, a pinto. I couldn't wait to see her every morning. Francisco would smile and shake his head. He didn't look much older than me and I wondered how he'd come to be here but we never talked about it. He was Mateo's nephew and so handsome he was almost pretty. The cowboys were constantly giving him a hard time, but Francisco held his own and he was so good with horses they all respected him.

All the men at the ranch had a story, but nobody was talking, at least not about their own pasts. They were a varied group, some of them pretty intimidating but they were always kind to us. At meals and around the corral they talked plenty, not caring if the stories they told were fitting for our delicate young ears, especially around the fire rings at night, when the tequila and whiskey flowed freely.

"Remember that night in Santa Fe when Andy McBurn took a knife to that muleskinner that always smelled like somebody pissed on him?" Joe Burke said and a few others laughed. Sparks from the fire danced upwards into the starry night, the smell of mesquite and pinon perfuming the air. "He carved him up like a Christmas goose."

Whitey Cogburn chuckled. "Sure as hell do. That muleskinner was livin' on borrowed time, after he beat up one a Madame Rita's whores so bad. Andy was always partial to that little gal cause she could suck the varnish off a chair leg, I swear. Heard she married some cowboy and went back to Texas. He was one lucky bastard." Whitey took a drink of whiskey and passed the bottle on, like they usually did.

I was too caught up in wondering why somebody's virtues

were counted by sucking varnish off a chair leg, but it didn't take long for Colin to enlighten me to that one and lots of others. Growing up on the streets of New York gave him insights I'd never had.

"The other night when McLowry was here, he told me some sheriff over to New Mexico shot and killed old Andy a few weeks back. I was sorry to hear of it," said Rinaldo Hernandez. For a moment in time silence reigned as if to pay homage to Andy McBurn. I was sad too and I didn't know Andy McBurn from a coyote but their regret was infectious.

"Sometimes, *compadres*," said Mateo, his voice soft, "I think we are all living on borrowed time." He strummed his guitar, a plaintive chord and then switched to a happier one. "So drink tequila, love the ladies and enjoy your stay, eh?"

So they drank and laughed some more and the stories flowed again, spun out into the desert night and the waiting ears, especially ours. This was a different kind of school and one with lessons we'd need to get on in this world. I appreciated every minute of it.

Colin was getting around so well Francisco and Whitey decided it was time for his further riding education. The first time he'd ever been on a horse had been the day he rode after our wagon in a panic and his ability to control the horse the least of his problems then. He'd been shy of horses since, understandably. Amy and I were perched on the corral fence watching as Colin swung his bad leg over the saddle and settled in with a triumphant smile. The smile disappeared with Old Mike's first step and he grimaced as his left foot tightened in the stirrup. Francisco stepped up and whispered something and gently guided Old Mike around, showing Colin how to show the horse what he wanted and after a time, he was doing it on his own, first walking and then trotting around the corral. Amy and I waved each time he passed by.

"That boy looks fuckin' terrified, I swear."

I jerked around. A man, no, a boy not much older than me,

sat on the fence beside me. I'd never heard him come up, silent as a desert wind. He grinned at me and I couldn't help but smile back. He gazed at me, his blue eyes merry, his cheeks rosy and his dirty blonde hair sticking out from under his dusty hat. I glanced down at the rest of him and his clothes were no less dusty than his hat but I noticed the gun he wore on his hip was shiny clean.

"Billy," he said, holding out his hand and I turned to him and shook it. "There you go. Ain't you just like some little fairy queen, with them green eyes, hair like sunlight and that little pointy chin, girl."

"Hello Billy," I said. "Where'd you come from?"

"Hell, honey I blow with the wind, don't ya know?" He laughed. "What's your name?"

"Josie Fallon." I leaned back. "This is my friend Amy, and that's Colin up there on that horse."

"Amy, huh? The little brown fox," he said, chuckling at his own wit. "Ol' Colin looks like he's never been on a horse afore. Where's he from, anyway?"

"New York City," I said. "And he hasn't, except to rescue Amy and me."

"Goddamn," Billy said. "I was born in New York City myself, so they tell me. Colin and I need to have a chat about that, he survives his ride."

Amy snorted and stepped down from the fence. "He'll survive just fine, fella. He's survived a lot worse than that." She stomped off, puffs of dust rising under her feet. Amy was never one for chitchat. I was no front parlor wonder at it myself but I stayed put.

"Billy!" Whitey Cogburn came over. "When did you get here? I ain't seen your squirrelly ass since Tombstone."

"Hey Whitey," Billy said. "How you doin'? I came in with Hiram just now. Need me a new horse, one a different color, you know?"

The two of them went on but all I cared about was he'd said

Hiram was here. I jumped down off the fence myself and ran to the house. There he was, just putting down a glass of water but I didn't care. I threw my arms around him, my head coming to rest just below his ribs. He smelled like horses, leather, safety and sunlight.

"Whoa," Hiram said, and put his hands on my shoulders. "Josie, it's good to see you, too."

I clung to his sturdy frame like a tick until he pried me away, both he and Mateo chuckling. "So tell me, how are things going?"

I felt a little silly but I didn't care. "Good, really good. I can shoot and ride and so can Amy and Colin and his leg is so much better and he's out there riding right now."

"Slow down." He held me away and peered at me. "You look like a different girl than the one that came to us just three weeks ago. Sally wouldn't believe it. You got some heft to you now, Josie, and you don't look scared of your own shadow."

There was an old silvery mirror in the bedroom and I knew my face was nearly as brown as Mateo's from being outside all the time and I felt much better but I hadn't really paid much attention to that. There were other things much more important.

Hiram eyed the gun on my hip. "Think you need to wear that around here?"

"Well, maybe not," I said, "but I sure do like the feel of it."

He rolled his eyes. "We got us a desperado here, Mateo." He steered me out the door. "Let's go check on the other two devils."

We went out to the corral where Colin was still riding around, getting comfortable enough to wave at Hiram and me as we put our arms over the top rail. Billy still sat there and nodded at Hiram.

"Josie, this's Billy," Hiram said.

"Oh, we met already, big man," Billy said. "'Course I'd notice a gal that sweet." He looked over at me and grinned and Hiram sighed and rolled his eyes. "Your friend is doin' better, not lookin' like he's going to fall off. He might make a horseman yet."

Colin trotted up to us, grinning widely at his prowess. "Good to see you, Hiram." He patted the horse's neck. "I'm getting the hang of it, I think." In his enthusiasm, he pulled the reins a little too tightly and the horse backed up abruptly, Colin's face surprised. "Whoa, there, guy." Within seconds, he figured it out and turned the horse, grinning triumphantly. "Ha, I'm getting this." He trotted off, his back ramrod straight.

Billy laughed. "Hey, New York, let's talk over some tequila now that you're a real cowboy. See you later." He jumped down and headed over to the bunkhouse.

"You watch yourself around that one," Hiram said to me, chuckling. "He's a goodhearted kid, but he's got a bit of a temper. On the other hand, he might just be somebody you can learn from if you're careful."

I stared up at him. "How's that?"

"He's an orphan himself. Got arrested stealing food when he was just your age, girl, and he's learned to survive by his wits which is something you're going to have to do as well. Ain't nothing to be done about that except prepare you best I can and that's just what we're doing right now."

I swallowed. It wasn't like I didn't know that but for a while here in this place with the first real freedom I'd ever known, I'd put it away in a dark place and hadn't thought about anything beyond horses, guns, tortillas and being with people I trusted.

"Thank you, Hiram," I said firmly and looked him in the eye. "I owe you, we all do. Trust me, there'll come a day when I can repay you, and I will."

He put his arm around my shoulder. "You know what, Josie Fallon? I damn sure think you just might at that."

CHAPTER 6

"Jesus God, girl."

The smoke was still thick in the air when I dropped the pistol back in my holster. The target Hiram had created out of a bale of hay and a sheet with rings painted on it was shredded in the bull's-eye area.

"Mateo wasn't kidding. You're a god-given natural. What you think, Billy?" Hiram said, turning to his companion.

Billy nodded. "You're good, Josie. Accurate. But I'm hear to tell you, honey, there's a hell of a difference in shootin' some bale of hay and shootin' a man. That's where you're gonna have a problem. When the crunch comes, women fold like a bad card. Right, Hiram?"

Hiram shrugged. "Some." He gazed at me. "Not all. There's Sally, remember?"

Billy snorted. "Hell, Sally's one in a million but you know that." He pushed his hat back on his head. "All's I'm sayin', Josie, is you got to be sure of what you want to do. Really, most people don't know what the fuck they're doin', so I guess it don't matter whether you're a woman or not. Sorry."

I didn't say anything, just took my gun out and reloaded. "Set 'em up again, Hiram."

"No point in wasting ammunition. Billy's right. You got it down, Josie. The real test will come if you have to shoot somebody and there ain't no practice for that, trust me, honey."

I did trust him and besides, my arm was sore. We trudged back to the house, Billy chattering to Hiram as usual and Hiram answering in his laconic fashion. Billy had his new horse but he didn't seem in any hurry to leave and seemed to be enjoying himself. I didn't mind, he made me laugh. Things hadn't gone much easier for Billy than they had for me, I'd come to find out. He wasn't shy of sharing his history, in bits and pieces.

A few nights later we were sitting out by the fire as usual, listening to the men swapping stories and Hiram was right in there with the rest of them, although he glanced over at the three of us occasionally and cut off some of the worst parts. He was not a man to brag and certainly the one that all the others paid deference to so he didn't have to. By and by, like every night, people left one by one until this night there was no one left but me and Billy.

Sparks flew into the clear desert night, circling like enchanted fairies from the stories I'd read, up to the stars that sprinkled the midnight blue sky above us. I watched, mesmerized, my mind swirling in patterns as random as they did. It was very still, only the occasional night owl hooting or a horse moving around in the corral. I looked over at Billy, who was staring into the flames.

"Where'd you come from, anyway?" I'd been curious about him from the first minute I'd seen him. I wasn't sure he'd answer, or if I was being rude, but I wanted to know.

"Truly was born in New York City, just like your boy Colin. I don't remember shit about it before we moved away. My momma made bad choices of husbands, sweet woman that she was," Billy said. "She moved us here and there and ended up in Silver City, a lunger and alone, after Antrim up and left. When she died I thought I'd die, too. I loved that woman."

Instead, I kept on best I could. There was barely enough

money to bury her and we kept on for a time but Jesus, it's hard to make a livin' when nobody takes you serious as a worker no matter you're just trying to get started. I started stealing from those self-righteous assholes who did nothin' to help us, just to get by. Just some food and clothes but you woulda thought it was diamonds and pearls."

He looked at me then and his eyes were watering and I didn't think it was the smoke from fire, curling up into the night. I took his hand in mine, squeezing hard.

"Billy, I'm an orphan, Colin and Amy too. We know what it's like when nobody gives a damn about you. I been living in that hell of a so-called orphanage for years, just ripening up so they could sell me for a whore."

He blinked. "What? Hiram said you were running but he didn't mention why. Bastards oughta pay, Josie."

"One of them did already," I blurted out. I blamed it on the whiskey Whitey had been sneaking to me earlier. "I didn't mean to kill him, but I couldn't let him kill Colin so I stabbed him. That's the whole reason we're here. The law's after us now, not just the orphanage."

Billy stared at me like I was something he'd never seen before and I thought he was going to get up and leave. Instead, he gathered me up in his arms and kissed me. I'd never been kissed before and I was thinking it'd be Colin that did it, but it was pretty nice and Billy's lips were soft against mine. It didn't last long because Billy was quite a talker.

"Jesus Christ girl, you could be my sister, but that's not exactly how I think of you, not with that face." He smiled his crooked smile and softly caressed my cheek. "We're two of a kind, Josie. I never started out wanting to hurt anybody but sometimes they don't give you no choice. That's sorta how it went with me."

We talked the rest of the night through, the words pouring out of both of us like floods that had been dammed up forever. The hurt, pain, shame and anger we'd had to tuck away that we'd both had to live with that seemed to last forever. It wasn't supposed to have been that way for either of us, but it had been. Once those cuts heal, the scabs form but the memories remain, creating resentment and a deep-rooted desire for satisfaction.

It wasn't revenge we thought about just before we fell asleep or in that shadowy time before we came fully awake, but justice on our own terms, a sort of retribution and a chance to live the life we were owed. A silent trust based on our common histories was born that night between Billy and me.

The cactus and mesquite trees became visible through rosy gold streams of dawn light when we blinked and came back to the reality of where we were. I stood up and brushed the dirt off the britches Mateo had given me. Billy curled up beside the remains of the fire.

"See you later," I said. "I need to get in there before anybody wakes up." Old habits die hard. Likely nobody cared but I thought of Hiram and wasn't completely certain about that. Billy smiled lazily and caught my hand, lids heavy over his eyes.

"We'll do some shootin' in the afternoon, Miss Fallon, if you're of a mind." He dropped my hand and his eyes closed. I crept noiselessly into the house and my bed, but probably Mateo wasn't fooled for a second. That man had a sixth sense that served him well. Still, it was worth it. I fell asleep smiling.

I'm not sure I'd ever done that before.

I DON'T KNOW IF IT WAS THE HORSES OR THE RAISED VOICES that woke me. I blinked and sat up. The sun was high overhead so it must've been around noon. I ran out to the main room but no one was there. Through the open door I could see Hiram on the veranda, six of his men around him. Five men on horseback were in the yard in front of the house, dust milling in the air from their hooves.

"Godamnit, Hiram. I'm here to do business and you're telling me to ride away? You lost your fucking mind?"

"No, Thornton. I'm telling you I don't have any horses for you."

The man in front, a dirty white hat on his head and a mean scar down his cheek, wheeled his horse in a circle. "Fuck you don't, Young. I can see 'em from here."

Hiram grinned and put his hand on the butt of his gun. "I didn't say I didn't have horses, Wiley. I said I don't have horses for *you*. Ride on."

"You still sore about that bank in Santa Fe, Hiram? Thought we put that behind us a long time ago."

I heard the sound of a shotgun being racked on the veranda and I held my breath. Wiley Thornton must've heard it too, unless he was deaf as a post.

"It wasn't just a bank, Wiley. You killed a woman and a kid in there for no good reason. That I don't forget. Now get the hell out of here and take your scum with you."

"Josie, get away from that door and get down," Billy whispered in my ear and I jumped like a rabbit. He stood beside me, his gun drawn. I'd never heard him make a sound from where he stood beside the window. "Right now."

I did as he instructed and lay prone on the floor. This didn't seem to be going well.

The first shot fired came from the yard, one of Thornton's men, aimed at Hiram but it was far from the last. A barrage of gunfire followed. My ears were ringing when the gunsmoke cleared and Billy was outside with the others. Thornton and his men were riding off except for one man who lay on the ground, his reins dragging beside the gun that had been in his hand, his horse crowstepping wildly and ready to bolt. I stepped gingerly onto the porch. Everyone there looked to be in one piece.

Hiram flipped the dead man over with the toe of his boot and stared at him. The man's face was somewhat marred by the bullet hole in his forehead.

"Anybody recognize him?" Hiram said, turning to the rest of the men.

Rinaldo Hernandez walked over and peered down. "Ah, *si*. He's the gringo who hangs around at the Nugget in Benson. Bad *hombre* this one. Likes to cut up people's faces with his knife." He reached down and took the man's knife from its scabbard, weighing the blade on his open palm.

"*Muchas gracias, pendejo*," Rinaldo said and sat down on the veranda to inspect his sharp new acquisition.

"No loss, then," Billy said. "Nice shot, if I do say so myself."

Hiram rolled his eyes. "What makes you so sure it was yours, kid?"

Billy gazed at him for a second, took off his hat and swiped a hand over his forehead before clamping the hat back on. "Because I always hit exactly what I'm aiming for, Hiram and you know it."

He grinned and Hiram laughed. "I'll give it to you."

Billy unbuckled the man's gunbelt and yanked it out from under the body, picking up the gun from where it lay. He shoved it back into the holster. "No point in burying this with him. Besides, Colin could use it."

They strode back up to the porch where I stood in my bare-foot glory, a little dazed by the last five minutes. Hiram made a tsk sound and guided me in the door.

"Sorry you had to see all that, Josie," he said as he sat me down on one of the chairs around the table. "You all right?"

I nodded. I wasn't lying, either. It really hadn't bothered me much at all to see that man gunned down. He was there to hurt people I cared about. Maybe there was something wrong with me, really fundamentally wrong. Then again, bad people meet bad ends, that's what I thought and it seemed fair to me. I was getting to like that kind of fairness, maybe because I hadn't seen much of it.

The atmosphere around the fire that night wasn't near as boisterous as it'd been on other nights. Oh, there was still the whiskey and a little joking, but the day's events had everyone in a more somber mood. Murmured conversations between two or three rather than anyone holding forth with a funny monologue seemed to be the case. Hiram stood up and threw another log on the fire.

"Boys, Thornton's likely to stir up some trouble for us any way he can and believe me when I tell you he's a mean snake with no regard for anyone or anything."

"We're none of us angels, Hiram," Whitey Cogburn said, "but Thornton's a rum one. He'd run over his mother with a pack of hogs just for fun. Never liked him and these boys he's runnin' with are no better."

Nods and murmurs of agreement went around the fire.

"Juan Silva told me they're calling themselves the Rovers," Rinaldo said. "Pack of *los hijo de putas*." He spit into the fire for emphasis.

"Point is, he got his own man killed today and he's not man enough to take the blame for that. He'll be looking for revenge," Hiram said. "Count on it."

When Whitey handed me the whiskey bottle I took a big swig. I handed it to Billy, his eyes glittering in the firelight.

He shrugged and took a long drink. "Way things are going, you might get a chance to aim at something besides a straw bale, Josie girl. Ready for that?"

"Those fuckers look like targets and that's all that matters to me," I said. "Anybody that goes after my friends is my enemy. It's very simple."

Hiram sighed and reached for the whiskey. I knew he didn't want this for me but he also knew I could handle it.

I grabbed the whiskey bottle back from him. "Abracadabra," I said. "It's magic, you know?"

"Well, it's something," Hiram said, "but I got a bad feeling it's not magic at all."

CHAPTER 7

Despite Hiram's dire predictions about Thornton, everything remained quiet. I kept busy, helping Mateo in the kitchen, as he was teaching me to cook with little success. I went riding and shooting with Billy who seemed to like hanging around.

I came to realize that I was the reason for that after a few more stolen kisses. Colin eyed him with some disdain, mixed with grudging admiration after shooting one afternoon. Billy had given him the gun and Colin took to wearing it just like I did. Amy steered clear of Billy altogether for reasons I couldn't fathom. After breakfast one morning, I asked her why.

"He's got something inside him," she said, "something that won't let him settle like normal people, Josie. An anger, or maybe just a grievance. I can't explain it, it's just something I know and it's not good for him or anyone he's around."

"Hmm," I said, handing her a plate to dry. "I know he's different, but then everyone I've met in the last month is different than anybody I've ever known before. He's sweet. I like him."

She snorted and slammed the plate down so firmly I was worried it'd break. "Everyone knows that, Josie. Especially Colin. You need to be careful."

I could feel my face getting hot and I concentrated on scrubbing the pan in my hands. I nearly blurted out that Billy and I had a lot in common but I kept it to myself.

Colin and Amy had been spending a lot of time together, just as Billy and I had, but I didn't mind. Colin had become more reserved with me, but still occasionally touched my hand or gave me sidelong glances and smiles. At present, our futures were a blank slate, the three of us, and I kept putting off talking to Hiram about what came next. He didn't seem to have any sense of urgency about it, even now that Colin's leg was as healed as it was going to get. Still, all three of us knew we couldn't hole up here on Hiram's ranch for much longer. Amy could always say Colin and I abducted her but he was just as likely to get hanged as a horse thief as I was for murder and there were witnesses to document both. We needed a plan but we were at a loss as to where to go or what to do next.

After supper that night, Hiram motioned us to stay with him on the veranda after the others wandered away puffing on their cheroots and laughing softly at each other's jokes. The sun was setting over the western hills, and it looked like the sky was on fire, a treat I'd come to look forward to each evening. Anyone who ever said the desert was ugly had never seen that. At the orphanage we were usually stuck in the house doing bible studies at that hour.

"Getting restless out here?" Hiram said.

"No," I said, "but I'm thinking you don't need us hanging around forever. Trouble is, I don't have the slightest idea where the hell we even are."

Hiram chuckled at that. "I know, which is why I've been giving all of you a little time to acclimate to what life really is outside the walls of Angel's Refuge." He lit up a cheroot himself, blowing the smoke into the darkening sky. "Mateo's got a map or two in there which I suggest you take a look at if you've not seen it yet. You're in the southern desert of Arizona Territory, and the towns around here are Tucson to the west, the biggest, and lots of smaller settlements, then to the east, there's Tombstone, Benson, Douglas and some others. Over to New Mexico, further east, there's Silver City, Santa Fe where Billy's from and other places. Your old friends at Angel's Refuge deal with quite a few people in damn near all of them, but there's a lot of good people who don't. It's a big world."

Well, some of that was news to me, not so much Colin or Amy, perhaps. Colin exchanged glances with me over Amy's head, his eyes sympathetic. He'd at least been on a train across the country and Amy had traveled with her family to the west. I'd studied a little geography but they'd been careful not to acclimate us to the surrounding area, likely afraid we'd try to escape. I think it was the fear of not knowing which way to go once I got out of sight of that hated house that kept me in it for so long. I felt foolish now and I said so.

Hiram chuckled. "Oh Josie. You been stuck in that place like a rat in a trap since you were four years old. I'd be surprised if you didn't think you were on the damn moon. No need to be feeling bad about that. You figure out direction as quick as you figured out that gun you're sportin', you'll be a force to be reckoned with."

Colin smiled and so did Amy, who put her arm around me. "Don't be shamed none, Josie. How could you know anything about the world growing up in that place? Not that I know much more."

That made me feel better but I still wished I'd gotten a better grasp of the world before now.

Hiram blew out more smoke and gazed at us. "It's not the geography you need to worry about anyway, least not so much. It's what you're gonna do when you leave here we need to figure on. After that the rest is easy. Course you might want to think about changing your names."

Colin jerked up at that. "What?"

"There's wanted posters up on you and Josie, son," Hiram said. "Haven't seen anything on Amy, but then she's sorta a bystander, as it were. Saw 'em in Tucson last week before I got here."

"Holy Christ," I breathed. My mind was reeling. "So I'm officially an outlaw? Wanted for what?" My stomach had plummeted to somewhere near my feet even though I was sitting down. I tried to take a deep breath and looked up at the purpling sky, trying to find a few stars to guide me or at least give me a sense of a world that still existed beyond this porch. I was pretty sure I already knew what he was going to say.

"Murder."

Oh god. I shouldn't have been surprised but hearing that word out loud when you're a sixteen- year-old girl is not something that happens very often and I sure never thought it would happen to me.

"What about me?" Colin said quietly. He looked at me as though awaiting a sentence he was dreading.

"Horse thief," Hiram said and took another big draw on his cheroot. "Doesn't matter if said horse is dead. Amy's not been mentioned. I might point out you can be just as hanged for a horse thief as a murderer around here. You all know this isn't a surprise, or at maybe you didn't. Only thing different is it's official now."

A scuff of boots and a skeptical snort announced Billy, who'd apparently been standing just inside the door. "That's fuckin' bullshit, Hiram, what they're tryin' to do to them."

"No disagreement there, kid," Hiram replied, clearly aware of Billy's presence. "Got any ideas?"

"Hell yeah, I got ideas, Hiram, but ain't none of them worth spit unless they want to get into even bigger trouble," Billy said. His smile was dangerous and his hand had gone to the butt of his Colt and rested easy there. "How about you?"

"A couple."

Even Billy waited for what Hiram had to say. Colin looked like he'd been kicked in the stomach, much as I likely did.

Hiram rocked back in his chair. "Way I see it is, you get out of here and head for California. Nobody over there, especially in the south, gives a damn about law and transgressions over here, at least so far. They got their own rules. I know a few people with some horse ranches over there, relatives of Mateo's, that would take you on with no questions asked. You're going to have to work hard and I wasn't kidding around with changing your names. After that, you can decide to follow your own path. How's that sound?"

Scary, I thought, but a lot better than dying. Besides, I didn't know much, but I knew California was next to an ocean and that was something I'd always wanted to see. I looked at Colin and Amy and they didn't seem averse to the idea either. Billy opened his mouth but Hiram put up his hand. Silence reigned on the veranda for a few minutes.

"Sounds like a plan," I said. "I still have to change my name?"

"Up to you, once you get there," Hiram said. "In the meantime on the road, I'd say yes."

I reached a hand out to Colin and the other to Amy. "What do you say?" They both grasped my hands and nodded.

"We're in," Colin said.

Amy squeezed my hand and smiled. "Yes," she said. "I hear it's nice there." Where she heard that, I had no idea but it didn't seem like the time to quibble.

"California," I said. There didn't seem to be much choice.

Billy took a long look at me and wandered off into the night. I watched him go until it got too dark to see but he never looked back. Hiram rocked back on his chair and finished his cheroot. He seemed satisfied but then again, I thought, he hadn't planned on getting saddled with three troublesome orphans in the first place.

And that, as they say, was that. We wouldn't be outlaws anymore but ranch hands and our future was California, which seemed like a good option, considering. I hoped it had nice sunsets. What it wouldn't have was Billy and I wasn't sure how I felt about that.

We went off to bed not long after that. After Hiram left, Colin, Amy and I sat on the veranda for while, but we found there wasn't much to say. We'd dug this hole we were in and Hiram's option of California seemed to be the best choice for us. Staying around here didn't hold any particular place in our hearts since all we had were bad memories and the reason we were in this fix to start with. Amy hugged me and went off to the bedroom we shared in the main house, her steps slow. Colin stood up and then, changing his mind, sat back down beside me.

"Josie. I want you to know I don't regret a minute of it." He took my hand. "I would've been next, a slave in some mine and God knows where you and Amy would be if I hadn't ridden out that day."

I threw my arms around him. "You were a hero," I said. "Just like in the fairy tales. But I'm no princess even though you were the white knight." My eyes blurred with tears. "I hope I haven't ruined your life along with mine. California sounds like salvation, Colin. It's the only way I can see."

He buried his face in my hair and his arms tightened around me. "Me, too, Josie. Thank god for Hiram."

We sat that way for a time, comforting each other, something we'd needed to do for some time now. It had been a rough few weeks and we'd found little time for that between the fear and the uncertainty as well as learning the things we'd need to keep us alive. This small moment was the first time we'd come together like this and I wished I'd made it happen sooner.

I kissed him on the cheek and made to stand up when he pulled me back down, kissing me on the mouth the way Billy had. I wasn't all that surprised but it wasn't the same. Colin was dear to me, but since this whole thing had started, things were different. I was different. I didn't want to give him reason to think otherwise. Gently, I pulled away and wished him goodnight.

Tomorrow was going to be quite a day, according to Hiram. Off to parts unknown on fast horses. I think my life was repeating itself, but I was no longer a child or even a frightened orphan.

⚜

I WOKE EARLIER THAN USUAL LIKELY FROM THE THUNDER. IT was just before dawn when I walked barefoot out onto the veranda, the air cool and spicy with sage, juniper and mesquite from the rain. It stopped with the sunrise, puddles everywhere, trees glittering as the sun touched their dripping leaves. To me it felt like a fresh beginning. We packed our few belongings, mostly some clothes like the ones we were wearing, extras donated by all the vaqueros, even the hats we wore. Hiram and Rinaldo Hernandez were going with us on part of our journey and all our saddlebags bulged with food and water. The horses milled around in front of the house, their hooves muddy. Colin and Amy said their goodbyes and were already on their horses but I hugged Mateo and found tears welling in my eyes at having to say goodbye to this man who had been so kind to me. He brushed my tears away with his thumb, and then packed a dozen tortillas into my saddlebag.

"*No lagrimas, una pequena,*" he said. "We will meet again. And my cousins will welcome you." He laughed. "You can shoot the rattlesnakes away from the stables and they will find that a great skill. Your tortilla making is not so good, but..."

I smiled. "I'll practice, I promise."

I looked around but I hadn't seen Billy since the night before and I didn't see him among the vaqueros that came to bid us farewell. I knew I was stalling but time was up. I reluctantly walked to my horse and took the reins from Hiram, who gazed at me and jerked his head towards my horse. I'm pretty sure he knew exactly what I was doing.

We never heard them coming. The wet ground left no dust trail and we weren't as vigilant that morning as we should have been. The riders, close to a dozen, came from two directions, guns drawn. It surprised everyone and the look on Hiram's face stopped me cold. He pulled the rifle from his saddle scabbard and turned to face them when the first shot whistled past my ear and Mateo staggered and fell next to me.

I dropped to my knees beside Mateo, but the light in his eyes dimmed as I touched his cheek. A rage like I'd never known coursed through me as I pulled the Colt from its holster. The yard became a melee of horses and men, shots coming from everywhere. I focused on a man I'd never seen before riding towards me and pulled the trigger. He tumbled from the saddle and I sighted on the one behind him with the same result. Something stung my ear and I felt warm blood trickle down my neck but all I wanted was revenge for the man at my feet and I sighted on a third rider and shot him in the head, his hat blowing off.

Men were standing and shooting at men on horseback, and Billy came up behind me, yelling at me to get down as he passed by, pistols in both hands. Colin had dismounted and was lying on the ground shooting along with some of the ranch hands while Hiram and Rinaldo spurred their horses towards the invaders. I recognized Thornton and aimed at him but Hiram's rifle took him first and he slumped in the saddle, his head near gone, his horse rearing in panic. I shot until I ran out of bullets, the gun too warm in my hand. I was digging more bullets from my pockets when the shooting stopped.

Hiram and Rinaldo rode off in pursuit of the remaining raiders, along with Colin and some of the vaqueros who jumped on the empty horses of those we'd killed. I was still frantically trying to reload when Billy put his hand on my shoulder.

"It's over, Josie."

I shook him off and finished reloading. He put his hand on my gun. "Stop. For now, anyway."

I blinked. Dust and gunsmoke filled the air but it was relatively quiet. I saw Billy put his guns back in their holsters and then I looked around. Mateo lay still beside me, and tears ran down my face as I closed his eyes and smoothed his hair. He wasn't the only one. His killer and a few of the raiders including Thornton, lay in the yard, along with three of the vaqueros. And there was one more.

Amy was on the ground ten feet away gasping for breath, blood seeping from the hole in her shirt. I knelt beside her, and put my hands under her arms, lifting her off the ground, while Billy took her feet, and we carried her inside to the bed we'd shared, laying her down gently. I looked at Billy and he shook his head.

"Get Whitey," I hissed. "Now." I knew from the stories I'd heard around the fire many nights that Whitey had learned how to deal with gunshots. Billy turned and ran, his bootheels staccato on the floor.

I sat beside her and smoothed her hair off her face, grasping her hand.

"Hang on, Amy. We'll fix this."

Her eyes flew open, staring at me. "Ain't no fixin' this, Josie," she whispered. "You take care."

I wasn't ready to believe that. I squeezed her hand tighter and kissed her cheek. It wasn't a minute later when her hand went limp in mine and I knew she was gone forever. My heart broke, what there was left of it. This girl, just beginning her life, had died because of my impetuous actions. If she hadn't thrown in with me and Colin that day, she'd still be alive and I had to take responsibility for that. Christ Jesus. Colin. Was he going to die today too?

I kissed Amy's lifeless forehead and ran out of the house, straight into Billy and Whitey Cogburn.

"How is she?" Billy said as Whitey ran into the house.

"Dead."

"Aw shit, no, Josie. Not the little fox," he said and pulled me into his arms. I felt his tears on my face but I could muster none of my own. I felt numb, with nothing but a wish to put every single one of those bastards in an early grave. For Amy, for

Mateo, for the others who lay around us, and for my own satisfaction.

Billy stepped back and looked at my face.

"You want to kill them all," he said and it wasn't a question but I answered it anyway

"Yes. If Hiram hasn't done it already, I will."

"Girl, you won't be alone." He flung his arm over my shoulder and led me back into the house. "You ain't never going to be alone in that, long as I'm around. I hate it when things ain't right."

CHAPTER 8

"I'm not going to fucking California."

Hiram sighed and took his boots off the table, the chair landing on its other two legs with a resounding thump. "Josie, you listen now. All this aside," he waved his hand towards the front door, "California's still the safest place for you and Colin. We'll take care of the rest of it, trust me. It's not your fight."

It was late afternoon. Hiram, Rinaldo and Colin had returned with some success but a few of Thornton's gang had escaped. We'd buried Amy, Mateo and the vaqueros, two whose names I had never known. Hiram had spoken over their graves and many of the hard men who stood beside me had unabashedly shed tears, even Billy. I could not, a cold rage and a festering need for revenge pushing out any other emotions. Now, we sat in the main room: Hiram, Billy, Colin, Rinaldo, Whitey and others, some on the few chairs while others stood against the walls or squatted on their heels. It seemed we found safety and comfort with each other and I couldn't fault that.

Whiskey bottles and glasses littered the table, toasts for those gone and respite for those here. Nobody had an appetite so neither my poor cooking skills nor anyone else's had been called to duty. I didn't have an appetite for anything but vengeance. Looking around the room, I didn't think I was the only one. The air was thick with anger. I could almost see it, seething around them, the dark red color of dried blood.

I stood up and finished my glass of whiskey, slamming it down on the table. "How can you say that to me, Hiram? Of course it's my fight. We buried Amy today, and Mateo and other brave men who defended us." Those who had ridden in to do their dirty work and died trying we'd dragged out into the desert and left for the buzzards. "I want every one of those bastards who rode in here and left in one piece to die for that."

"I know. I know that, Josie," Hiram said, his voice imploring. "But you aren't the one to do it. Leave this to me, like I said. For God's sake, you're a child."

"No, Hiram. I am not a child. Not anymore. I can thank you for that, along with a few others, one of whom we buried this afternoon."

He shook his head and sat back down heavily on his chair. "Christ on the cross, what have I wrought?"

Nobody had an answer for that one, nor any more words for some time, but glasses were refilled, more than once and glances exchanged, along with raised eyebrows and shoulder shrugs.

"Any of you know their names, these men who got away?" I said. "Or do I have to ask around?"

"I do," Billy said. "At least I didn't see them among the bodies. I know where to find 'em too."

I eyed him skeptically. "Oh, do you?"

"Yes." He sounded sure. "And I'll ride with you."

Hiram slammed his fist on the table. "Stop this right now, both of you. Josie's not going after those men. They'll kill her sure." He glared at Billy. "I'm going to kick your ass for even encouraging her, kid. What the hell you thinking? You keep this up you can ride out of here right now. Alone."

"He's not riding alone." Colin poured himself a glass of whiskey and took a healthy drink, his eyes on Hiram. "I'm going with him." His face was streaked with dirt and sweat, like all of us, and his jaw was set. He stared at Hiram and surprisingly it was Hiram who looked away first.

Well. He'd healed up, all right, and those afternoons shooting with Billy hadn't gone to waste. The boy had turned into a man and I'd missed it.

Whitey broke the tension. "Hell, Hiram, you got a mutiny on your hands here," he chuckled. "The cub turns into a lion. I don't think California's on his plate either."

Hiram didn't bother to offer a reply. He turned on his heel and went outside. It had been a long bad day and the silence stretched into a long ribbon of despair, anger and regret while boots shuffled and shoulders shrugged.

After a few minutes, I followed Hiram out the door, and Colin and Billy went with me. We stood on the veranda and watched Hiram, leaning against one of the corrals, his head on his arms. I knew this had been a terrible day for him just as it had for the rest of us and that he took the blame on himself for not recognizing how much of a threat Thornton had been.

"If you're going after them, I'm coming with you," I said, looking both Billy and Colin in the eye. "Don't give me any nonsense about I'm just a girl. I killed three of those men myself."

Billy nodded. "You got no argument from me, you know that. I don't have any plans that need disruptin'. Hadn't thought I'd be doin' some vendetta ride, but I'm in if that's your fancy." He gave me his usual lopsided grin. "I don't want none of those bastards ridin' away free from this shit here today."

"What's your thoughts, Colin?" I said.

"Josie, we been together since this whole thing started," he said, and put his hand on my shoulder. Billy's eyes flicked towards us and just as quickly away, his face motionless. "You want in on this, it's fine with me. You can handle yourself."

That was all I needed to hear. I walked over to Hiram and put my foot on the lowest fence beam. He looked down at me.

"I already know what you're going to say, Josie."

"Expect you did, Hiram."

He turned to me, one hand on his hip. "If this is what you want, I won't stop you." He gazed into the setting sun and sighed. "I wanted to give you a future but I think I made the wrong choices. Bringing Billy here was a serious mistake to my way of thinking because the two of you were like twins and I didn't see it. I didn't know I was teaching a girl with an appetite for vengeance how to go about getting it. Sally warned me and I didn't heed it."

"Sally's a smart woman," I said. "She saw it even before I did. Don't blame yourself, Hiram." I put my head on his chest and he didn't push me away. "There's something in me. Something that got woke up that first day away from Angel's Refuge. It was just waiting for a chance to surface. Being here gave me a chance to learn and I needed that. After today, I truly know who I am."

He took hold of my shoulders and pushed me gently away, gazing into my eyes.

"Who is that, Josie Fallon?"

"Somebody who makes it right, Hiram, no matter what it takes," I said. "I aim to do just that. They can name me anything they want but I'm that person and that's the path I'm following."

He sighed and pulled me back into his arms. "God knows you've earned it, Josie. I can't fault that. For God's sake, try not to get yourself killed, cause riding with Billy has had bad results for some people. I told you in the beginning to be careful of him because the minute you two laid eyes on each other, I saw trouble. No accounting for the heart and I'm way past giving advice on that. I take responsibility for the opportunities I've offered you, good and some would say bad, but not that one." He took my face in his hands and kissed my forehead. "Remember, your own mind is what'll save you in the end and know that Sally and I are always here for you if you need us."

WE RODE OUT EARLY THE NEXT MORNING, BILLY, COLIN AND me, before anyone was stirring. I didn't want to see Hiram again because there was a niggling part of me that was worried I'd change my mind and stay right here if I did. After the first mile or so, Francisco caught up to us, spurring his horse to catch up, saddlebags bulging as ours were.

"Hey boy, what you doing?" Billy said as he pulled up beside us.

"Coming with you," Francisco said, his face determined. "Mateo was my uncle. I have a duty to avenge him. It's our way, we are Montoyas."

Billy snorted and I ignored him.

"You sure about this?" I said. "It's not going to be easy. We're like as not going to get ourselves shot."

Francisco shrugged his slim shoulders. "As God wills it."

We rode east into the rising sun, the land coming awake around us. A few pronghorn bounced across our path and a few coyotes here and there but we saw no other signs of life except for the small animals who scurried away at the sound of the horses' hooves.

Billy said the two we were after, Mort Clendon and Ben Short, usually holed up near Bisbee near a place called Mule Gulch, doing gold mining when they weren't out killing people. He knew a lot about a lot of bad people, Billy did. The reasons for that were a little cloudy, and I'd learned enough in the last couple of weeks to know they weren't always ones that exonerated him. Still, I trusted him. He hadn't set out to be a killer any more than I had. Life took you down strange roads.

We stopped around midday after crossing a lot of empty desert with no dwellings in sight. We let the horses cool and graze a bit on the sparse grass while we munched on tortillas and beans.

"How about a little practice, Colin?" Billy said, finishing his tortillas. "Can't do no harm."

Colin grinned and followed him a ways off and soon Francisco and I heard their shots. I repacked the saddlebags and sat down to wait. I didn't need any more practice and neither did Francisco, I knew. It wasn't long before they came back, Colin with a big grin and Billy smiling.

"This boy, he's got it, Josie," Billy said. "We're ready."

"Feeling pretty good about that gun, Colin?" I said and he nodded.

"I sure am." Colin swung himself into the saddle without a hitch. "Never thought I'd be wearing one but now that I am, I like it. A lot."

I knew the feeling.

Nearing dark, Billy led us towards a ranch with some buildings that seemed to materialize out of the land around us, the first evidence of habitation I'd seen today. There was a flickering light in the window of the weathered house. We rode up to the place, and Billy jumped down from his horse, holding the reins.

"Susie, it's Billy Bonney," he called "You home?"

The door opened and a woman toting a shotgun stood silhouetted against the feeble light from inside.

"Thought you was dead," she said. "Come closer."

Billy did so and as he stepped onto the porch, she lowered the shotgun and put her arm around him. It was pretty dark and his hat was in the way, but I think he kissed her.

I felt a surge of pure jealousy and Colin chuckled. "That boy gets around."

All I wanted to do was turn around and ride out of there, but within minutes we were inside that house, sitting down at Susie's table while she filled our plates with some stew whose ingredients I didn't want to know but I was so hungry I didn't much care.

Susie and Billy conversed in low tones while we ate. Colin glanced at me now and then but we hadn't said much since we'd come in and I was in no mood to do so now. Francisco was quiet as usual.

Susie stood up and gathered our empty plates and Billy turned to us. "We can spend the night here. It's safe."

"How do you know?" I muttered. Colin gave a strangled cough.

Billy gave me a little smile. "Cause I know Susie, that's why."

"Well, that's obvious," I said. "Old girlfriend?" I couldn't stop myself.

Susie came out of the kitchen and set four glasses down, along with a bottle of whiskey. She poured and handed them around.

"Let me tell you a story," she said. "I think," she looked at me, "it's one you need to hear."

When I was fourteen, my pa found me foolin' around with the cowboy he'd hired that year." She smiled wistfully. "He was a good-lookin' man, that one. Lookin' back, it was damn near worth it. Anyway, my pa kicked me out with just the clothes on my back and I ended up in Silver City. I was hungry, young and stupid. I made money the only way I could for three years and it wasn't pretty. One day, this kid showed up and became my best customer for a few days." She flicked her eyes to Billy but he didn't even blink, sipping his whiskey. "He told me to find a rancher who needed a wife and get out of the game soon's I could before it wore me down. I took his advice."

Susie took a drink of whiskey and flung her arm out. "So here I am. Charlie's over to Benson picking up supplies but he's been good to me. This ain't no Chisum ranch, but it's all right." She patted her belly and for the first time I noticed the healthy bulge beneath her apron. "Charlie'll be a good pa to this one too, even if the man's a little older than most." She leaned over and kissed Billy on the cheek. "Y'all are welcome here anytime. Any friend of Billy's always is."

After listening to that, I felt both better and worse. The world wasn't kind to women, but in my limited experience it wasn't kind to anybody.

The four of us laid our blankets down on the floor and slept like the dead that night. Colin, Francisco and Billy were snoring softly long before my eyes closed. I listened to the plaintive songs of the coyotes outside for a time before the whiskey and some peace of mind did their work. Where was I going? I asked myself for the tenth time that day. But I thought I knew the answer and that didn't bring me any solace either. Out of sheer exhaustion, I slept.

Morning brought Susie's pancakes and bacon, which were excellent and before the sun was high, we were back on the road, heartfelt thanks and goodbyes all around. I meant it, too. I found I liked Susie a lot and not just for her hospitality.

Around mid-afternoon, we stopped and munched on Susie's cold pancakes. Francisco finished first and stood up, stretching.

"Where we going anyway?"

Billy swigged down some water. "Mule Gulch. Guessed you missed that part, comin' late an' all. If they ain't there already, they will be soon and we'll wait."

Francisco nodded. "How far?"

"Not very." Billy hated useless questions and to him, that one fit the bill. We rode on until after dusk, nearly stumbling across a camp before we saw it. Their campfire was a low glow in the gathering dark, where half a dozen men sat around in a circle, eating from the pot that hung over the coals on a makeshift tripod.

"Hello. We're friends," Billy called from aways out.

"Can't know that 'til you show yourselves," a voice responded. "Come closer and we'll see if you're a thieving liar or not. Slow, now."

Slowly we came, getting off our horses at Billy's direction, while he shook hands with the big man with suspenders who'd answered. After a brief discussion, he gestured us towards the fire.

"You're welcome to what's left, if you're hungry," he said. We wasted no time, digging out our tin plates and forks. I don't know what was in that stew either, but once again it tasted fine and I didn't care.

"Dave Eddy," the big man said. "This here's my crew." He didn't offer up any names which was just as well, as I wouldn't have remembered them anyway. "We're prospectors. Y'all are welcome to bed down for the night. You lookin' for gold, or passin' through?"

"Haven't decided yet," Billy said, shooting me and the others a glance. "On our way to Silver City unless something special turns up."

Dave Eddy snorted. "Ain't nothin' special here, just a lot of hard work so far. But who knows? Tomorrow could be the day. We always say that around here and sometimes it works out."

We ate in silence for a few minutes. The other men melted off into the dark one by one until only Dave Eddy sat by the dwindling fire.

"Seen Ben Short or Mort Clendon around?" Billy said, chewing nonchalantly.

Dave Eddy shook his head. "Don't know Mort but Ben Short rode in this afternoon. They got a place just east of here, Ben and some friend of his, could have been Mort. You friends of them?"

Billy shrugged. "Not really. Overheard them talkin' last week about a rich vein here a while back. Hard to tell if that was true, but hey, thought it might be worth checkin' on. How's it been?"

Eddy eyed him suspiciously. "You're green at this, ain't you, boy? We don't talk about where or what we find there. You better learn that fast if you think you're stayin' around. It's every man for himself here and no fucking favors." He looked over at me. "Not a good place for a girl, neither."

"She's my sister," Billy said. "Where I go, she goes. Don't worry, she can pull her weight, and so can my friends."

Eddy's skepticism was evident but he didn't say anything more, just shrugged and wandered off, mumbling a vague good night.

Colin watched him go. "Friendly fella. Still, it's not like we're looking to make friends, is it? Only long enough to get to Short and Clendon."

"Every day that goes by lets them tell others about what happened at the ranch and it's best there's no witnesses, even if they were the ones started it," Billy said. "Aside from the fact they deserve to die for what they did."

Francisco nodded and so did Colin. There was no disagreement among us on that score. Colin gathered up our plates and cleaned them off, and Francisco followed as they left to care of the horses. Billy made to follow, but I pulled on his arm.

"Wait a second. So, we look for them in the morning and just shoot them? Doesn't sound like the best plan if we want to ride out of here." I was having some second thoughts about this. Not about killing them, but about having witnesses to it. I was already wanted for murder, but I didn't need to add more to the official tally.

Billy smiled. "Tends to work for me, especially when the people I shoot deserve it."

"No, it doesn't," I said. "This isn't Hiram's ranch and some wild shootout. You've managed to get yourself quite a reputation, so I hear. I know I just got out of an orphanage, but I haven't been deaf and blind the last few weeks and I was never stupid. We need to do this smarter than that."

I knew I'd chosen the wrong word or two when I saw his eyes flare and he jerked away and turned his back. I waited a minute and then put my arms around his waist, my head resting on his back, listening to his breathing. He smelled of sweat, wet cotton and just Billy.

He turned around and gathered me up. "Josie, I swear you'll be the death of me. We need plans now? Christ almighty, I been living without one for a long time."

"I'd prefer it," I said, and it sounded prim even to me.

He kissed me and I kissed him back. I'd been hungry for this for some days but there hadn't been time or opportunity. He stopped for a minute and looked down at me. "Prefer it, would you? I'd prefer this, Josie, and a whole lot more."

He kissed me again and his arms tightened around me. A muffled cough sounded behind us and Colin dumped our meager bedrolls on the ground. We broke apart, my cheeks flaming and I thanked all the saints the light was so dim.

"Horses are hobbled near some grass," Colin said. Francisco loomed up beside him.

"Time for sleep, no?" He spread his blankets out on the other side of the fire. "*Buenas noches, amigos.*"

We all followed suit, laying down on our blankets but it was a long time before I fell asleep, in spite of Francisco's good wishes.

CHAPTER 9

A second night on a cold hard bed was taking its toll on me. I sat up and my bones creaked like I was an old woman, not a girl of sixteen. I stretched and listened to my backbone crackle like the green wood Rinaldo used to throw on the fire. It wasn't quite light but I made out the prone forms of my three companions, still sound asleep. Just as well. I made my way to what served as a privy, an open trench and easy to find by the smell of it, and then down to the creek to wash off the worst of the last two days' dust and grime. It was peaceful down there, just birds waking up and twittering amongst themselves as the sky lightened, the air fresh and cool.

As I came back up to our makeshift camp, Colin was squatted down, working on building up the coals of the fire and fiddling with a pot of coffee. I took some tin cups from our saddlebags and squatted down beside him to wait for the water to boil. I nudged him with my knee.

"Not quite where we figured we'd be, is it?"

He gave me a rueful grin. "Not really." He nudged me back. "Better than Angel's Refuge so I don't give a damn, truth be told, Josie. I was going crazy in that place. Since then, I been shot at, learned to shoot back and I'll be damned if I'm going to let Amy or Mateo go unavenged."

He stared at me and his eyes were dark. "Billy's got that part right. These bastards deserve killing and I don't care who says different, law or otherwise."

I patted his knee. I didn't know what else to do. I agreed with him but I still harbored some hope we could do what we came here to do and get away clean. That hope was fading as fast as the pre-dawn light. It was going to be a bright sunny day and our sins would be on full display, I feared.

I fried up some bacon and beans, which we wrapped in the last of Mateo's tortillas. We cleaned up, packed and saddled the horses but left them tied to a mesquite tree and instead walked into the more populated areas of Mule Gulch, Billy in the lead.

I hadn't seen miner's camps before but I had a sense this is what most of them looked like. Tents, shacks, bedrolls and campfires were scattered here and there perched amongst the surrounding hills and gullies, all leading down to the stream that flowed in a healthy spate through the whole area. There were some bigger tents, one with a board that said "Assay Office" and another "Supplies". As far as anything else went, they seemed to be on their own when it came to restaurants, saloons or female companionship. I guessed they had to go into the nearest town for that, likely Benson or Tombstone, but I wasn't sure. The whole place reeked, from the trench latrines and the stench of unwashed men and garbage. A couple of skinny dogs slunk here and there, chased off repeatedly by the men who emerged from their tents and blankets to start another day of looking for gold.

Nobody seemed in charge and there was no law enforcement of any kind that I could see. 'Course I wasn't sure what that would look like anyway, but everyone I saw seemed to be doing exactly what they wanted with no direction or fear of retribution. Kind of a perfect place for men like Short and Clendon and I could see why Billy wasn't worried about the law, although quite a few of the inhabitants were carrying guns. Hopefully Short and Clendon didn't have many friends here.

We strolled nonchalantly around, stopping at the tent that said "Assay Office". A man sat inside at a table and looked up as Billy ducked under the tent flap. We stayed outside watching for any sign of the two men we sought. There had been such confusion and gunsmoke at the time of the fight, I wasn't sure exactly what these two looked like, to be honest, nor even certain that either one of them had shot Amy, Mateo or the others. Francisco said he saw the man who shot his uncle but he didn't know his name. It didn't matter to me. They'd made their choice when they rode in with Thornton and as far as I was concerned anyone in that pack of wild dogs didn't deserve to live.

Colin knew what Ben Short and Mort Clendon looked like, as he'd chased them and their friends for quite a ways, with only these two escaping. "I'll know them," he said, peering around from under his hat brim. "Don't have a care about that."

Billy came back out of the tent. "Says Short's got a claim further east along the creek, maybe the sixth or seventh camp in. Saw him yesterday getting supplies."

"Let's go then," Colin said, turning into the sun.

Billy grabbed his arm. "I say we give it a little bit, see if he and Clendon come around."

"What the hell for?" I said. "So we can shoot them in front of all these people? I'm with Colin on this, Billy. Maybe you don't care, but I do."

Billy shook his head. "No, Josie. Because it's rough terrain up there and there's not a miner in his right mind that doesn't have a gun close by when strangers come sneaking around his claim. I know these dirt farmers. They're mean."

"Shit, we know that already," I said. "He rode with Thornton." I stepped up beside Colin.

Billy's eyes flashed. "Stop this right now. You wanted to ride with me on this, you're gonna listen to me. Nobody here gives a shit if we blow the brains out of half of 'em, much less those two. Less competition is how they see it."

"What makes you such an expert?" Colin said. He hadn't heard much about Billy but I had. This was no time for arguing.

I put up my hands. "You're right. We'll hang around."

Billy smiled. "Good. We don't see these roosters by noon, we'll hunt 'em down. How's that sound to you boys?"

Colin and Francisco exchanged glances and nodded. "Deal."

I sighed with relief. We wandered down what passed for a main street in Mule Gulch, exchanging greetings with the men we passed, many of whom looked twice at me. I was thinking it might be a good idea to stuff my hair under a hat or even cut it off. Too late now.

An hour passed and still no luck, according to Colin and Billy. We were getting hot and thirsty, to say nothing of conspicuous. We ducked into the supplies tent to get some shade. It took a minute or two for my eyes to adjust but when they did, I was amazed at the stock inside. I'd never been to a store before and in this unlikely tent in a gulch there was an array of goods like I couldn't have imagined. Mining tools from pans to picks to shovels were on the shelves, along with clothes, candles, pots and pans as well as flour, sugar, coffee, bags of beans, tins of fruit and even a jar of penny candies. The man behind a counter made of a plank and two blocks of wood, gave us a welcoming smile and held out his hand. Colin took it, smiling absently.

"Good morning, friends," he said. "I'm Charlie Oppenheimer. Got everything you need to set up, right here. We can even arrange credit if you need it, based on your claim rights. Feel free to look around."

"Got any water?" Billy said. "Getting warm out there."

Charlie smiled. "Surely do, right over there in that barrel. Dip in."

We wasted no time in doing just that, drinking from the metal dipper in the water. Sated, we did as he suggested and looked around, while Colin wandered back outside to keep watch for Short and Clendon.

Billy bought some ammunition for his pistols and tucked some bullets into my pockets too. Charlie seemed stocked with everything. Weapons were as prevalent as cooking pots, both of which I guess were necessities around here. We wandered around for a few minutes and I was fingering a nice broad-brimmed brown hat when Billy picked it up and plopped it on my head.

"Suits you fine," he smiled, adjusting it down further over my eyes. "Like it was made for you."

I so wished for a mirror but I could tell he liked how I looked and that was good enough for me. It did seem to fit well, too.

Colin poked his head in. "They're coming."

We pushed through the tent flap, following him closely. Francisco stood a few paces up the street and was staring at the two men who walked towards us. I didn't recognize either of them, but Colin had. They came a few steps closer and one of them stopped, his hand on his companion's shoulder, whispering something.

"Hey *cabron*," Francisco said, his hand on his gun. "*Justicia por Mateo, bastardo.*"

The shorter man looked up and Francisco's shot took him in the chest. He fell backwards, dust puffing up around his body. Before I could even blink, Billy and Colin both shot at the second man. He jerked sideways and ran like a rabbit between two tents while we ran after him like wolves eager for dinner. Men were yelling and running for cover, some of them throwing themselves flat on the ground.

We followed him relentlessly as he dodged between tents and firepits, jumping over piles of equipment and boxes, but he finally ran into an overhang, crouched down and fired at us. I felt a bullet whine past my ear and heard Colin roar something that sounded like "no more", shooting rapidly at the man as he stood up to run again. The bullets took him in the leg and the shoulder and he fell, the gun clattering on the rocky ground beside him. Billy strode up and kicked the gun aside.

"Remember me, Ben Short? You always was a dumb fuck."

"It was just a job, Billy. Thornton said y'all needed to be taught a lesson." He began to blubber, snot running from his nose. "I didn't know you were there. It was Mort, he was the one who kilt that gal."

Colin stepped up beside Billy. "No, he didn't. I saw you aim at her."

Billy shrugged and took a step back. "All yours, Colin."

Colin hesitated but only for a second. "For Amy."

He shot Ben Short right between his shifty eyes, holstered his pistol and turned to me. My gun was in my hand and I wasn't even sure how it'd gotten there. He patted my shoulder.

"It's done, Josie."

Well. That part was anyway. We wasted no time in retracing our steps to the main path. Men stood around, murmuring to themselves but nobody drew a gun or tried to stop us until Charlie Oppenheimer stood in our way, arms crossed and face determined.

"You didn't pay for the hat," he said. "That'll be two dollars. It's a nice hat."

Charlie Oppenheimer was a very brave man. I gave a second's thought to just shooting him. It seemed like the way the day was going. Then Billy flipped him some coins and Charlie smiled.

"Nice doing business with you. Hope you enjoy the hat, Miss."

"Oh, I believe I will. Good day, Mr. Oppenheimer." I tipped said hat in his direction as we made our way up the hill to our horses. We rode quickly and silently away from Mule Gulch, a place I hoped to never enter again. Mission accomplished. Where we were going from here I didn't know.

CHAPTER 10

I absently turned the rabbits on the fire, watching Colin clean his gun, following Billy's instructions. Francisco was doing the same. We were new at this. Since I hadn't even fired my Colt, I didn't bother. Besides I'd already learned how to do that. I wiped my greasy fingers on my pants. They were pretty grubby already and a little more wouldn't make a difference. I was learning about life on the trail.

It was dark by the time we'd stopped, having ridden throughout the day. There was a stream and some cottonwood trees so it was a good place to camp. Billy had said we ought to get as far from Mule Gulch as we could, and nobody disagreed with that. By the middle of the day it had been hot and uncomfortable but my new hat shaded my face even if I was sweating underneath it. The country we'd ridden through was hilly, filled with pronghorns and coyotes but not any houses or places to stop.

We were tired and hungry, the horses were tired and hungry and there wasn't much conversation. We'd just killed two people and even if they deserved it, it wasn't an everyday occurrence for any of us, except maybe Billy. We polished off the rabbits and a pot of beans and when Billy pulled out the whiskey bottle, we passed it around a few times.

"How you all feeling about what we did today?" Billy hunched forward towards the fire, gazing at each of us in turn. "Been pretty quiet."

Colin took another long pull. "Pretty goddamn good. I think my sainted mother would be proud. How about you, Francisco?"

Francisco grinned, his teeth very white in the darkness. "Justice, *muy amigos*, justice. Mateo will rest easier now."

"How about you, Josie?" Billy said, throwing another branch on the fire.

"I got a really nice hat but I didn't get to shoot anybody." I said. "'Course tomorrow's another day."

Billy laughed. "Josie, you're something special, you are." He flung his arm around me.

Well, he was right about that. Whether I was something really special to him was what was going through my mind. Colin and Francisco's keen glances weren't helpful when it came to any privacy but I was hoping for later. I grabbed the whiskey bottle from Francisco.

"Speaking of another day," Colin said, "we better figure out what's next."

"Well, there's California," I said. "Staying around here sounds like trouble. I'm already wanted, and after today, you two may be as well." I turned to Billy. "You've got a reputation, have you got the law after you, too?"

He grimaced. "I hear one or two sheriffs know my name and such."

I couldn't help but roll my eyes. "Or there might a jail or two you left."

Billy laughed. "I heard that too. Thing is, that doesn't have to be the way it is for you all. What happened at Mule Gulch was fast and nobody knew who you were. Place like that, there's no law and nobody wants them anyway. Ben Short and Mort Clendon didn't make many friends there, trust me, and nobody'll miss them. Only problem we got here is you, Josie. You killed that driver and there's already wanted posters up. We need to figure that out."

"She did it for me," Colin said. "He would've killed me." He grabbed my hand. "I owe you, Josie. Forever."

"We were in it together, Colin," I said. "It just happened the way it did, that's all." I'd tried to feel some remorse but I didn't and I didn't want him to feel any either. I took a healthy pull on the whiskey bottle and passed it to Billy.

Francisco had been silent but his dark eyes had been watching this exchange. "It doesn't matter to me," he said softly. "You are now my *compadres*. I go where you go."

Billy finished off the whiskey and threw the bottle into the desert. "Let's get some sleep. We'll figure it out in the morning."

We made our beds and it wasn't long before I heard soft snoring from Colin and Francisco. It was quiet, just the snap of the branches as they burned down to coals and the occasional hoot from an owl. It was peaceful and I took a few deep breaths of the sweet night air but sleep wasn't coming for me. My mind was swarming with possibilities, each more improbable than the other. Hiram was right, though. The safe choice would be California. I looked over at Billy's blankets but if he was there, I couldn't tell. I felt abandoned for some reason but I guess I shouldn't have. A few kisses didn't mean a thing.

"Josie." A nudge on my foot startled me. Billy stood beside me, that crooked smile on his face, holding out his hand. I took it and he gently pulled me to my feet, cocking his head towards the trees behind us. My heart lurched in my chest. I'd been waiting for him to say or do something but now I wasn't sure what I wanted.

We walked a few hundred yards away from the fire and sat down on the blanket he spread on the ground. For a time neither of us said a word, staring into the starlit sky. Then we both turned towards each other at the same time and clung together like it was the last thing we'd ever do. We'd kissed a few times but this was different. This time I meant to see it through. To what, I wasn't sure but I knew there was more because my whole body was tingling and pulsing like I'd never known, so there must be a good reason for it and wasn't just some kissing. He laid me down on the blanket and unbuttoned my shirt as well as his. It felt like my skin was on fire and so was his. His kisses trailed down my neck and his hand was gentle on my breasts. I leaned into him and after a time, he groaned.

"Josie, listen." Billy pulled away and the night air was cool on my body. "I've never felt like this before." He brushed his hand over his eyes. "I mean, I been with whores before but this is different. You're different. You make me think of things I haven't thought about in a long time and it was like that the first minute I laid eyes on you. I been on my own it seems like forever, even caring for my mama before she passed. You're messing with my head, girl, but not in a bad way. It's just a way I can't make sense of yet. A way I'm not sure how to find."

Oh god, I thought. My blood was fizzing in my veins. I knew from the first minute I saw him that we were destined to be together, just like one of those fairy tales I used to read. He was certainly no prince on a steed, but this boy, no...this man, was special to me. His courage, his kindness, his charm and that goofy smile that lit up his eyes when he looked at me had enchanted me. That he was dangerous only added to his allure because I knew that I was too, and that I'd never have to explain or justify myself to him.

"What you trying to say to me, Billy?"

His eyes glittered in the starlight, staring straight into mine. "I ain't never said this before but I think I love you, Josie Fallon." He stilled, like a boy in the schoolroom who thinks he may have blurted out the wrong answer.

"I think I love you too," I said and put my hand on his neck, pulling his mouth to mine. "Maybe we need to make sure. Let's see what we can do about that."

He kissed me again, my mouth, my neck and down my belly,

and further, shucking off my pants. We were in a fever is all I can say. The first time was fast and reminded me of Jim Avery but that was a memory I'd buried forever and I put it back in its grave. The second time was much better. I didn't care about any women he'd been with because they'd taught him well. We did things I didn't even know people could do and I didn't care about the little rocks that ground into my back and my knees because it was worth every second.

We lay back on the blanket, gazing into the fading stars, the sweat cooling on our bodies in the cool night air. Dawn wasn't far away. I could already hear the mourning doves cooing in the trees. I turned towards him and put my hand on his chest.

"Billy."

"Josie?"

"We're together now, no matter what." It wasn't a question.

"Yes," he said.

And that was how it was.

CHAPTER 11

I lay on my blankets, turned away from the ashes of the fire. It was almost light but no one had stirred. Billy and I had returned an hour before to our respective beds and I could hear his snores, as well as those of Colin and Francisco. I couldn't sleep though. It wasn't just the pleasurable ache between my legs, but the thoughts swirling in my head, some because of that but more so, what the day before us might hold, and a lot of days after that.

Who was I? A runaway orphan? A killer with a wanted poster? Billy's girlfriend? I squeezed my eyes shut until spangles swam in the blackness. All I'd wanted was to be just Josie Fallon, a girl with a future that was something to look forward to, a safe haven or a job that would let me discover the rest of my life and put the memories of Angel's Refuge behind me. That was gone forever now. The world out here was no less a cruel place than the orphanage had been, in fact, much worse. Surprisingly, though, it had its virtues, at least for me. I knew so much more than I had two months ago. Nothing I could have learned from a book, but only from real life. I thought about the books I'd taken, the Shakespeare and the fairy tales. Those stories were wonderful but I'd never wanted to be the princess in the tower or the maiden in the village, but rather the knight who rode in to rescue them in their time of peril. Peril had become real, and I'd become my own version of the knight. I had no sword like Henry V, but I had a Colt.

MEMORIES TUMBLED AROUND LIKE FIERY SPARKS IN THE WIND. I knew how to shoot, how to ride, how to make love and how to kill and ride away knowing I'd done the right thing. It wasn't the usual finishing school Mrs. Higgins had told us about, but it sure was one I'd taken to and looking back from that first wagon ride to just hours ago, I didn't regret a single damn thing. I thought about my last conversation with Hiram. Something had awakened in me, nurtured by deprivation and injustice and I didn't have the least desire to put it back to sleep. Damned I might be, in the eyes of some, but not in the eyes of those I cared about. My eyelids relaxed and I felt my fingers unclench themselves from the blanket. No shame, no recriminations, self or otherwise. I slept.

The smell of bacon woke me and I sat up, blinking in the bright sunshine. Colin was bent over the skillet set on a trivet over the fire. A pot of coffee sat in the coals and he glanced over at me.

"Coffee, Josie? Looks like you could use some."

I nodded and he handed me a tin cupful. I wrapped my shirt tail around the handle and took a sip, the hot liquid so good against my dust-parched throat.

"Thanks," I mumbled and drank some more. Yellow hair stuck out from an immobile mound of blanket across the cookfire but Francisco was nowhere to be seen.

I finished the coffee and Colin put some biscuits in the bacon grease to soften. I poured another half cup and sat back on my heels.

"Quite the cook you are," I said.

Colin shrugged but he looked pleased. "Learn or starve, I guess. I sorta like it."

I thought of my many botched tortillas in Mateo's kitchen and for a second didn't know whether to laugh or cry. "Good," I said. "Cause I'm no damn good at it."

Colin handed me a warm biscuit with a slice of bacon in it and I found I was ravenous, polishing it off in a few quick bites. He really was quite the cook.

"Something smells good." Francisco walked up, drops of water from his still wet hair on his fresh shirt. "Little creek down there if you're looking to freshen up, Josie." He tucked his old shirt into his saddlebags and squatted down beside Colin, taking a biscuit from the pan.

I grabbed a clean shirt myself, along with a little towel, some soap and a hairbrush and made my way through the mesquite trees. He was right. A fast running stream, studded with rocks lay at the bottom of the hill shaded by cottonwoods. It wasn't deep enough to do more than a sponge bath but it was more than adequate for that. Anything else would have to wait. I brushed the tangles from my hair and braided it into one long tail. Now that I had a hat, it would be easier to tuck the braid up and pass as a man, and I had a feeling that might be necessary soon. It was peaceful there and I sat for a while on a flat rock, listening to the doves coo and the water as it bubbled past.

I could hear the boys laughing as I walked up the hill.

"You hit him so dead center he went down like he'd been hit with a cannonball," Billy said. "You pulled fast, too, faster than me even."

"We will practice, *amigo*," Francisco smiled. "We may need it."

"That's the damn truth of it," Billy said.

I briskly skirted around them and put my stuff on my blankets, rolling them up. They all stared at me silently. I put my hands on my hips and stared back.

"Morning, Josie," Billy grinned. "Sleep well?"

Colin coughed, got up and busied himself cleaning the skillet and Francisco looked as though he'd been turned to stone. I was glad I don't blush easily but if I'd still had that coffee in my hand, Billy'd be wearing it. I guess shooting people wasn't all they'd discussed or maybe they hadn't had to. There wasn't going to be any secrets in this crew, clearly. Maybe that was for the best. I shrugged and sat down beside Billy and Francisco.

"Well enough," I said. "So what's next? Our vengeance ride over for now? Maybe we need to think about the future a little if we want to have one."

Colin plopped down beside me. "I know there's a couple more of those snakes that slithered away but I don't know their names or where to find them. Do you?" He directed this at Billy, who shook his head.

"No. I might recognize them if I saw them again, but that's about it. For now, I guess we need to think about taking care of ourselves."

Nobody said anything for a minute or two, pondering that. Finally I jumped in.

"I don't have a lot of choices, and neither does Colin. Wanted posters sort of take away your options." I looked at Francisco. "You could go on back to Hiram's. 'Course you did shoot that guy in the middle of Mule Gulch yesterday and those people weren't blind, even if they didn't know who you were."

Billy laughed. "He sure the fuck did and they'll be talking about that for some time, I believe." He looked over at Francisco, who was wearing a rather distinctive Mexican vest, pants and spurs. It was like he'd put on his Sunday best to go chase down his uncle's murderer. People were going to remember that, no question. "Y'all got outfitted real pretty for family vengeance there, Francisco."

Francisco looked at each of us in turn and shrugged. "*Si*. I am a Montoya. Fuck them all."

Well, there was no arguing with that. Wasn't likely he was getting out of this clean either. Colin turned to Billy.

"Since all of us are wanted or soon to be, that leaves you. I have a feeling you're not so clean either. What were you up to before you came to Hiram's?"

Billy gave that lopsided grin I'd come to love. "Well, I had a little problem with a blacksmith in Benson a while back, but I ain't heard nothing about that in some time, so it's likely blown over. Things are a bit testy over in New Mexico, I admit, so it's probably not the best idea to cross that border. I do believe there's a wanted poster or two that has my name on it, and a few people looking for me, just to be clear with y'all."

My backside was getting sore and I stood up and stretched. It was approaching noon and we'd been sitting here way too long for people who'd just killed two men not that far away. They all looked at me as though I had some answers which I surely did not.

"Gentlemen. What the hell do we do now? Doesn't look to me like we have a lot of options. There's California, or Mexico, and don't look at me for any damn thing else because I been stuck in an orphanage all my life, and the rest of you don't exactly look like world travelers either. All I know for sure is I'm not hanging for anything I've done, and I don't want any of you to be dangling on the end of some sheriff's rope either."

Billy clapped his hands together a couple times and after a second Colin and Francisco did too.

"She's right, boys. Where you want to go?" Billy said. He brushed off his pants and stood up, too, as did Colin and Francisco.

"California sounded good in the original plan, before all this shit went down," Colin said. "It sounds like a long ways though."

Francisco nodded. "My uncle has a place. I'm in."

Billy looked dubious. "It's a long way, I know that much." He glanced at Francisco. "What kind of place your uncle got there anyway?"

"I can't say for sure, but I know it's a big spread and he's doing well, so Mateo told me." He smiled for the first time today.

"And you can see the ocean, he says, and there's whales in it. I've always wanted to see the ocean."

Billy looked at me. "Josie?"

I didn't have to think about it for long. Hiram had suggested it for a reason and there was no law following us there. Besides, an ocean was a powerful draw for someone who'd been locked in a house in the desert for twelve years. Just the thought of it made my heart sing.

"California," I said.

Billy smiled at me. "California it is, then. Before we saddle up and ride out of here, there's just one little thing."

"What's that?" Colin said.

"I'm down to my last few dollars and you don't have any. I don't know about you, but I don't think we're going to get too far on jackrabbits. Since we're wanted anyway..."

Colin gave a harsh laugh. "So we add robbery to the list?"

"Hell, boy, they want to hang us all for murder. Robbery ain't nothing."

He had a point. On the other hand, we weren't exactly practiced in the art of stealing, even though there was no doubt we could kill people. I didn't want to add innocent shopkeepers to my trail of bodies. It was growing longer by the day.

I sat back down in the dirt. "So what do you suggest?"

They all joined me around the cold ashes of our fire. The sun was now high overhead and I was getting nervous.

"Where the hell are we anyway?" I said. Any direction I could see was just empty high desert, studded with rocks, cactus and an occasional lonely tree.

Billy looked around. "Somewhere on the Bobacomari. It's a big cattle ranch. I know some old boys got a horse operation around here, the McLowrys, but I haven't seen them in a while. Nobody's likely to bother us. I steered us north out of Mule Gulch, thinking no one would think we'd go this way."

"So if we're going to get some money and rob somebody, who'd you have in mind?"

Billy pondered this. "Well, stagecoaches is stupid, unless they got a payroll on 'em, otherwise it's penny ante stuff, pocketwatches and such, and I don't know the schedules. Then there's assay offices and banks, but that's risky, going into the main streets and all. We did that yesterday. It's not like we need a huge stake, but then if we're going to do this at all, we might as well get as much as we can. Hitting the general store hardly seems worth it."

"Well," Colin drawled, picking his teeth with a mesquite stick, "seems to me there's a couple kinds of places that do brisk business just about everywhere around here, not that I've had the opportunity to visit either one. Billy seems to be pretty familiar with both, though. In his wild past, of course." He looked pointedly at me and I couldn't help but laugh, and they all thought it was pretty funny too. "Some places just deserve to be robbed, you ask me."

And that is how we decided to rob a saloon and whorehouse. The devil, as Mrs. Higgins used to say, is in the details.

CHAPTER 12

Those details proved to make all the difference, before and after. We stayed at our campsite on the Bobaco-mari through the day and that night working them out. Colin shot a couple more rabbits and between that and stale tortillas, we made do.

I wasn't happy about the whole idea, nor was anyone else, really. We'd put ourselves into a place where we didn't have any options. When your name and face are on wanted posters, waltzing into town and getting a job doing anything exposes you to people doing their civic duty and who would turn you in, so there was no road to doing honest work for an honest dollar. Like Billy said, we were already wanted for murder and horse thievery, both hanging offenses, so robbery was nothing in comparison. I didn't have much experience with the outside world, but it sure hadn't proven to be very forgiving. We were set on a course there wasn't any turning away from.

Choosing which place to rob was the biggest problem, but after weighing the options between Tombstone, Tucson and Benson, it pretty much boiled down to Tucson, not the closest, but much closer to California, as well as the biggest. Then all we had to do was figure out which place to rob. Since three of us hadn't ever been there, we only had Billy's experience to rely upon. That, surprisingly enough, wasn't all that extensive.

"So which one's the best bet?" Colin said, chewing on his hard tortilla. "Anything stand out to you, Billy?"

"Well," Billy said. "My experience ain't all that broad, contrary to what you might think." He shot a glance at me which I ignored. "'Specially in Tucson. That's an expensive place compared to, you know, other towns."

"So?" Francisco rarely said anything but he emphasized his words this time. "*Verdad, amigo.*"

Billy shrugged, shooting Francisco a look. "All right, all right. There's a lot of places, but only one I been to. I was told it was the best and I believe that's true. It's big, a cantina and saloon, and lots of girls and all." He seemed to be caught up in his memories and there was no way I wasn't going to stop him, not only for our current purposes but learning more about the man I'd just spent the night with, cause I sure didn't know much.

"It's run by this woman, Elena Alcazar, and she calls it 'Stella' like a star. It's got a big saloon and gambling tables, and she lives up on the second floor with the rooms for the girls. There must be twenty rooms up there, and her place too. It's busy all the time, but especially on Saturday nights when the cowboys come into town. I can't see how it doesn't make a lot of money, which is perfect for us."

Francisco nodded. "Even I have heard of this place. Stella is special. My uncle has told me. You have been there, Billy?"

Billy nodded and didn't look at me. I figured this was a good time to take a walk. I surely did not want to hear of his adventures at Stella's. I stood up and brushed off the seat of my pants.

"Carry on, gentlemen. This may not be a topic I care to hear more about. I'll be back."

I wasn't surprised when no one objected. Colin was my friend, as was Francisco but Billy was now my lover. If he meant a word of what he said the night before, he didn't want me listening to this, so when no words were said, I felt a little better.

I walked through the mesquite trees and down towards the creek and then stopped.

What was I thinking? If I couldn't hear this, I wasn't ready to rob the place. Besides, while they were all as handy with a gun as I was, especially Billy, I was a better planner than all of them, from what I had seen so far. I crept silently back to the campsite, screened by the mesquite trees and a tall saguaro cactus.

"Jesus, Billy," Colin was laughing. "Hope you had some money on you. This is some place from what you say. The whiskey prices alone would clean you out."

"Well, yeah, I did," Billy said. "But I'm glad I saved some because I spent the whole night with the prettiest damn girl I've ever seen. Her name was Isabella and she had this long chocolate brown curly hair and the saddest eyes I've ever seen. If we take this place down, she'll be happy to see Elena Alcazar lose her money, from what she told me."

I didn't give a damn about secrecy or anything else, bursting through the mesquite trees and grabbing Billy by his shirt, nearly pulling him to his feet.

"What did you say her name was?"

Billy grabbed my hands and sat me down firmly. "Stop it, Josie. What the hell's got into you?"

I batted his hands away and stared at him. "What did you say her name was?"

He took a deep breath, glancing over at Colin and Francisco who were motionless with shock.

"Isabella. That was her name, Josie. What difference does it make?"

I stared at all of them, and when it came to Colin, I saw a glimmer of recognition in his eyes.

"It makes all the difference in the world," I said. "She was my sister, my best friend in the world, gone for two years. Now I know where she went and what she's had to live with."

I glared at all of them, all these young men who couldn't know what it was like to be a girl with no choices, orphaned or not but subject to the lust and whims of men, whether it be whore or even a so-called wife, and only if they were that lucky. Being a woman, especially in the west, was a chancy business. Men held all the cards and there were few Sallys out there, even she had paid her dues before she married Hiram, and there were even fewer men like him. I hadn't been out in the world long, but I had learned fast. Right now, I couldn't even look at Billy.

He, however, didn't have any problem looking at me. He put his hands on my shoulders and looked into my face.

"For god's sake, Josie," Billy said. "I didn't know and I didn't put her there. I'm sorry. That's all I can say right now. It's in the past. Can you live with that?"

I dropped my hands. Of course he couldn't know, and a lot of girls could be named Isabella, so it might not even be her. I knew in my heart, though, that it was.

Colin stood up and put his arm around me. "Josie, I remember her, and I know what you're thinking. God knows, this could turn out to be a good thing, if in fact it's our Isabella from Angel's Refuge."

I sat back down. "Maybe." I felt sick inside, thinking about what she'd been through the last two years while I sat at Angel's Refuge doing nothing to help her. This could be the chance I'd been waiting for. They all looked at me as though they were waiting for permission, and I came to realize that maybe they were.

"It doesn't matter if it's my Isabella or not," I said finally. "Whoever the hell she is, she doesn't deserve to be in that place if she doesn't want to be. Given that, I say Stella's is our target. Now, what's the best way to do it?"

We spent the rest of the evening figuring that out. Billy thought waiting until around three in the morning when most of the patrons were gone, drunk, or upstairs was the best option. We'd go in, two in front, two from the back entrance, and anybody that objected, we'd knock out or shoot. The money was in Elena Alcazar's rooms above and we'd go up there and get it, in and out in five minutes and ride away fast. There were a couple of variations on this lunacy that I listened to before I ventured my own idea.

"Listen to me," I said. I was getting downright cranky with this nonsense. Men were so wanting to charge headlong into whatever it was they wanted to do. Sometimes that worked but this was not one of those times.

"First of all, there will be no shooting anybody because the minute we do, people notice, even on a Saturday night in Tucson and it's not going to be easy to then find the money and leave, since we don't know where the hell it is exactly anyway. There's no point in killing people," I glared at them all, "even though you've all gotten some experience with that and seem to have an appetite for it, just because they happened to wake up at the wrong time in the wrong place." I held up my hand as all three of them opened their mouths to protest.

"I've got a better idea."

❧

WE RODE INTO TUCSON ON A SATURDAY EVENING JUST AS THE sun was setting. Pink and orange streaks made a panorama in the sky as dusk fell and suddenly, the way it always happened in the desert, it was dark.

We were down to our last tortillas and just enough money between Francisco and Billy to get drinks at Stella's saloon. It was only a two day ride from the ranch we'd been camped on, and I marveled to myself how close things really were. For years, I'd thought of the outside world as a huge and frightening place. Even the day we left Angel's Refuge and managed to find Hiram and Sally was forever imprinted on my mind. It had felt then before we saw their lights as though I was at sea in a strange land where I could wander forever, lost and eventually dying, my bones joining those of the skeletons of dead cactus or the coyotes whose bones sometimes littered the ground.

Much more reassuring now was the company of my friends, a couple of whom did know which direction to take without a road to travel on, and who would never abandon me. It was comforting but at the same time, I knew I had lots more to learn.

Tucson was, at least to my mind, teeming with people, buildings and traffic. Two story buildings, some wood and others stucco, mingled together, blending their styles of architecture between that of America and that of Mexico, and the people on the streets, whether walking or on horseback and wagons, seemed to be a blend of the same.

"So, New York," I said, nudging Colin who rode beside me, "what do you think of this?"

He laughed. "Well, they're industrious, I'll say that. They've made something out of damn near nothing, when it comes to this desert. Quite the metropolis."

I didn't know, but I'd take his word for it. In the last ten minutes I'd seen more people in one day than I had in ten years. I couldn't begin to imagine what New York was like and I wasn't sure I'd like it, at least from what Colin had told me. I thought he did, though.

"Do you miss it?"

He paused for a minute. "I miss my mother and my brothers, but the rest of it? Not really. It's all I knew, before this." He waved his hand. "There's something different here. The air's clean, the sky endless. I remember days when I couldn't even see it in New York from coal smoke." He shrugged. "To tell the truth, Josie, I like it better here. Even given, well, you know."

He reached over and squeezed my hand. "We're going to be all right."

I squeezed back. "Yes," I said, because any fears could only be detrimental to what we'd planned this night. It was going to work simply because it had to. I had become a determined person who knew believing in yourself made a whole lot of difference. Maybe all of it. I loved Billy but I knew most of the time he didn't know why he was doing the things he did, but what he had was confidence, that boy. I think he was passing it on to me.

We rode slowly down the street, past businesses, mostly shuttered now, and a lot of saloons that were getting crowded, making our way further into town, and eventually we came across Stella's. It wasn't difficult. The place shone like the star it was named for, torches burning outside the entrance. Two stories of creamy adobe stucco, the walls painted with vines and flowers with flowerpots hanging outside in the verandah. It was a charming facade that gave the lie to the sort of goings on that were the main enterprises inside the doors.

We ambled by, and turned onto the next street, following that a block or so to a vacant lot where we had a clear view of the back of Stella's, including windows, its haphazard balconies and stairs. The place was big, taking up most of the entire block both ways and it did have a back door, I guessed for deliveries and such, as well as a back staircase from the second floor. That shouldn't be a problem for us, and in fact it was just what we'd been hoping to find. Clearly the delivery door was left unlocked, as men appeared from time to time, dumping boxes and trash, the door flapping on its hinges as they came and went, music and laughter wafting into the air. Occasionally women appeared on the narrow upstairs porch, taking the air but they didn't stay long.

It was dark and quiet back there, and we waited a time to see if anyone had business nearby, but it seemed none did. There was nothing back there but some storage shacks, trash and the empty desert beyond. It didn't smell nice, but the usual evening desert wind helped a little as did the sagebrush that littered the place.

"Ah god, that feels good," Billy said after swinging his leg over his horse, shuffling his boots in the dirt. We all did the same and he was right. I put my hands on my lower back and stretched. I swear I could hear the bones crack but no one else seemed to, maybe because they were doing the same thing. Colin and I were not used to being in the saddle for hours on end, but we were learning. I had a feeling it never got a lot better.

Billy pulled some dusty-looking jerky out of his saddlebag, and a bottle of whiskey, both of which he passed around. Nobody complained about either one. I knew there was no point in cautioning anybody about the whiskey and I took a healthy swig myself. It was going to be a long night.

It was early, much earlier than we needed it to be, and we sat on the ground and watched as silhouettes appeared against the curtains on the second floor rooms. It was early, yes, but active. Good lord, I thought, these cowboys were a randy bunch. Then again, I didn't have a lot of experience in this area. Maybe they were all like that, but the only one I knew about didn't seem to share those shortcomings. I glanced over at Billy and he grinned back, passing me the whiskey bottle. Well, he hadn't grown goat horns on his head yet. I figured he likely never would.

"How long, you think?" Colin said, laying back and cradling his head on his arms. "This could be a long night."

Francisco laughed softly. "*Verdad, amigo*. Patience is a virtue, no?"

"That's just your belly talking, friend," Billy said. "Course, money don't equal food, so we're going to have to wait on that, once we got it."

I snorted. "Maybe we should've hit up the general store instead."

Billy cocked his head. "Maybe, but I don't like to take from people that make an honest living. Stella's is another story. But we only got one shot, Josie. I'm trying to think ahead more'n two days, like we talked. Besides, there's the other thing." He shot me a glance, his eyes gleaming in the fading light.

Oh, well I knew. "Yes, there is definitely that," I said. I could tell these hours were going to pass agonizingly slow. With these boys, that could be deadly. "Why don't I tell you a story?"

And so I did, just like Scheherazade in the fairy tale book I'd stolen. I started out with a few I already knew, like Snow White and the evil queen, King Arthur and the round table, and then I just started making them up. Not a one of them had heard stories like this before, just like me, and it was like opening a portal to another world for them, full of dark forests, magic caves and white castles on cloudy mountain peaks.

We sat there in the dirt behind a whorehouse and saloon, tired, anxious and planning on violence, while I conjured up heroes, princesses, villains, witches and other worlds for these young men whose lives, like mine, had been bereft of all of that. For a little time, they left that dirt and sorrow like the children they'd never really had the chance to be, along with me. No loving parents, no caresses at bedtime, no full stomachs and no assurances that the next day would be safe and wonderful.

"And they lived happily ever after," I said for the tenth time that night. I looked up and the moon was high overhead. "It's time, boys."

CHAPTER 13

Billy and I sauntered through the front door of Stella's like we were familiar customers, taking a seat at one of the round tables near the staircase in the rear. The air was thick with cigar smoke, whiskey and the smell of too many people too long in an enclosed space. This late, half the tables were empty, but still a couple of dozen patrons were seated at the bar and other tables, talking and playing cards while some pretty girls in brightly colored dresses wandered here and there. The piano player was sitting on his bench, taking a break with a glass of whiskey while a man with a guitar sang a plaintive song in Spanish. I liked it, in spite of what we'd come here to do and took in everything like the first-timer I was. Billy glanced over at me.

"Nice place, eh, Joe?" he said. "Kinda thought you'd fit right in."

I nodded, grinning back at him. "Sure do, pal."

Billy went over to the bar to get us some drinks and I leaned back in my chair. I checked my hair, tied up with a piece of leather and stuffed snugly under the brim of my new hat. I'd rubbed some desert dirt on my cheeks to look like stubble or at least cover up my lack of it. I'd been wearing Francisco's old pants, boots and shirts for weeks anyway at the ranch so I was fine there and I wasn't all that pretty to start with especially with my hair hidden, so I figured I could pass as Billy's little brother looking to get to know a girl for the first time. All we had to do was find the girl.

Under lowered lids, I perused all the girls flitting around the saloon but none were Isabella. This made me a little anxious, because she was the foundation of our hastily patched together plan. The other options were going to be a lot more dangerous. Billy returned with our whiskies which we sipped slowly.

"Spot her yet?" he said, "cause I ain't."

"No." My fingers twitched on the glass. I was tired, hungry and hoping this wasn't a really bad idea. The general store was looking better all the time.

We sat for a time, nursing our drinks. Conversation, some murmured and some louder, punctuated by laughter and cursing at cards, flowed over us. We attempted to chat but both of us were too nervous to do much talking. Occasionally, girls would ascend the staircase with a man in tow, while others came down one by one to join the ebb and flow of the patrons below. After a time, only a few men were left in the bar, and one of the girls came over.

"Evening, gentlemen. I'm Molly." She was blonde, in a tight purple dress and pretty although her eyes looked as tired as mine. "Interested in some entertainment tonight?"

"Ain't you a pretty thing," Billy said, smiling at her with that grin he had. Molly looked enchanted but then that was her job, so I refrained from kicking either one of them.

"Thing is, gorgeous, I brung my little brother here in for his first time," Billy continued, clapping me on the shoulder so heartily I nearly lost my hat. "Last time I was here, I told Isabella I wanted her to introduce him to life. She around tonight?"

Molly's smile faded a bit. "She's here, but she's been busy, friend. Could I fill in?"

"Honey, if it was me, you'd be mine tonight." Billy pushed back his hat and stared at her as though he was looking at cherry pie. Now I really wanted to kick him. "But Isabella and I made a deal already and I never back out on a deal. Tonight's for Joe here. Any chance you could check on her? It's gettin' late, you know?" He took her hand. "Next time I'll be looking just for you."

Molly sighed, pushing her hair off her face, pulling her hand away from Billy's reluctantly. "I'll see what I can do. Next time, sugar." She winked. "That's a deal, too."

She made her way up the stairs and once again we waited. The remaining whiskey in our glasses was getting dangerously low. We didn't have either the time or the money for more. Robbing people was a tedious business so far. I thought about Colin and Francisco waiting out back and hoped they hadn't fallen asleep, but they were likely as twitchy as I was.

A cowboy at the next table threw down his cards in disgust and pushed his chair back. On his way past us, he stopped.

"Ain't I see you somewhere before?" He peered owlishly at Billy. "You sure look familiar."

Billy shrugged. "Not that I recall, friend. Just got here from Denver."

The cowboy blinked and staggered a little. "Huh. Coulda sworn." He lurched his way to the door and left.

"You know him?" I said.

"Uh, yeah, he was in Silver City for a time," Billy said. "He's so drunk he won't remember but we need to get this done. Now." For the first time, he looked not just nervous but worried. That made me worried too and not for the first time, I thought we should just hit the general store and get the hell out of here because it was too dangerous and the girl here probably wasn't my Isabella anyway. There was only a couple of patrons left in the place. Then she walked down the stairs, her red taffeta dress rustling with each step.

She stopped at our table. She looked beautiful, as always, her lustrous curls falling on her shoulders, but her eyes were clouded and a bit vacant and the makeup on her face couldn't hide the paleness.

She gave us a big smile, nonetheless. "Molly says you were asking for me."

Billy got up and pulled out a chair beside me. "Yes, ma'am. I brought an old friend of yours with me tonight."

She turned to me and if I thought she was pale before, now she turned ghost white and her eyes went wide. "Josie?" she whispered.

I grabbed her hand. "Yes."

Tears welled in eyes. I squeezed her hand in mine. "Hold it in, Bella. You want to get out of here, girl?"

"God, yes. But there's no possible way." She glanced over at the bartender and the man dressed in black who stood at the end of the bar. "They'll kill us."

Billy laughed softly. "Not tonight, honey." Then, louder for the benefit of anyone listening, "Sweetheart, my little brother Joe here is a virgin so you treat him good. You two go on upstairs and I'll be along shortly."

Isabella looked at him and seemed to come to a decision. She pulled me out of my chair and smiled back at Billy. "Come on, cowboy. We'll have us a time."

We silently ascended the stairs, leaving Billy at the table. She led me wordlessly down the hall to a room and closed the door. The décor was spartan, just a bed, and a chest with a washbasin and ewer on it. A filmy red curtain was draped over the window, the only effort at décor. I guess at Stella's the whores didn't need fancy. We sat on the bed and she hugged me, my hat falling off.

"It really is you," she said, her hands on my face. "You said you'd find me and by God, you did. How'd you get here and how'd you know I was here?"

"Long story," I said, "which I'll be happy to tell you tomorrow. Right now, we got business to do and that includes taking you with us, if you're agreeable."

Isabella gave a laugh, which ended in a choking sob. "If I'm agreeable? Holy Christ, Josie, I'd kill the mother I never knew to get out of this hellhole."

"Well," I said, taking out my gun, "it's not your mother we may have to kill, but I hope you're up for anybody else. We're also taking their money. Which way is Elena's room?"

Soft footsteps that stopped outside the door signaled Billy's arrival. I opened it and he stepped in and closed the door behind him.

"So, she in?"

Before I could answer, Isabella did. "Hell, yes." Her eyes were no longer vacant but fierce. "Elena's room is the last room on the left. The old bitch never locks the safe because she's got Dade Patterson sharing her bed every night when he's not sniffing after me. Nobody goes up against that bastard."

Billy grinned. "Well, right now he's downstairs holding up the bar and hustling drunks, so we got to be fast, don't we?"

Isabella pulled the taffeta dress over her head and threw it in the corner. She rummaged around under the washstand and quickly donned a pair of britches and a shirt, then pulled a pair of dusty boots from under the bed. The whole transformation took less than a minute.

I couldn't but stare in awe. "Where in hell did you get those clothes?"

She snorted. "Traded them with a cowboy I know for favors. Figured they'd come in handy and here we are."

"Well, shit," Billy said. "I like a person that thinks ahead."

Isabella glanced at me. "I didn't before when I should have, as Josie knows and that's not a mistake I'm making again." I didn't answer but I knew the last two years had been very hard for her, much more so than me.

We crept down the hallway to Elena's room and Isabella opened the door. Even in the dim light, my eyeballs nearly exploded. The entire room was decorated in purple and yellow, from the velvet settees and wallpaper to the fringed lampshades that illuminated a large woman in a purple lace outfit. Elena Alvarez lay like a queen on her curtained four-poster bed, snoring loudly. The room reeked of a cloying perfume that smelled like rotting roses. Somewhat reluctantly, I shut the door to the fresher air softly behind us.

Isabella put her finger to her lips and guided us into a small annex, where a desk, two chairs and a large safe, the door ajar, sat in the gloom. Billy pulled a sack from his pocket and opened the safe door wider. Bundles of paper money, gold coins and pokes of silver and gold dust stuffed the two shelves and he hurriedly stuffed it all into the bag while Isabella and I watched Elena sleep from the annex doorway, not wanting to get too close. I had a sixth sense whenever anyone was around me when I slept, and I suspected I wasn't alone.

Just as we were ready to leave, the door to the hall opened and shut firmly. We melted back into the darkness of the annex and stood still as statues, hardly daring to breathe.

"Sweetheart?"

Billy gave a nearly inaudible groan. Dade Patterson brushed back his waistcoat and sat down on the bed beside Elena. Her eyes flew open and she smiled, holding out her arms. He leaned over and kissed her, holding up a bag.

"A good night, then?" she said, her words slurring.

He laughed. "Hell, yes. It was a Saturday. Sorry you had a headache and had to miss it, but it was even better than usual. I've already been to the girls' rooms and collected." He frowned. "Except for Isabella. You seen her?"

Elena sat up, staring at him blearily. "No. Where the hell could she be? She didn't have a date outside, did she?"

Dade shook his head. "Nope. Last time I saw her she was going upstairs with some kid. That's weird, now that I think about it. Didn't see him around again either."

The man was like a wolf scenting prey and I sensed Billy stiffen beside me. He knew it too. Patterson stood up and stared into the doorway to the annex, pulling his gun from its holster.

He hadn't taken two steps towards us when Billy shot him twice in the chest.

"Godamnit, I didn't want to do that," he said, standing over Patterson's body. Isabella and I burst out of the annex in time to see Elena Alvarez pick up a derringer from the bedside table and aim it at Billy's face.

"You're going to die for that," she said but before she could pull the trigger I shot her in the head, her blood splattering those purple bedcurtains before she fell onto the floor. I didn't want to kill her or anybody else but I couldn't just let her shoot Billy.

Three gunshots in the relatively quiet night were at least two too many and we heard shouts from below, likely the bartender closing up. I grabbed Dade's bag from where it lay beside the bed and the three of us ran down the hallway to the back staircase, practically falling over each other before we reached the ground, Billy carrying the bag from the safe. Colin and Francisco had the horses at the bottom of the stairs and we jumped on them, Isabella holding on tight behind me. We tore out of Tucson towards the open desert.

We didn't stop for maybe three miles, looking behind us all the time. There were no lights and we couldn't see anyone following us. That wasn't going to hold true, though. Tucson wasn't some gold camp. There'd be a posse for sure and we needed to ride a long way before morning light if we had a prayer of getting away from the law that was surely after the monsters that had unleashed the horror at Stella's. Nobody had seen what happened, but they would think back to who was there sooner or later and we couldn't afford to be around once they did. So we rode on, hungry, tired and scared, but satisfied, too. We had money and we had a future now. The moon was high, and the shadows of the cactus and mesquite trees dappled the desert floor as we galloped by. Isabella held on and in the beginning, laughed with exhilaration which took a turn into the relief of sobs. After a time, her head fell onto my shoulder and I knew she was asleep. I held one of her arms to make sure she stayed in the saddle.

Thing is, to me the real horror at Stella's was the girls forced into slavery and the madam and her lover who'd profited from their shame and degradation. I'd have shot the old whore again and again if it meant I could save a girl for each bullet. At least I'd managed to take the one I cared about and for now, that was enough.

CHAPTER 14

Dawn found us out in the desert, safe and alone but hungry. Money we had, food we didn't. I started thinking about our plans and stopped when I realized how short-sighted we'd been. You could pretty much rob anybody, but you had to transfer that to what you needed. Here we were, miles from nowhere, plenty of money in our pockets but nowhere to spend it and no food or store to buy any. On the other hand, we had Isabella.

We'd stopped at a small creek with a few cottonwoods and hobbled the horses, all of us stretching out on the ground and falling asleep almost instantly under what would become shade, except for me. I watched as my companions closed their eyes. Isabella lay beside Francisco who hadn't taken his eyes off her since we'd scrambled down the backstairs of Stella's. They could've been sister and brother, both of them so beautiful, with their dark eyes and hair. The thought of the two of them together made me smile. Time and circumstance would tell, I guess.

Billy snored softly beside me and Colin rolled onto his side, coughed and lay like a statue on the desert floor. It'd been a hard day and night and we could go no further without sleep. I lay down, my head pillowed on my arms but my mind wouldn't shut down. I closed my eyes and saw Elena Alcazar's head explode again, her blood so red against those purple bed hangings. Who had I become? A killer, for certain, but not one who enjoyed it or looked for opportunities to do so. I was a killer of circumstance, I told myself. A killer who only took lives from those who had hurt others or one that had been given no choice when it came to survival.

The little voice in my head, the one that had been in there for a while now, laughed. *Josie Fallon, you made choices and they didn't have to mean killing anyone so stop the excuses. You like it. You like your brand of justice. Admit it and then maybe I'll let you sleep. You could use it.*

"Yes," I said out loud but it was cold comfort.

EARLY AFTERNOON SUNLIGHT BORED INTO MY EYES AS I blinked and rolled sideways. There would be no more shade from the cottonwoods. My mouth was a dry as dust and I swallowed, grit coating my throat. Billy was sitting up, his head on his knees and Colin coughed, lunging to his feet and heading beyond the rocks, the first to go while Billy and I waited for our turns. Isabella and Francisco sat by a small fire, and the coffeepot was nestled in the coals. Thank god.

Coffee is a wonderful thing, not only for waking you up, but the sheer relief of a hot liquid in a parched mouth and throat. We sat silently and sipped and nobody said a word for some time. Billy got up and wandered over to the horses, peering out towards the east and south.

"Looks good. No dust trails, but then it's damn flat and I can't see all that far. Still."

"So no posse, then?" I said.

Billy shrugged. "Don't look like it, Josie. Although, I have to say, I'm pretty sure that bartender or the poker player at Stella's recognized me. It wouldn't take much to put things together, even though nobody saw us once we went upstairs. Pretty clear things went to shit after that and they need to look at somebody."

My stomach growled. "We need provisions."

"I'll say," Colin chimed in. "Any towns between here and California, Billy?"

"Well, I hear there's a couple of spots, but this is new territory for me," Billy said. "And you and Josie sure don't know much when it comes to geography." He laughed. "What about you, Francisco? Been to your uncle's place in California before?"

"Only once, as a *nino*," Francisco said. "I don't remember any towns on the way, and there may not be any."

Silence descended once again while we all considered options. The stores in Tucson were not one of them. The sun poured down and the horses shuffled down to the creek. They wanted to be gone as much as I did.

"I know a place that has lots of provisions," Isabella said. We all turned to look at her.

"And where would that be, pretty girl?" Billy said. "Stella's?"

Isabella shot him a look of pure disdain and I nearly laughed out loud.

"No." She stared at me. "It's a place that could use a good cleaning out, and not just food. I have some debts to pay."

I stared back and we both smiled at each other, terrible smiles. It seemed Isabella had some very dark tendencies of her own.

I stood up. "Excellent choice. Tonight we're eating well-deserved roast chicken, boys, and it won't cost us a penny, just a little hard riding on empty stomachs. We can do that. What do you say?"

It was late that night before the big frame house rose up before us, silhouetted against the half moon. There was a tiny light on in the adobe house where the Mexican workers lived, but the big house was dark and silent as we rode slowly towards the compound, as were the barns.

Isabella rode beside me, and I could see her teeth gleam in the moonlight as she grinned at me before we dismounted and tied the horses to the post beside the barn. Even though I'd stabbed Bob to get away from the clutches of this place, she had even more reason to be seeking justice for the two years she'd endured at Stella's, thanks to the mercenary proprietors of Angel's Refuge. While I was a little concerned about my own morality, given that inner voice, Isabella had no qualms at all, it seemed. I decided I couldn't condemn her no matter how this turned out, but I had a hope to temper the worst of it, not knowing exactly what that might turn out to be. I'd buried those memories of Avery deep and in the last few weeks it was like it'd never happened. Maybe we'd just steal some food and chickens and I hoped in my heart that was going to be all the mayhem we might exact this night.

We crept towards the house. I knew Joanie Higgins and her man Avery's rooms were on the first floor and I'd be surprised if Avery at least didn't sleep with a firearm at hand. Stony was a bigger concern but he usually stayed in his rooms above the barn. I didn't think the Mexican women that worked in the house would intentionally turn on us, but then again, they didn't know who we were, especially coming around in the dark of night. They might be just as invested in stopping intruders as their bosses were.

I turned the knob on the front and was surprised to find it locked. They'd never bothered before. I guess I couldn't blame anybody but myself for this change. Stealth was our best ally so I shook my head and shooed them around to the kitchen in the back. As I suspected, the kitchen door was open, as the cooks and the maids went in and out late and early both. We rummaged around and quickly filled sacks with coffee, sugar, flour, tinned food and pretty much anything we might have a need for. Quietly wringing the necks of a few chickens was our last target, in case they put up a fuss. As we toted the sacks out towards the horses, Rosa, the head cook, appeared in our path, her white nightgown a billowing sail in the night breeze. Before I could say a word, she let out a scream that tore through the night.

Colin dropped his sack and put his hand over her mouth. "It's all right, Rosa, it's all right, it's me, Colin. You remember?"

She struggled in his grip but within seconds recognized him and quieted, but it was far too late. Lights appeared in the downstairs windows and we heard a door slam. We were in it now.

Rosa ran back to the adobe house and slammed the door tight. I looked around. Everyone had put down the sacks of food and drawn their guns, except for Isabella, who of course didn't have one. Instead, a butcher knife gleamed in the moonlight, gripped tightly in her hand. She hadn't wasted her time in the kitchen.

"Hell, Josie, you said there's only three of them, maybe only two, right?" Billy said, his voice hoarse. "We can just tie 'em up and get the hell out of here." He looked over at Colin and Francisco. "No need for gunplay." He glanced at Isabella. "Take it easy, girl."

Jim Avery burst through the kitchen door, a pistol in his hand. "Stop right there, whoever you are." He stopped short when he saw five figures in the yard, and crouched down, his gun leveled at us.

"No need for that," Colin said. "We just came for some food, and we'll be out of here in no time. Put down the gun, Avery."

The fact that Colin had said his name startled him.

"Who the hell is that?"

"Colin Donnelly, remember me? Put down the gun. We can all walk away from this just fine."

"Not you, you ungrateful little shit," Avery said and shot

wildly towards Colin. He missed but Francisco didn't and Avery fell facedown into the dirt, groaning.

"That's enough. Take the sacks and let's get the hell out of here," I hissed. "Now."

Billy grabbed one, as did Colin and I, stumbling towards the horses, but Isabella stood still as a fencepost, Francisco beside her.

"Come on," I said. No sooner were the words out of my mouth than a shotgun boomed and Isabella screamed. Joanie Higgins now stood in the doorway, in a flannel nightgown, her hair wild, loading more shells into the shotgun she carried.

"Stop, or I'll kill you," I said, dropping the sack and leveling my .44 at her. "We're leaving and you're not stopping us."

She looked up at the sound of my voice. "Josie Fallon, you murdering little bitch, is that you? I always knew you were headed for a bad end, much as I tried to teach you the ways of the Lord."

"Ways of the Lord? Wonder what he'd think about sending girls to be whores?" Isabella said, stepping towards her. "Remember me, Mrs. Higgins? 'Cause I sure as hell remember you." Before Joanie Higgins could cock her shotgun, Isabella's knife flashed more than once and our old tormentor fell beside her partner, their blood mingling in a black pool in the moonlight. So much for those dreams of San Francisco, I guess.

I can't say I didn't feel some satisfaction and there was no doubt Isabella did. She wiped the knife off on Joanie Higgins' nightgown. The boys hadn't moved a muscle, staring at us and I guess waiting to see what we'd do next.

Isabella turned to me. "There's a lot of money in there, Josie. We aren't leaving here with just food. Come on."

"You're bleeding," I said, as I trailed after her into the house.

"I know. The old bitch nicked me with some buckshot from that shotgun," Isabella said. "We'll find something to wrap it up." If I'd had any doubts about her ability to adapt, they were long gone. This was a girl who knew what she wanted.

We made our way to the office and she flung open the door. I looked down the hallway and saw some of the kids standing stock still on the stairs in the dim light from the hall candle sconce. Their faces were pale and frightened and I recognized April and Maryann's among them, staring open-mouthed at us.

"It's all right," I said. "Tomorrow you can do whatever you want. Tucson isn't that far. Take the wagons, turn right onto the road and keep going until you find it and the sheriff. Or, take some of this money and hightail it out of here on your own. I know most of you pretty well and I know you'll take care of each other. If you don't, we might have to come back. Tonight, go back to bed and forget you saw anything."

They scurried wordlessly back up the stairs. Isabella opened the strongbox and whistled. "Christ, they were loaded. What the hell kept them here? Making kids miserable?"

She grabbed a carpetbag from beside the desk and began stuffing stacks of bills into it. I looked around and on the desk was Higgins's ledger book. I stuffed it into the carpetbag beside the money and put my hand on her shoulder.

"Hey," I said. "We've got plenty. All those kids up there?" I jerked my chin towards the ceiling. "They're going to need it more than we do. Leave some for them."

Her eyes were a little wild and her hands were stained with Higgins's blood. She studied me for a second or two. Then she reached into the carpetbag and put back some of the bills. "All right, Saint Josie. You got your wish."

We ran back down the hallway. As we came out of the house, I saw that Colin had led out one of the horses from the barn, and they were tying sacks of food onto the saddle. From the looks of the feathers on the ground, we really would be having roast chicken. There hadn't been a sound from the adobe cottages or the barn, so we'd gotten lucky, or Stony Logan had, being away on one of his usual forays. Higgins lay very still as I passed but Avery stirred and his eyes opened.

"Josie girl," he said, blood running down his cheek. "Remember? Help me."

"Of course," I said and shot him in the balls. I didn't give him so much as a backward glance as we rode away into the night.

CHAPTER 15

Iwoke to the smell of roasting chicken, salivating like a starving dog who'd not had a good meal in days, which was a pretty good comparison, really. I decided right then that whatever else my life was going to be from here on, it sure as hell was going to include good food when I needed it.

We didn't get all that far from Angel's Refuge the night before. Far enough, though, before we found a good place to stop. There would be no posse after us, and with any luck, that would hold true for some days, at least until Stony returned or some odd passersby happened upon the place, which was unlikely as the entire time I'd lived there, I'd never seen a single soul stop by. No one there, from the children to the Mexican women, was likely to raise an alarm. I strongly doubted there would be any regret among either of them for the deaths of Higgins and Avery, and we'd left enough cash and supplies to be sure people would be provided for. We were flush with our two successful raids and so tired we threw caution to the winds, and had just enough energy left to take care of our horses and gratefully fall asleep on the desert floor.

"Josie." I blinked as Billy's face swam into view. He smiled

121

and pulled me to my feet. "Come on. Chicken and biscuits for breakfast, girl."

I licked my fingers and dropped the chicken bone onto my tin plate. We hadn't spent much time talking, just stuffing ourselves for the first time in days. Francisco and Isabella had gotten up early and cleaned and spitted the chickens, even making biscuits and we ate every crumb and morsel. I think it was the best meal I'd ever had, no offense to Sally's or Mateo's cooking, which until now had both been at the top of my meager list. They say hunger whets the appetite and I can verify that is true, especially with nobody slapping your hand if you reached for more. My companions looked as satisfied as I was. Angel's Refuge had finally provided, even if took death to do so, which I'd always sort of thought it might.

Colin and Billy cleaned up the plates and, shooing me away for which I was grateful, so full I could hardly move. I looked over at Isabella, combing her hair.

"Where'd you put the carpetbag? I want to get a look at Higgins's journal I put in there last night."

She gestured languidly towards the sacks of supplies we'd taken and I found the carpetbag, the journal stuffed down among the money we'd stolen. I walked away towards the creek and sat down under the shade of a rock formation, opening it up.

I didn't know anything about accounting or ledger books, but it didn't take me very long to discover Joanie Higgins's methods. She had three sections, fairly simple: money in, money out were the main two. After all, that was her concern, not the welfare of those she was supposedly caring for. The third section, longer, listed names. I found mine among them, along with many others, where they came from and where they went. It was interesting that she would keep such a damning account of the orphans she took in and that she disposed of. I paged through the book and went back to the accounts. Money out was for food, linens, clothing and services, like Stony and Bob, and supplies, which frankly seemed overly generous in those categories. There were salaries for her and Avery there too. Money in was from saloons, brothels and mines in Arizona and New Mexico as well as a few individual names. There was about the same money coming in as going out, except for one listing that intrigued me in the "out" section: somebody listed as R. MacNeil, in Prescott, Arizona. Whoever this was, he was paid regularly and paid very well. I remembered the conversation Isabella and I had overheard and how Joanie had mentioned his name. MacNeil was the boss of this operation, the man they resented because they had to pay him.

I was comfortably full and warm there in the sun, and I shut the book and closed my eyes, thinking. Whoever MacNeil was, he was making a lot more money than Higgins or Avery did. Maybe he had more than one orphanage where he took in children and sold them when they'd grown enough for his purposes. The more I thought about it, the more unsettled my thoughts became. What kind of a person did this? Joanie Higgins and James Avery were bad enough, but what if there were more just like them, places all run by someone who was even worse?

"Hey, sleepyhead. Let's go for a walk."

For the second time that morning, I opened my eyes to Billy, his blue eyes bright and his quirky smile engaging. I put up my hand and he pulled me to my feet once again.

"Sounds good," I said, and we wandered away from the campsite where I could hear Isabella laughing at some story Francisco and Colin were telling, towards the cottonwoods trees that bordered the creek.

"How you doin'?"

I hesitated just for a second. "Good."

He stopped and pulled me into his arms, holding close. "I think you got somethin' on your mind." I could feel his heartbeat next to mine. "I think I do, too."

We stood there for a minute, and I wrapped my arms around him. It was a good feeling and one I didn't want to end. But it did, because he was right.

"You go first," I said, because I was pretty sure what it was.

"Your friend Isabella. She's a pretty girl, all right." He hesitated just for a second. "But she seems a little angry." He pulled back and held my arms in his hands. "I don't think I've ever seen anyone, 'specially a woman, stab somebody and seem to like it so much."

I couldn't disagree. "I know. But, you have to understand, Billy. We grew up in that awful place and put up with Joanie Higgins and James Avery telling us what to do, beating us, feeding us rotten food and treating us like dirt for years. Isabella's time at Stella's was even worse, having no choice but to be a whore every damn night for every damn man that came in that door. Is she angry? Hell yes, and she's got every right to be. What she did to Higgins was the end result of all of it."

I stared into his eyes. "I shot Elena Alcazar for the same reasons, so Isabella didn't have to, so I can't condemn her. That said, I admit she could calm down some."

Billy sighed. "Well, it's over and done, and can't say they didn't deserve it. Worries me some when people get too bloodthirsty. I've made too many mistakes myself to not see trouble in somebody else. Just thought I'd get that off my chest." He stared into the distance, chewing on a cottonwood twig. Pensive Billy was one I'd not seen before.

"Francisco seems quite taken with her," I said, and took off my shirt. He needed distraction.

"That boy is in love," Billy said, shaking his head. "From the first minute he saw her, there was no stoppin' him." He looked over at me then, for the first time since we'd sat down and grinned. "Can't blame him, because that's how I am about you, Josie. And I know damn well Hiram told you to stay away from me, but it didn't stop you none, did it?"

"No," I said and kissed him. Before I could take another breath, we were laying down beside that creek and had the rest of our clothes off. If anyone came by, we sure didn't hear them.

The sun was at full noon and beating down on us. Billy

propped himself on his elbow. "Josie, I swear I can't get enough of you."

"That's good," I said, and headed for the creek. It wasn't deep but it was enough to wash off in and Billy joined me. We splashed around and even ducked our heads in the shallow water, laughing like the happy children neither of us had ever been. Now was what we had and now was enough.

When we got back to camp, the three of them were counting money. We had the sacks from Stella's and the carpetbag from Angel's Refuge and between the two, they'd made quite a stack, Isabella giggling, and Colin and Francisco both seemed quite happy as well.

"So what's the take?" Billy said and sat down beside them.

"A lot more than I thought," Colin said. "From Stella's, we got around $6,000, but from the orphanage, we hit the jackpot, even though Isabella said you made her leave half of it." He stared balefully at me. "Even with that, it's close to $20,000."

Billy whistled. "Christ, it's like we robbed a payroll train or something. That's a lot of money."

It was a lot more than I thought, too. We were a bit stunned and we'd gotten away clean, at least so far. I didn't know much about robbing people, but I knew that wasn't always the case and sometimes robbers get killed, if not by the people they were robbing, the law got them afterwards. In our cases, we'd done the killing with minimal witnesses at least none left alive, so if we were smart and kept moving, there'd be no law either.

I pulled out the ledger book and held it up. "I want to show you all something. At least half the money Higgins and Avery were taking in at Angel's Refuge went to some man named MacNeil in Prescott."

"Yes," Isabella said, excitement in her voice. "I remember the day we overheard them, Josie. He's their boss, I think."

"Apparently," I said, opening the book. "I've been thinking a lot about this. I think he runs more than one Angel's Refuge. I can't say that for sure, but why would he stop at just one, if you think about it? This needs to stop and I'm pretty sure there isn't anybody within the law who'd make that happen. They pass themselves off as upstanding citizens doing their Christian duty for all those poor children they take in, and the horrible part is, I think Higgins at least thought she was teaching us Christian virtues, even if the only reason was so we'd be able to survive the trials ahead or if we didn't," I looked pointedly at Colin and Isabella, "we'd die thinking Jesus would hold our hands and send us to heaven."

I threw the ledger book into the fire and sparks cascaded before the flames began eating the pages. Colin grabbed it back out, throwing it onto the dirt and stamping out the flames.

"Shit, Josie, we might need that," he said. He was right. Nobody met my eyes and I couldn't blame them.

Billy put his arm around me. "You all right, Josie?" His eyes were concerned and I guess they had a right to be.

"Yes. I'm fine. Just . . . mad is all."

"You got a lot to be mad about, girl."

I looked up into his eyes, so blue it made my heart ache. "I guess I do, Billy Bonney. I guess I do."

We roasted the four remaining chickens so they wouldn't go bad, and boiled potatoes and carrots and had another hefty meal as the sun went down. We packed the rest for the road. After dinner, we passed around the full whiskey bottle Billy had grabbed from Elena Alcazar's nightstand.

"You're a forward-thinking lad, Billy," Colin said and held up the bottle in a toast before passing it to Francisco. "There's more to life than money, eh?"

Darkness fell, and while we talked about a great many things, we still hadn't had a conversation about what to do or where to go next. Restlessness was settling in for all of us, because we couldn't stay still and wait for fate to happen. We had to decide if we didn't want to caught unawares, and nobody knew that like Billy.

Colin laughed and drained the last of the whiskey, throwing

the bottle into the desert. "So we're desperadoes now, don't you think?"

Billy shrugged. "Depends."

"How's that?" Colin said, peering at him owlishly. He was drunk but I was the last one to lay any judgment on him for that, as I was pretty far gone myself. I stared up at the sparks rising from the fire into the night sky as though they were omens that foretold the future.

"Depends on what you want to be," Billy said, staring at Colin. "You got enough money now to hightail it to California with Josie," he glanced over at me, "which was the original plan, since you're both wanted in Arizona. Ain't no doubt about that."

He glanced over to me. "I was sorta thinkin' I'd tag along. You know, start a new life in a new place and all. I'd really like to see that ocean. I hear tell there's whales, spoutin' water way up into the air. You ever seen a whale in New York, Colin? I hear there's an ocean there too. I was born there but I don't remember much."

Colin smiled. "No, I was too busy trying to stay fed back then, whales was the last thing on my mind. Don't know if they even come around there, it's so cold. I hear California is always warm and they even got weird palm trees everywhere. And oranges..." His voice trailed off, eyelids fluttering.

"I think we should go find Mr. MacNeil," Isabella said. "There's man who's got some explaining to do. He's also got some money, and I'll bet Josie's right. If Angel's Refuge wasn't the only orphanage he'd started up, I'd like to find out." She pulled another bottle of whiskey out of the bag she'd carried from Stella's and handed it to me.

"What you think, Josie?"

I uncapped the bottle and took a drink, passing it to Billy. "I think there's some people got a reckoning coming, that's what the fuck I think."

Billy set the bottle down and gazed at us all. "Now, I ain't one to be telling people what to do, never have been. Gets people's gander up, I find. On the other hand, my mama used to chide me for gettin' in fistfights at school with bullies pickin' on little kids. Can't abide that."

He sighed and picked up the bottle, taking a long swig and passing it to Francisco. Billy looked around at all of us and nudged Colin's foot with his boot. Colin's eyes flew open and he stared at Billy.

"What?"

I snickered and he zeroed in on me. "What'd I miss?"

"Not much," I shrugged. "Just a little planning and justifying going on here, and consideration of the wonders of California versus the joyous possibility of bringing yet another rotten human being to justice to account for his sins." Whiskey didn't seem to deaden my ability to talk intelligently, but it may have had a much worse effect on the decisions I made while imbibing it.

"I gotta pee," Colin announced after a long thoughtful pause, and headed into the cottonwoods. Of course he did and it sure wasn't his bladder. I knew him well enough for that. I also knew he'd heard every word we'd said.

"I will go with Isabella," Francisco announced. "She is a woman who knows her mind."

"Huh," Colin said, stepping back into the firelight. "She surely does and it's a bloody one at that. You still got that knife you killed Higgins with, honey?"

Francisco stood up and glared at Colin, fists clenched. This whole discussion was going into dangerous territory and some of it was my fault. I stood up and waved my hands.

"Stop it." I yelled, just to get their attention and I did, miraculously. I stood up, wobbling just a little and I wondered just for a second how I got to be the spokesperson for this decision. "We got two choices here and they're pretty clear. One, we go to California, like we planned all along, and that's probably the best option, in spite of what I said earlier. It's safer, gets us away from the law, and we can start over. That's something we all need." I looked around at my companions and saw I'd gotten their attention so far.

"I know we all been drinking whiskey and thinking about past hurts, but we have to consider what's the best choice for us, vengeance aside. We've done some of that already. Maybe enough of it.

"Second choice, go to Prescott and find MacNeil. Bringing him to justice is silly, since justice doesn't care. Killing him is what we really mean, and maybe going even many steps further, and liberating orphans from other orphanages if we find them, which likely means more killing, no question. They aren't any more likely to say, 'Oh I'm sorry, please give these children a good life, will you?' than Joanie Higgins was. Some of us, like me, Colin and Isabella, have a stake in that. Francisco and Billy do not. So that's our choices, my friends. You want to sleep on it, or do a vote now?"

"We sleep on this and have the same choices in the mornin' along with more discussion, and that likely wastes another day, which I don't think we can afford. People might be comin'. I say vote now," Billy said. "Then we can decide if it's all in, or not, and be ready for tomorrow."

He stared at me and I met his eyes. I couldn't tell which option he was leaning towards and I wished with all my heart that I could. Billy wasn't a come-along guy. He went his own way, I knew that from the beginning. But then there was me, and I knew that he thought some differently than he had.

I sat down and grabbed the whiskey bottle.

The vote didn't take very long. The way north to Prescott was much longer but that's where we went and at the end, there weren't any goddamn whales.

CHAPTER 16

"Good god, I didn't think it was this far."

Isabella walked beside me into the brush, rubbing her backside. We'd been riding for days, heading north and I was heartily sick of her whining, since the whole damn thing had been her doing in the first place. Well, not entirely if I was being completely honest. I'd like to see MacNeil get what was coming to him too, as would Colin, but dragging Billy and Francisco into our revenge raid didn't seem quite fair. Still, people did that for people they loved, I guess. At least they did in stories and it seems those stories weren't wholly made up, since here we were. That didn't change the fact that I'd like to stop up Isabella's mouth with a tight bandanna and a wad of cornmeal. I knew I wasn't alone and even Francisco rolled his eyes sometimes when he didn't think anybody was looking. Lord, that girl could talk, and I wasn't very happy about most of the words coming out of her mouth. I wasn't alone.

"What, the creek or Prescott?" I said, pulling down my britches.

"Prescott, of course, don't be stupid," Isabella said, doing the same. "Josie, I swear you are getting cranky with me. Tell you the truth, I'm tired of that, too."

She finished and pulled up her pants but before she could fasten them up, I shoved her into the dirt, straddling her.

"Shut up, Isabella. Just shut up."

Shocked, she stared up at me, her eyes wide.

"I don't want to listen to your complaining for one more minute, and neither does anybody else. We're going to do what we decided to do. Nobody said it was going to be easy. I know you didn't have any idea how far away Prescott was, no more than the rest of us, but we're all damn tired of hearing from you."

She started to protest and I tightened my grip on her shoulders. "I'm not fooling around here. You're the only one who hasn't proven herself, 'cept to stab Higgins to death and that was a crazy thing nobody wanted to watch.

"I worry about how you're going to handle yourself once we get where we're going, and so do they." I glanced behind me. "We don't need some loose goose running her mouth and her knife hand. We need a little more grace than that. And everybody's backside is just as sore as yours. Do you understand what I'm saying?"

She nodded, tears running down her cheeks. I didn't think it was regret, it was more plain scared, but I didn't give a damn. I loosened my grip and she sat up, brushing dirt out of her hair.

"Damn, Josie," she sniffled. "You got mean."

I sighed. "No, Isabella. I learned how to survive." I turned her to face me, my hands on her shoulders. "We rescued you, because we knew how, and we didn't have to." I stared at her. "I'm not the same person I was before and I'll never be that girl again. But I learned you have to be smart about it, and that's what I'm trying to tell you. If you don't listen, we're all at risk. Do you hear what I'm saying to you?"

She brushed the tears off her cheeks. "Yes." She threw off my hands. "Yes, all right?"

I stood up, brushing dirt and pine needles off my britches. I wasn't fully convinced but at least I'd gotten my point across for the time being, or at least I hoped so.

We walked back to the boys, hand in hand like we were best friends in the world and Isabella didn't have a word to say, which lately was unusual. Both Billy and Colin looked hard at me and I knew what they were thinking. I smiled sweetly and Colin turned away, a smile twitching on his lips.

"We stopping here for the night, amigos?" Francisco said. "I can start a fire."

"Sounds good," I said, looking at the sun descending into the pine trees. "Prescott can't be all that far away, since we're in the high country. We should be there tomorrow." I sounded like I knew where I was, but I had no more idea than the rest of us.

I wasn't that far off the mark since we rode into Prescott mid-afternoon the next day. We began to pass quite a few farms and ranches the closer we got. One look at Prescott's courthouse square and the prosperous shops and businesses that surrounded it along with the treelined streets and pretty houses set up a longing in my heart, one I didn't quite know how to deal with. *What would it have been like to grow up in a place like this?* I thought, as we passed by laughing children chasing each other around the green grass on the square. If I ever had a child, I'd want this for her, something I'd been cheated of. Hell, I wanted it now, we weren't that far from being those kids ourselves. I glanced over at Colin and Billy, and I could see I wasn't alone. Billy set his face and stared straight ahead and Colin blinked rapidly, busily reknotting one of his reins. No words passed between us and we plodded gamely on, searching for a livery and finding one a couple of blocks from the square. The sign, such as it was, said Prescott Livery. Original.

"Hey there, travelers." The skinny livery man spat a glob of tobacco juice into the straw in the first stall. He needed a bath worse than we did and his eyes were disturbingly close together. "Need a place for them lovelies you got?"

He held out a grimy paw and Colin leaned over and shook it.

"Justis Pence. I run the best livery in the territory, friends. You've come to the right place."

We got off our tired horses, taking the saddlebags and sacks. Billy handed Pence twenty dollars. "We need 'em fed, brushed and stabled for a couple of nights, *friend.* Know a good hotel close by?"

"Sure do, son, sure do," Pence stammered, quickly pocketing the money. "Try the Palace over by the courthouse, or the Prescott House. They're real nice." He took the reins of two of the horses. "What's the name responsible for these beauties?"

"Billy, uh, Smith," Billy said, giving me a little sideways smile. "You take good care of them, Justis. I'm countin' on you. We'll be real grateful and all."

"Yessir," Pence said, spitting another glob of tobacco juice. We all picked up our baggage, which also contained our guns, and walked back towards the square.

It was a busy afternoon in Prescott. Women walked by carrying baskets, children in tow and wagons were pulled up by the stores, men loading supplies. Like Billy had warned earlier, we had taken off our gunbelts and stowed them, since no guns were allowed in town. Saloons were doing a brisk business, horses tethered outside and music and talk spilling out on the street as we strode by.

"Quite the sweet proper town," Billy said. "What say we stop in and get a drink somewhere?"

I'd braided my hair and stuffed it under my hat, but Isabella looked, well, like Isabella, her dark hair curling around her heart-shaped face. We'd have to do something about that, I mused.

Colin shrugged. "Why not? It's been a long day."

We turned into the next saloon and sat down at an empty table while Billy went to the bar. He returned quickly with a bottle of whiskey and five glasses. He uncorked the bottle and poured, holding up his glass.

"To Prescott."

We drank. Prescott, indeed. We were here for a lot more

than seeing the sights, sweet as they were. Before long, we struck up conversations with some of the other patrons. They were a friendly bunch for the most part, offering lodging advice. The Palace was expensive, as I figured from the name, but the general recommendation was a place called the Range Hotel, catering to cattlemen and such. Well, money wasn't our problem, but we certainly didn't fit in with the suited men and fancy dressed women I'd seen on the streets. Maybe we'd need a day to reconnoiter and get some new clothes before we attempted such genteel digs as the Palace. I nudged Billy with my knee.

"The Range sounds about right for now," I said and he nodded. "I need a bath, some food and a bed. We can take care of the rest tomorrow."

"I was thinkin' the very same thing," he said and threw back the rest of his whiskey. We followed suit, gathered our stuff and headed out.

We followed the directions we'd been given at the saloon. It wasn't far. The Range was a two-story building, and we crowded into the small lobby while Colin walked to the desk and got three rooms. I sidled up to him as he signed the register.

"We need baths," I whispered in Colin's ear, and for another ten dollars, the clerk was eager to arrange for that as soon as possible. He suggested we wait in the restaurant, pointing to an open doorway.

We didn't waste any time on that one. We devoured steaks, potatoes and the best chocolate cake I'd ever eaten, like wolves tearing at a carcass. Truthfully, I'd never eaten chocolate cake before, but damn it was good. I smiled at Colin, my teeth full of chocolate and he grinned back, his teeth the same.

I stuck my toe, covered in soapsuds, out of the bath water and wiggled it at Billy, who was sprawled on the bed. "Get those clothes off, cowboy, before the water gets cold, and hand me a towel, would you?"

"I can do better than that," he said. "Stand up." He held out the towel, arms wide. I stepped onto the wooden floor and he enveloped me in the towel. Meager as it was, it was bigger than anything I'd ever had before and I pulled it around my shoulders. I dried off while he shucked off his clothes and sunk into the tin tub, sighing contentedly. I curled up under the patchwork quilt on the bed and listened to him busily scrubbing himself. We'd none of us had a bath since we left Hiram's, except for the occasional creek. I'd even washed my hair and it was likely going to be a few shades lighter. Desert dust had sunk into every part of my body and soul, it seemed. I'm sure Colin was doing the same in his single room, as were Francisco and Isabella in theirs. That relationship had seemingly been fated the minute they laid eyes on each other. I couldn't fault them for a second, since it seemed Billy and I had been the same, although with a few ups and downs.

I had nearly dozed off when I felt Billy's weight on the mattress beside me. I opened my eyes to find his, wide open and six inches away. He pulled me into him.

"So. Prescott."

"Yes." In the end we'd all voted for it, but I knew his heart wasn't in it. He'd done it for me and I knew I had to make that count. Had to make sure he was safe. This wasn't his fight. For him and Francisco both, they were here because of me and Isabella, and Colin.

I ran my hand down his cheek, and onto his chest. "I know. I owe you." I kissed him. "Just loving you isn't telling you near enough, Billy Bonney, but I'll do the very best I can to show you how much." I threw my leg over him and moved slowly up and down his frame, while he groaned softly and grabbed my hips.

His bright blue eyes bored into mine as his arms clasped me tight. "Ah god, Josie. I don't know if you're the death of me, or just the beginnin' and I don't give a damn, either way."

The sun rose in Prescott like it did everywhere else, slanting in through the flimsy curtains in our room at the Range Hotel. Billy was pulling on his dirty pants and shirt, grimacing.

"Get up, Josie," he said. "We got things to tend to. These

clothes are making me sick. We are outfitting ourselves today and it's past time we did. We sure as hell got the money for it."

We met up with Colin, Isabella and Francisco in the restaurant. We finished our steak and eggs, drinking two pots of coffee, and the place started to fill up. We paid the bill and wandered out to the street. How we were going to find MacNeil without attracting attention to ourselves was worrisome. You can only sit around in saloons asking questions for so long before somebody gets curious but we had another pressing concern this morning. Businesses were opening, and a store that displayed clothes and hats in the window caught my eye.

In we went and within an hour, we emerged, looking like upstanding citizens or at least clean-living ranchers from the area. We damn near bought the place out and the storekeeper was delighted. Billy and Colin explained we'd been caught in some range war north of here, barely escaping with our lives and needed to outfit ourselves top to bottom. He was more than happy to oblige.

Isabella and I had opted for some skirts that had a split that allowed us to ride, a new innovation according to the shopkeeper, along with shirts and two pairs of pants each in case that didn't work out, much to his disapproval. It was so good to have clothes that were clean and fit me, truly mine for the first time. I felt like I was becoming the person I'd always wanted to be, even if I'd taken a road slicked with blood to get there.

The boys fared just as well. New pants, shirts and jackets and in Colin's case, boots that fit him for the first time since he'd been in the west. Given his New York city background, I thought maybe they might be the first time any boots had fit him, let alone clothes. He grinned at me, stomping onto the boardwalk outside the store.

"Great boots you got there, Colin," I said. "Like 'em?"

"Shit, yeah," he said, pulling me into a twirl. "You look pretty nice yourself, Josie."

I did too and I knew it. My newly washed hair spun around

my face as did my twill skirt, inches above my boots, the ones Hiram had given me. I still wore my hat from Mule Gulch. Billy smiled at us and took my hand as we continued down the board-walk. We were ready to take on Prescott now. All we had to do was find MacNeil.

It didn't take long.

CHAPTER 17

Prescott this fine morning looked much like it had the previous day. Shopkeepers were sweeping off the wooden boardwalks in front of their stores, the bank was doing a brisk business, and I'd heard the schoolhouse bell ring while I was trying on clothes. We nodded hello to one and all, feeling quite happy with ourselves, all bathed, fed and clothed. It felt like we could even have a life here, if we kept our heads down, but I knew that was a sad illusion. Colin and I both had wanted posters out for us, and if they weren't here in Prescott yet, they would be. Billy had a issues on that score as well. Our appearance had changed some and I usually tucked my hair under my hat and passed for a boy. But still, once news of the killings at Stella's worked its way northwards, Isabella was likely to be wanted, at least for questioning, since she'd conveniently disappeared.

That fact in particular had been worrying me. With that distinctive face and hair she stood out like a flame among ashes and all it would take was one person to recognize her or see a poster for any of us and we were all at risk.

We passed by a barbershop and I grabbed Isabella's hand and pulled her inside. The place had two chairs, both empty at the moment. The air reeked of bay rum and big mirrors sat on the wall in front of the chairs. The proprietor gaped at us and then grinned.

"Ladies, I think you've come to the wrong establishment," he said, smoothing his white apron over his ample belly. "I shave and cut gentlemen, or at least what passes for it." He laughed uproariously at his own joke and I giggled obligingly.

"Sir, I understand that," I said, smiling sweetly as I could. "But my sister here has a problem we were hoping you could help us with. We'd be happy to pay double your usual rate."

"For what?"

"A haircut, sir," I said and squeezed Isabella's hand hard when she gasped. "See, my sister here is looking to get away from a cattle rustler who's taken a fancy to her. If that beautiful hair wasn't on display, we might have a chance to slip away from him." I let a tear slip down my cheek. "It could mean the difference between life and death, sir."

He eyed us like we were foreign creatures that had somehow crossed his threshold. "Well, I don't think I can help you, and besides, that could spell some trouble for me. So, no."

"Forty dollars help you with that trouble?"

He blinked. He probably didn't make that in two weeks. He whisked out a clean white towel and shook it.

"Set the little lady down right here," he said, pointing to the closest chair.

Isabella hissed at me like a goose who eggs I was trying to steal. "Damn you Josie, I don't want my hair cut."

"Maybe not," I whispered. "But if you care about Francisco and the rest of us, you know I'm right. Besides, you're still beautiful. Nothing can change that." I had a few ideas about that as well, most of which included dirt, but that was a topic for another time.

Mollified, she sat down and allowed him to wrap the towel around her neck. It didn't take long. We emerged from the barbershop half an hour later, Isabella looking like delicate-featured teenage boy on his first excursion into town. We would need to get her a hat though. Mine was firmly in place with my braid tucked inside. I'd left the barber his forty dollars although when he'd been engaged in clipping off Isabella's lovely curls, I'd pocketed a straight razor and a nice pair of scissors because after all, fair's fair. Besides, they might come in handy. Billy's hair looked like a haystack most of the time.

The boys were lounging on chairs in front of the shop but sat up and threw their cigarettes into the street. Colin grinned and clapped Isabella on the back. She still looked beautiful, her dark curls framing her face.

"Hey there, Izzy, you sure are a cute-looking young lad. Good thing I prefer ladies or I'd be pledging my undying love, wouldn't I?"

We sat off back down the street in high good spirits. We were having fun, perhaps for the first time as a group, without the aid of campfire whiskey. It was a feeling that I know I hadn't had often in the past, nor, I suspected, had my companions. For that brief moment, we were just young people having a grand time on a pretty morning.

We sauntered down another block, and another brick two story building but this one had a metal sign beside the door. It read "Children's Rescue Services" and below that, "R. MacNeil, President". I'd almost missed it, as had everyone else.

"Stop." I think it was the sharpness of my voice that halted them in their tracks. "See that sign?"

We went to the nearest saloon to discuss our strategy, which wasn't terribly complicated. That sign left no doubt about where our quarry was located. We all agreed Colin seemed the most mature-looking, his six foot frame, sunbleached strawberry blonde hair and handsome face the very picture of the new Western rancher, fresh from the East. We cooked up a story about some orphans from our fictitious range war that needed a home and how he'd heard such good things about Children's Rescue Services that he knew they were the very people to help.

"I like it," Billy said, and poured us another round. "Only I got a suggestion. Josie, you oughta go with him, like his sister. You two look alike, and between all of us, you're the most persuasive bull shitter I've met in a long while."

Everybody laughed at that one, even me, although I didn't think it was all that funny. I'd never thought of myself as dishonest, and Billy's comment stung a bit.

I grabbed the bottle and poured another shot. "Thanks for the compliment, sweetheart. I'll be sure to remember it. You might find your humor cold comfort in nights to come."

Everybody laughed again, except Billy who wouldn't meet my eyes. I took pity on him and kissed his cheek. He perked up but I could tell we'd have some discussion later. Right now I didn't give a shit. We had work to do if we ever wanted to get on with our lives. This whole Prescott venture, new clothes and chocolate cake aside, was starting to give me a headache. I'm not good when I'm worried and I was getting damn worried.

"Let's do it," I said, and pushed back my chair. "Catch his ass before lunch."

We trooped out of the saloon and back to the building with the plaque beside the door which led upstairs. The downstairs was a feed store doing a brisk business, wagons double parked outside.

Billy, Isabella and Francisco wandered down the street, but not too far and Colin and I went up the staircase to the second floor. A short hallway had doors, all inscribed with a business name, but the first one was Children's Rescue Services in gold paint on its frosted glass. Colin opened it an into the lion's den we went.

A small desk with an officious looking man sitting behind it were the sole furniture and occupant. A large bible rested on the desk. The brass nameplate beside it read Mr. Obadiah Jones. Colin stepped forward, clearing his throat.

"Good day to you."

The man looked up, adjusting the spectacles on his nose. "And good day to you as well. How may I help you?"

His hair was slicked back on his balding head and he looked like a suspicious bird as he peered at Colin. His pale face didn't crack a smile.

Colin was magnificent. He smiled and held out his head. "Justin Truegood. I'm from up north a bit. I was hoping you could help us with some orphan children. Everyone says you all are the people to talk to."

Mr. Jones sniffed as though he smelled something going off. "Everyone?"

Colin's smile didn't falter. "Well, some of the people in town and around."

"Hmmm." Mr. Jones shuffled some papers on his desk. "Orphan children, you say?"

"Yes, sir. You see, there was this range war up north and there are three children, ages six to ten, whose parents got killed and they have nowhere to go. I heard you people take children in when they are in dire straits so I was hoping you could help us." He turned to me. "This here's my sister Sally. She's been looking after them best she can, but we're headed to Colorado and we can't take care of them any more."

I smiled sweetly. "Please, sir. We surely would appreciate your help. Those poor children need a good Christian upbringing. They mustn't be allowed to go astray."

Jones stood up, eyeing us up and down. We seemed to pass his inspection. "Wait here." He went through another door behind him, shutting it firmly.

Colin blew out a long breath. "Well, that was interesting. Think we'll get anywhere?"

I patted his arm. "Justin, we're going to be just fine." There had been a flicker of greed in Jones's beady little eyes, one I'd seen often on Joanie Higgins's face.

The door opened and Jones gestured us into the interior office. The well-fed gentleman behind the desk looked twice

Jones's size. His dark hair was cropped short but the odor of the pomade he'd used to tame the curls on top suffused the room. His embroidered waistcoat and the round gold watch tucked halfway inside a pocket gleamed as he leaned back in his chair, staring at us. His eyes were penetrating and even I flinched a bit at his perusal. Jones left, shutting the door with a click.

"I'm Roger MacNeil, Mr. Truegood." He held out his hand, not rising from the chair, and Colin leaned over to shake it.

"Pleased to meet you, Mr. MacNeil. This is my sister Sally, sir," he said, glancing over at me. "We're so grateful for your time and I give praise to the good lord for the safety of these children that need your help."

I nodded and felt MacNeil's eyes crawling up and down my body. I can't ever remember taking such an instant dislike to anyone before but then I hadn't met all that many people in my life. Even so, this man shot to the top of the list.

"We may be able to work something out, Mr. Truegood. Tell me more about these unfortunate waifs."

Colin spun his story about the range war and dead parents while MacNeil busied himself cutting the end of a large cigar and lighting it up. I looked around the office. It was spare, just the desk and the chair MacNeil sat in, with a small bookcase against the wall beside me. There were a couple of side chairs, but he hadn't invited either of us to sit down. A photograph of some children lined up in rows was on one wall, everyone looking stiff and focused at the camera. I couldn't help but take a few steps to make out the writing on the bottom. "Angel's Refuge, Arizona" and I looked closer yet. My own ten-year-old face stared back at me, hair shorn and sticking up in spiky tufts and I remembered the day Joanie Higgins had lined us up outside the orphanage and some man had come and taken our picture. Colin himself was in the back row, taller than most others, and he didn't look all that different than he did at this very moment.

"You're a curious one, aren't you, Sally?"

I started and stepped back to Colin's side. "Sorry, sir, sorry, but I just couldn't help notice the children in the picture. They look so well cared for."

"Of course they are." MacNeil got up from behind the desk and walked over to the frame on the wall. "This is one of our homes for the unfortunates. It's called Angel's Refuge and it's a wonderful place where boys and girls are cared for, educated and groomed for worldly experiences after being brought up with the word of the Lord."

Colin coughed and to me it sounded like he was choking but MacNeil didn't seem to notice. He'd turned his gaze back to me and rested a meaty hand on my shoulder. I'd left my hat with Billy and now wished I hadn't when his hand moved on to caress my hair.

"You two certainly have been well cared for yourselves. Swedish ancestry, perhaps?"

I turned and he dropped his hand, still towering over me. MacNeil was a big man, tall and very well fed himself, unlike the children in the picture before us.

"No sir," I said. "My mother was Dutch and my father's Irish. They've passed on but we're headed for Colorado to live with my uncle Liam."

"Ah." He drew on his cigar and the smoke circled around the room.

I grabbed Colin's hand and squeezed hard. I wish I'd tucked my gun into my pocket this morning or I'd have grabbed that instead and ended this nonsense right here and now. Probably a good thing I didn't.

"That's why we're here, sir, to find a place for these children we can't take with us. I surely do hope you can help," Colin said, shooting me a warning glance. He squeezed my hand back so hard it hurt.

"Well, I think perhaps that can be worked out," MacNeil said, settling back down behind his desk. "I have a lovely children's home not far from here that may have some room. Why don't you check back with me in the morning and we can visit it to be sure it's to your liking. It's called the Sanctuary. It's not far from here, just over in Prescott Valley. I'm sure you're busy preparing for your trip to Colorado, Mr. Truegood. While you're taking care of those arrangements, Miss Truegood here can accompany me to be certain it's acceptable and that problem will be off your mind and you can travel on without a care."

This time it was me that squeezed Colin's hand so hard he winced because I felt the anger emanating from him in red waves. It amazed me that MacNeil didn't pick up on it like a magnet attracting angry iron splinters.

Instead, MacNeil smiled benevolently and stood up. Our interview was over, apparently. We thanked him profusely and assured him I'd be by at ten o'clock the next morning to head to the Sanctuary.

By the time we reached the street and shut the door behind us, Colin was quivering with fury.

"Godammit, Josie, that man is a monster," he spit out. "Besides all the other shit he does, he's planning to rape you tomorrow and likely throw your body to the coyotes. We should kill him today and be done with it."

"Calm down," I said and tried to put the feeling of MacNeil's hand on me out of my mind. "I don't feel any different than you, Colin. If I'd had my gun I would have shot him in the face the minute he touched me. I just don't want us to end up in the Prescott jail, which looks quite substantial. There's a better way."

He stopped and grabbed my shoulders. "If you think you're going with that man on your own, I won't let you do it."

I gently removed his fingers from my shoulders and stepped away. "Colin, I'm not stupid. Trust me. MacNeil will die tomorrow." I stared into his eyes. "The only question is who pulls the trigger first."

I put my hand in his once again and we walked on down the street to meet our friends.

CHAPTER 18

Another bright sunny day full of new promise dawned in Prescott, Arizona. As decided, I was outside MacNeil's office at ten o'clock. The door opened before I could do it myself and Roger MacNeil emerged, smiling. His black suit was immaculate, his cheeks clean shaven and glistening, and he held out his hand.

"Ah. Good morning, Miss Truegood. We have a lovely day ahead of us."

I doubted that but I smiled too. "I'm so looking forward to it, Mr. MacNeil."

"Call me Roger," he said. "We're friends now."

He gestured towards the buggy harnessed to two horses pulled up on the street. "I thought perhaps we would be a little more comfortable in this conveyance than on horseback. After all, you're a tender young lady. While the Sanctuary isn't far, I've found it's always better to travel in comfort when you can. I'm sure you agree."

"How thoughtful." He helped me up the steps and within seconds we were off.

The seat was small, providing space for two people. One of

us was taking up most of the space and my thigh rested beside MacNeil's with nowhere else to go. This was going to be a ride that I'd want to forget.

Within minutes, we'd left the confines of Prescott itself and were headed into open country, pulled efficiently by the two carriage horses who knew their business. It was pretty country, rolling green hills, the vegetation a confusion of cacti and pine trees, the entire landscape seeming to fight for its place, not knowing exactly which to adopt for its own, the high or the low desert.

MacNeil handled the reins expertly but his driving skills weren't my primary concern. I watched him closely. Perhaps we'd been wrong about his intentions towards me but I was wary. I'd learned to smell treachery like a coyote with spoiled meat and to me, he stank of it, fancy suit and bay rum included.

We'd gone maybe four miles when he slowed the carriage and turned to me.

"I was thinking, Miss Truegood," he smiled, "that you might enjoy a spot of early luncheon under the trees there." He gestured towards some cottonwoods that formed a shady enclave, likely near a creek, as I'd learned. "I had my people pack a basket with some refreshments. I find travel to be much more relaxing when you bring the right supplies, don't you?"

I said nothing but smiled at him as he helped me down from the carriage seat. So it was to be here. I surveyed the country-side. There were no dwellings or any other travelers on the road, likely why he'd chosen it. Sometimes people made their own graves in spots that appealed to them.

He picked up a basket from the back of the carriage, along with a blanket, which he carried to the grove, shaking out the blanket and spreading it on the ground in the dappled shade of the trees.

"Miss Truegood, please," he said, settling himself down on the blanket and opening the hamper. "Join me."

"Delighted," I said and settled down on the blanket. It was a nice one, a red plaid. Very festive.

To my surprise, he pulled out a bottle of wine, uncorked it and poured two glasses he unwrapped from the hamper.

"I thought we could use some refreshment. I understand this is a choice vintage," he said condescendingly. "Assuming you are unfamiliar, Miss Truegood, allow me to introduce you to French wine."

How fortunate can a girl be. Although I'd never heard of it before, my first sip of something called *Sancerre* was very nice. It was a good thing I'd filled up on eggs and toast early this morning and was used to whiskey or my head would have been reeling after one glass of that stuff. I have to say it was a most wonderful wine. True to my most virginal role, however, I looked up at MacNeil misty-eyed as he poured me another.

"It's lovely," I said. "I've never had anything quite like it before."

MacNeil smiled. "I'm sure you haven't, but a lovely young lady like you deserves the best." He reached into the basket and produced what he called a strawberry tart, sugar glistening on the berries. I'd never tasted a strawberry before either, but there was no point in not doing so now. We had a little time.

That tart exploded on my tongue and it was the tastiest thing I'd ever eaten in my life. Angel's Refuge didn't specialize in desserts, needless to say, and between this, that chocolate cake, and Mateo's cooking, I knew for certain there was a world of food out there that now I had time to explore, along with a great deal more.

MacNeil seemed to enjoy watching me eat that nearly as much as I did the taste of it. I brushed the crumbs off my skirt, which I'd bought yesterday that came in handy for this occasion.

"Oh, Mr. MacNeil, that was delicious," I said. "How thoughtful you are. Thank you."

He smiled and pulled me gently down on the red plaid blanket and I gave him no resistance. He loosened his jacket and belt buckle, which I pretended to ignore and leaned over me.

"Miss Truegood, you are an enchanting young woman," he said, running his hand over my hair and cheek. "I'm so happy that you've come with me this morning."

He kissed me and I didn't resist. After all, I'm supposed to be an inexperienced young woman, inebriated on wine who is impressed with this influential man to whom my brother has entrusted me.

When his hand ran up my leg and moved my skirt up, I began to protest, as any virtuous young woman would. He shushed me and leaned closer, his voice hoarse.

"It's fine, it's all fine," he whispered, moving his hand reassuringly up and down my thighs. Then he shifted his body over me, his knees separating my legs. "I'm your friend, my dear. Just trust me to know what's best for you."

I pulled my knife from my skirt pocket and stared into his eyes when I pricked the end of it into his neck. His eyes flared wide and he froze.

"No, MacNeil. Trust me to know what's best for you," I said and tensed my hand.

Before I could push it in further, he twisted like a snake and knocked the knife from my hand, and it went spinning into the grass. He moved much faster than I thought he could've, given his age and size and for the first time that morning, I knew I didn't have the upper hand.

He loomed over me, his hand around my throat and his body pinning me down. His voice was a snarl. "Who the fuck are you?"

"Your destiny," I forced out. "I grew up at Angel's Refuge."

"Well, then you should know what you're worth, little orphan." His hand tightened around my throat and I gasped for air as he squeezed much harder. Everything was going dark but I saw Billy behind MacNeil.

"I can tell you what she's worth," Billy said, his gun pressed to MacNeil's head. "The whole world." The pressure around my throat eased but not before the black shadows claimed me.

It was the clink of the shovels against rock that roused me. Colin and Billy were busily digging a fairly large hole.

"Please tell me he's not dead yet," I croaked. I sounded like a frog and I coughed to little avail. "We need him." I propped myself up on an elbow.

Billy dropped his shovel and knelt beside me, pulling me into his arms. He kissed the side of my head.

"Christ, Josie, I don't know why we thought this was a good idea," he said. "We hadn't shown up when we did, that bastard would've killed you, just for spite."

Colin stood beside us, leaning on his shovel and staring at me. "He's sure right about that. Sorry we weren't as close as we should've been." He glanced over at MacNeil's body, laying under a cottonwood tree. "He's not dead." He smiled and it was a terrible smile, especially for Colin. "He's going to have lots to tell us, don't worry about that."

I rubbed my neck. Besides that, I felt fine. "Any more of that French wine around? That was very nice. You guys should taste it." I stood up, holding onto Billy's arm. "And those tarts? Amazing."

I brushed the dirt off my skirt. I could see Billy and Colin exchanging glances. They thought I was delirious or possibly drunk but they couldn't have been more wrong. I knelt down and picked up my knife and crouched down beside MacNeil. Blood ran down the side of his head from where Billy had clubbed him with the butt of his gun. I jabbed my knife into his side and was quickly rewarded with a yip of pain as his eyes flew open.

"Hi there," I said. "Remember me? It hasn't been that long. Here I thought we were friends."

He blinked and jerked upwards, but when I held up the knife, he lay back, panic in his eyes.

"Listen, Miss Truegood, I think you've mistaken my intentions," he babbled. "You and your friends here." He jerked his eyes towards Billy and Colin, then back to me. "Let's just call this a mistake. I can pay you all for your trouble if we just get back to Prescott."

I smiled. "No, Mr. MacNeil. I need something else from you besides your money. Tell me about the orphanages you manage, please. How many and where they are. Can you do that?"

He frowned. "I don't see why you need to know that. What is this?"

"This," I said, "is come to Jesus time, as your pal Joanie Higgins used to say. Tell me what I want to know or," I jabbed the knife into his side again and he screamed, "I'll have to keep doing this. I kind of like it. Do you?"

He tried to swing his fist at me, but it was short lived, since Colin stepped on his arm and Billy loomed up at his other side.

"Quit wasting my time, MacNeil," I said. "You've got none left unless you tell me what I want to know. The orphanages, how many and where?"

I leaned in close, picked his head up and whispered in his ear, where no one but the two of us could hear. "They're going to kill you in one more minute, you stupid man, if you don't tell me what I want to know. I won't be able to stop them. In fact they'll likely make me do it. I'm your only hope."

MacNeil closed his eyes, then opened them and despair was written on his face. "All right. There's four. Angel's Refuge you know. There's another six miles from here in Prescott Valley, another in Globe, and a newer one near Tombstone."

He sagged against my hand and I lowered his head.

"Is that it?"

"Yes," he breathed. "That's all."

"Records? Where can I find those?"

"Obadiah Jones, in my office. He's got them all."

"Excellent." I nodded at Colin and Billy. They both stepped forward but I waved them off.

"You know, Roger, there's something about the scent of bay rum that puts me in a very bad mood." His eyes went wide.

I drew my knife across MacNeil's neck, the crimson line so very satisfying and his eyes so very astonished. There was no need to tell him why because he knew. Justice was just beginning to be served and there was so much more to be delivered, so many lives to be avenged.

I can't say it didn't feel good. "Little orphan" indeed.

CHAPTER 19

We debated for a few minutes on what to do about MacNeil. Since they'd already dug the grave, it seemed a shame to waste it. We unharnessed the horses and turned them loose and left the buggy overturned by the creek. We'd thought about staging an Indian attack, but it wouldn't really work without bodies, and those we didn't have, his or mine. For now, all we needed to do was get back to Prescott and take care of Mr. Obadiah Jones before anyone missed either one of them.

I opened the door of Children's Rescue Services, Colin and Billy behind me. Jones looked up in surprise and pushed his chair back. We were sweaty and dusty from the ride and he couldn't help but notice, his expression wary.

"Miss Truegood," he stammered, "and Mr. Truegood. I didn't expect you back so soon."

"You didn't expect me back at all, Jones," I said. "Funny thing though, here we are."

His face paled and when he reached for the drawer in his desk, Billy leveled his gun at him.

"Don't do it."

Billy kept his gun on Jones while Colin walked around the

153

desk and opened the drawer, taking out the pistol inside. He gave a hard shove onto the chair and Jones's head hit the wall behind him.

"What do you want? I didn't do anything. I'm just a clerk. I got nothing to do with anything," he whined, blood dripping onto his starched shirt collar. He put his hand up and jerked it back, looking at it in horror. I think he would've kept babbling forever but we didn't have the time or inclination.

"Files, Mr. Obadiah Jones. We want the files on all the orphanages. Just give them to us and we'll take up no more of your time," I said. "Mr. MacNeil said you could help."

He wasn't a smart man but he was smart enough to know he was going to die if he didn't give us what we wanted. He gestured towards a cabinet on the far wall and I opened it to find file drawers, full of neatly labeled folders. Angel's Refuge, The Sanctuary, St. Mary's Hope, and Lambs of the Lord. Behind each of the primary folders were financial records and much more, but those I left behind. They were damning, I was sure, but all I was concerned with in the little time we had was the primary information on each of the orphanages MacNeil ran. A brief look at Angel's Refuge told me the place, proprietors and number of children, and that's all we needed to find the rest of them, as the rest were likely the same.

Hopefully, although I wasn't counting on it, law enforcement of some sort would find these and know what monsters MacNeil and his assistant Jones were, along with everyone that ran these horrid places. Maybe there would be some sort of exoneration for us in that event, but for now we had what we needed.

I threw open MacNeil's office door and found a leather briefcase I'd noticed the day before. I shoved the files into it while Billy and Colin kept Jones at bay. I turned to the boys.

"Got what we need. Let's get out of here."

"What do you want to do with him, Josie?" Billy said, jerking his gun at Jones. Colin looked at me expectantly as well. When did I become the queen of this group? I guess I missed that part.

I thought it over. I didn't have any particular grudge against Obadiah Jones. Then again, he'd been MacNeil's assistant in this nasty business for a long time from the look of things. And, if we left him alive, he'd call he law down on us within minutes. He'd made his choices in life impelled with lots of money long ago. There really wasn't much of a decision to be made unless we were sentimental and silly enough to make the wrong one. I didn't want to kill him, I'd had enough of that for today, but I knew there was no choice.

"Shoot him."

They both stared at me while Jones continued to whimper. Billy held his pistol skyward but Colin had no such compunction. He shot Jones in the head, looked at me and nodded.

"Let's get the hell out of here," Colin said. And so we did before anybody showed up to investigate. Prescott seemed like the kind of town where someone would so we took the back stairs.

I burst into Isabella and Francisco's hotel room. "Get your stuff, we're leaving," I said. "Now."

They didn't ask any questions or waste any time once they took a good look at my face, and we met up at Justis's livery and got the rest of our horses and gear. I regretted leaving the relatively soft bed but I didn't regret anything else.

We took the same road towards Prescott Valley we'd traversed earlier, passing by MacNeil's grave without any mention, just a look exchanged between me, Billy and Colin. We rode on until twilight and made camp in a secluded little valley hidden among some sycamore and cottonwood trees, surrounded by a rock outcropping, almost like a small fort. It felt like a safe spot.

We made a meal from our replenished supplies including some canned peaches Francisco and Isabella had bought at the store that morning. They had anticipated something like what had happened and I was very glad they had.

"These are good," I said, wiping the juice from my chin, as

everyone else nodded and did pretty much the same. Needs satisfied, and escape momentarily accomplished, we filled them in on the events of the day.

The sky turned purply-black and stars began to pop out and still we sat around the fire, propping ourselves up on saddles, knees and even rocks. I leaned back on Billy's side. After Colin finished, for a time silence reigned in the clear desert night.

"Josie," Isabella said and reach for my hand, folding it into hers. "What do you want to do?"

I looked around at the rest of them. "It's not just what I want to do. We all need to think about that. We might get away with Prescott, and even Angel's Refuge, but we're leaving a trail." Billy nodded. "Even if we think we're not. Somebody's going to figure this out, it's just a matter of time and one smart sheriff. On the other hand, maybe we'll get lucky." I smiled, with no trace of humor. "That hasn't been my experience so far, not without bloodshed."

Colin reached for another biscuit, blowing on his fingers. "Important people have to know about MacNeil and his operation. Likely they been paid off, law wise. But is it worth it for them to go after his killers? And if we go after more orphanage managers, how many until they decide it's their civic duty to do something about it?" He chewed on the biscuit, raising his eyebrows and gazing at the rest of us. "I'm not so sure leaving Prescott so quickly was a good idea, even. It sort of points the finger at us."

Francisco, who'd been fairly quiet for days now, gave a raspy laugh. "I can set your mind at rest on that point, *amigo*. When we passed the jail and the post office this afternoon, there were some brand new wanted posters inside and out." He took a long pull on the tequila bottle we'd been passing around. "I think the timing was good, *claro*?"

Billy shot up from where I'd been leaning on him. "What you saying, friend? Why didn't you say something earlier? Who was on those wanted posters?"

Francisco didn't even blink, I'll give him that. "You, for one. Five hundred dollars for "Billy the Kid", does that sound familiar?"

"Shee-it." Billy stomped his feet and turned around in a circle, still stomping. "Those damn posters are getting everywhere now."

I'd never seen him like this before, but then I didn't know he was wanted even in Arizona, either. I'd thought all this time it was just me and Colin. Hiram had warned me so I couldn't blame anybody but myself. Truthfully, I didn't much care. I'd done just as bad, likely worse, considering.

I stood up and put my arms around him. He was shaking from anger and whatever else brewed inside him. "Calm down. Nothing we can do about it."

He glared at me, but sat back down, seething. I passed him the tequila bottle.

"Who else, Francisco?" I said.

"You, for murder, and Colin too, along with horse thieving. Likenesses were pretty good, except for Billy's. His looked like some *cabron* been out in the desert too long."

Jesus, I thought. *Looked like we hadn't gotten away with shit. Likely Mule Springs and even Stella's, from the sound of it. God knows what they'd make of our activities in Prescott. Maybe the leftovers we'd missed from the ranch raid were having their revenge. My regret about killing Jones was fading quickly. We'd been moving fast but living on borrowed time, time we didn't know we'd been lucky to have.*

"They didn't have Isabella or me," Francisco said somewhat apologetically. "Guess they figured I was just some drifter Mexican and she was kidnapped and killed, like a lot of those girls." He realized what he'd said the minute the words left his mouth, and put his arm around Isabella, kissing her cheek. "*Lo siento, my amor.*"

Billy was silent, thinking rapidly, I could tell. I sort of felt like getting on a fast horse and riding until I hit the ocean but I shook that thought out of my head. We'd gotten this far and we had a mission, or at least we had once. Now I didn't know what direction to go. Billy put his hands on my shoulders, his fingers clenching. I felt his lips touch the top of my head.

"I got to get back to New Mexico and sort this shit out," Billy said, "or I'm a dead man. They'll never leave me alone, especially that damn Garrett. He'll go anywhere, even California, and I know it's him pushing this here." I felt my heart lurch. I'd only just found him and I didn't want to lose him now.

Colin snorted. "Sounds like you're not the only one. They're onto us quicker than I thought they would be." He stared at me. "Us orphans," he glanced over at Isabella, "we have some thinking to do. You want to raid orphanages like some fucking avenging angels, or should we be smart and head for those whales and palm trees before even there isn't far enough?"

"Isabella?" I said. She'd been staring at the fire like it held the secrets of life. She looked up, the flames reflecting in her dark eyes. A night hunting owl hooted above our heads and the plaintive sound echoed against the rocks.

"I can only speak for myself," she said. "You all sacrificed a lot, saving me. Joanie Higgins was one, but there's more like her, and a lot more kids like me and Josie and Colin who will go on to even more miserable lives than the ones they already have. MacNeil was the head of the snake, but parts of it still live and they could be even worse . I never thought I'd have the chance to do anything about that, but you all gave me that second chance. I'm going to take it, with or without you."

She walked away into the trees and Francisco followed, like I knew he always would. I looked at Colin and he met my eyes, his face somber. He stared at Billy.

"Billy," he said, "I understand what you have to do, and I know this isn't your fight anymore, if we go on with it. It's Josie's, mine and Isabella's. We been pretty slapdash so far and things have gotten a little out of hand, especially back there at the Refuge and Prescott. I'm sorry."

Billy shrugged. "We do things sometimes we ain't thinking

right about. Sometimes we think about them way too much and that leads to trouble, too." His arms tightened around me. "I never thought I'd feel this way about somebody," he put his head against mine, "but I do and I can't change that. I can't change what I've done in the past, neither. None of us can. But I got a friend has a ranch near Lordsburg who maybe can talk to the Governor again. I shot two men getting out of Lincoln but I didn't have no choice. He's got to understand that. If I go on with you all right now, it'll lead you down an even darker path, and that's one I been down already. They're offering a lot of money for me now and they won't quit. You'll go down with me if I can't stop this so I need to give it one more try. I don't want that for you, and I sure don't want it for Josie."

I'd never heard Billy talk about himself this long before. I thought my heart would burst. I swung around and looked at him. "I'm already on that dark path, Billy. I know you haven't been happy about what we've done but you've been right there with us at every minute, taking care when you could, because that's who you are."

I turned back around and stared at Colin. "You want to go on with this, no matter what? We're looking to get killed if the law follows us, you know that? How bad you want revenge anyway?"

Colin shook his head. "It's not revenge, Josie. It's justice for those kids, kids just like we were, so they don't end up in a whorehouse or killing people to survive. They deserve better and if there's a chance we can do that for them, I have to take it. I'm with Isabella on this. You have to do what you think is right."

I couldn't dispute a word he'd said. I'd gone this far and I wasn't giving up now. I couldn't.

I sighed, just a little. "Justice it is, then. But we're going to have to get smart, not just lucky."

I felt Billy stiffen against my back and then put his arms around me. He'd known exactly who I was from the first minute we saw each other, and he wouldn't have done anything different if he were me. We were the same that way.

"All right then," Colin said softly. "See you in the morning." He took his bedroll and walked slowly into the trees.

Billy and I laid our blankets down beside the rocks, the fire dying. Isabella and Francisco had silently picked up their own bedrolls and made their own camp back in the trees as well.

I kissed him gently and he responded like I'd struck him with lightning, his mouth on mine, then my throat, his hands moving over my body, pulling my skirts off. We made love like two starving people, hungry for each bit of skin and sensation we could taste and feel on each other. He hugged me to him at the end as though if he just held on, nothing would ever change, and I clung to him with the same intensity, but the tears on my cheeks told me it already had. I looked at the night sky studded with stars and watched one streak across the expanse. *It got loose,* I thought, *just like I had. I wondered what happened to a falling star.*

"I know you and I know why you do what you do, just like me. Something inside us, I don't know what, but we're the same that way. That's why I love you, Josie Fallon." Billy pulled me close.

I ran my hand through his hair. "No more than I love you, Billy Bonney."

I meant it and he did too.

Then.

CHAPTER 20

We gathered at first light around a small fire, sipping coffee and eating Francisco's biscuits stuffed with some ham Isabella had picked up before leaving Prescott. Between waking, dressing and the usual ablutions, nobody had much to say.

"Listen," Billy put down his cup. "I gotta leave for New Mexico and make things straight down there. They don't have much on me as far as anything we done here so far, and I want to keep it that way, for all our sakes." He looked at me, then gazed at everyone else. "I got a reputation, I guess and it won't do no good for the rest of you to be connected to that." He laughed and it turned into a cough. He shook his head and sipped some coffee. "You got enough trouble as it is, 'specially my girl here." He put his hand on my shoulder.

I couldn't disagree with that, nor could Colin, who'd done a lot of the shooting since this whole mess started. Billy had been the planner and the quickest to draw, saving us many times but not the first to kill. That dubious honor would go to us orphans, Isabella included. I looked over at her and her face, as usual, was as devoid of any emotion as a pretty glass plate. Colin raised any eyebrow, looked at me and shrugged. Looked like I'd have some work to do there.

Surprisingly, Colin stood up and came around to Billy, embracing him. "I'll miss you, man. I've learned a lot from you and I plan to use it, keeping her," he glanced down at me, "and everyone else safe. We all have to do the things we have to do. When it's done, we'll be together again. California and those whales aren't something we can pass up, my friend."

When Francisco and Isabella followed suit, murmuring things in Billy's ear that even I missed most of, my eyes were beginning to tear. Billy was like our guide, our leader and always knew what to do in any situation, even though he wasn't all that much older than we were. We trusted him, and I loved him. Being without him felt like a piece of me had been torn away but I respected his choice and knew he had to go. I sat as still as a statue through all of it, not trusting myself to say a word. I'd said them all last night anyway.

We doused the fire, packed and readied the horses. Before Billy climbed on his, I stood beside him and the others took some distance, thoughtfully. I flung my arms around him and he held me just as tight.

"You come back to me, Billy."

"I will, Josie, I promise. You and I have a future, girl." He smiled down at me. "From the first minute I saw you, I knew that," he propped his finger under my chin, "and you did too, much as you tried to ignore it back then." He smiled and I thought my heart would break.

"I'll get this business wrapped up, one way or another. I'll meet you all right back here in this same spot in a month, how's that? We need to stay out of towns much as we can from now on, especially after you all get done with your business further south. We can't afford to be hanging around down there."

I kissed him. "You better be there."

He grinned. "Only thing that'll stop me is if I'm in jail, and then it'll just take a little longer."

I didn't watch him ride away in the opposite direction from us. We were headed to the Sanctuary to do some business. I hope his turned out as well as we hoped ours would.

❧

PRESCOTT VALLEY WAS A BIG PLACE, WITH NO TOWNS, JUST occasional ranches and farms here and there. By noon, we hadn't come across anything that resembled Angel's Refuge or any houses big enough to hold a bunch of children. I was getting irritated.

"Colin, give me that file we took from MacNeil's office," I said, pulling beside him. "Let's take a break."

We stopped, giving the horses a break and munched on some bread and cheese. I looked at the file on the Sanctuary. There was no address, just a route number, the road we were on already. Maybe it was time to ask around. We stopped at the next farm we came upon. I went up to the door, braving the barking dog and knocked. A young woman answered, a baby on her hip.

"Hello," I said brightly. "Hoping you could help me find the Sanctuary, a children's house?"

She looked at my companions and then at me as though I'd grown two heads. "I ain't never heard of such a thing." She slammed the door.

Well. Maybe the next place.

Two miles later, we tried again. This time, we sent Isabella to the door. It slammed just as quickly. This was going to be a long day.

The next place was bigger, a horse ranch from the look of it. We rode in between fence rails that kept in maybe a dozen or more nice-looking horses. I went up to the porch and knocked on the door of the substantial adobe and beam house. This time a man answered, hatless but weathered-looking. He smiled.

"Hey there. I'm Ham Sturgis. Help you?"

This was a pleasant surprise. I smiled back. "Hi, sorry to

disturb you, Mr. Sturgis. I'm looking for a place called the Sanctuary, a children's home. You know of it?"

He eyed my companions and seemed to come to a decision, stepping out onto the porch. "Well, seems I do."

Progress. "I'm glad to hear it. Is it near here?"

"Yes. So I've heard." He looked at me carefully. "Once in a while, we've had a kid show up here but they always come to take them back. It's an orphanage, so they say, but godalmighty those kids are skinny."

I knew when to keep my mouth shut. I pushed my hat back a bit and waited.

"Not much of one, you ask me, but then nobody ever has."

I stared at him. "I am asking. And I don't like to see skinny kids either."

He gave me directions, and it wasn't far. I thanked him and as we rode out, he still stood on his porch, the slight smile of satisfaction still on his face. *Thank you, Ham Sturgis, you're a good man,* I thought.

Even without Ham Sturgis, we couldn't have missed the place. It loomed up in the distance, a big two story clapboard house that could've been a twin to Angel's Refuge.

"Christ," breathed Colin. "Another mausoleum just like the one we lived in."

We rode down the trail to the house. A dozen or more children, ranging in age from four to maybe fourteen, were working in the gardens and raised their heads in curiosity as we passed, and we stopped in the yard between a barn and some smaller outbuildings. I glimpsed more of them inside, busy at various tasks. We got off our horses and wandered into the barn, my eyes blinking in the dimness after the bright sunlight outside.

"Hello," I called, but no one answered, the children staring at us like we were from another world. I could understand that, if this place was anything like Angel's Refuge. We never saw hardly any outsiders much less talked to them in all my years there, so I wasn't surprised.

Inside the barn, a little boy looked at me in wonder, leaning on the broom he'd been sweeping out a stall with, and then his eyes got even wider, staring at something over my shoulder.

"What the hell you think you're doing?"

That was a voice I'd never thought to hear again and I whipped around, as did Colin, his hand on his gun. Stony Logan stood three feet behind us. Francisco slid silently into the gloom of an empty stall and Isabella stood with her back to Stony, staring into the barn, but her right hand gripped the gun hidden in a fold of her skirt. She knew that voice as well as I did. I never knew exactly what it was Stony did for Higgins and Avery, but I knew it wasn't anything good. He was the enforcer and took care of any problems. He would come and go frequently and now I realized he probably did the same for the other orphanages as he'd done for Angel's Refuge.

"Well, well. Didn't think I'd ever see the two of you again," Stony drawled. "Quite the desperadoes aren't ya?" He didn't seem in the least afraid of us, no matter what he may have heard. "Here because you want to come back into the fold?" He laughed, but the shotgun in his hand never wavered. "Might be a tad late for that, kids. You been pretty naughty."

"Fuck you, Stony," Colin spat. "If you were half as smart as you think you are, you'd put that shotgun down right now. Times have changed."

Stony laughed. "No, son, they haven't. Put your guns down on the ground. Who's your friend?" He gestured towards Isabella. "Turn around, honey."

She did and shot him in the leg. Isabella hadn't had a lot of practice. Stony fell, the look of disbelief on his face priceless, and the shotgun dropped onto the ground. I quickly snatched it up. Isabella smiled and stood over him.

"Remember me, Stony? The girl you raped in that wagon while the other girls watched on the way to my "new life"? Been waiting to see you again, since you made such an impression."

She looked up at Colin and me. "Any objection?"

We both shrugged.

Isabella was a much better shot up close.

The back door of the house slammed shut and I heard the bolt shoot home. This entire encounter was not going quite as well I'd hoped. Francisco came out of the barn and shooed the children from the gardens inside, and they were only too happy to go, eyes wide with shock. He shut the doors and looked at me and Colin.

"The *ninos* are out of harm's way. Now what, *amigos*?"

"The house. Stony's not the head of this place," I said. "Whoever is, they're inside and now they're very aware we're here and we're not friendly. Stony wasn't here by accident."

Colin nodded. "Front door?"

I shook my head. "I'm sure it's locked by now, too. Maybe we ask for a talk?"

He shrugged. I started towards the front porch when a bullet knocked my hat into the dirt. I crouched and ran back towards the barn, as did the others. So much for a chat. Another shot ricocheted off the barn door. This one came from a second floor window and I was pretty sure the first one had too. I was reluctant to shoot back for fear of hitting one of the children but Colin wasn't. He waved his hat around the corner of the barn and when another shot rang out, he shot back and we heard a cry from inside the house.

That was enough for me. Next thing you know, we were going to shoot some kid. I put my hand on Colin's arm. "Hey," I yelled. "We just came to talk. Stop shooting at us and maybe we can do that."

"Go to hell," a woman's voice yelled back. "You killed Stony."

"We didn't have a choice," I said. "But you do. Make the right one before anybody else gets hurt."

Minutes passed. No more shots and at last I heard the bolt shoot back and the back door opened. A bearded stout man stepped out, a shotgun in his hand, but lowered. A woman lingered behind him, her arm wrapped in a bloody bandage.

"Who are you and what do you want?" the man said. "We're just a children's home. We ain't got no money. You lookin' to rob people, you come to the wrong place."

I stepped out from behind the barn, and Colin, Isabella and Francisco slowly followed. The woman whispered something in his ear and the man's hand tightened on the shotgun.

"You Josie Fallon?" he said.

"Yes," I said and held up my left hand when he raised the shotgun. "Don't."

He hesitated and lowered it. "We heard about you."

"Well, I can see that. But maybe we can talk this out."

"Maybe."

Colin wasn't having it. "Throw that damn gun out here, right now. You too, lady, cause I can see that rifle in your other hand behind your skirts. There isn't going to be any more talking if you don't do that."

They hesitated, I'll give them that. But in the end, they both raised their guns and we shot them right there on the porch. Goddamn, people can be stupid.

❧

THEY WERE MARRIED, OR SO THE CHILDREN SAID. MARY AND Joshua Wiggins. We buried them out behind the barn, along with Stony and nobody mourned at their gravesides, none of the twenty-three children here at the Sanctuary, from four to sixteen. Truthfully, I'd been hoping the Wiggins's weren't the same as Higgins and Avery, but that was a feeble hope and I was quickly learning most hopes were only fairy wishes. Maybe we'd have better luck with the next two places. Right now, we had other problems on our hands, twenty-three of them, to be exact. At Angel's Rest, we'd been in a hurry and I hoped those kids had fared all right, but I didn't intend to leave here before I made sure, this time. It was one thing to liberate, but leaving them worse off than they were wasn't what we'd come to do.

We corralled them all in the yard, after searching the house. Some of the little ones had been hiding in closets or under beds and it broke my heart. Colin, Isabella and I talked to them about growing up just as they had, and what we'd done, leaving out the bad parts but what we'd done here was difficult to get around. After an hour, most of them still looked at us like we were about to shoot them as well. If there's anything an orphan will never have, it's trust in authority. One of the older boys whispered something to the girl beside him. She wore an apron and clearly worked in the kitchen, her hands reddened and her hair lank and smelling of grease. For all that, she was pretty but her eyes were hostile, although she'd had nothing to say so far. Few of them had.

"That's a sad tale you're telling and I guess we got no choice but to listen," she said. "What makes you any different from them?" She gestured towards the barn. "Besides, you ain't no older than me."

I sighed. Up until now, we'd left out the worst parts, but there was no getting around it now.

"What's your name?" I said.

"Wanda," she eyed me suspiciously. "Least that's what they told me. I was little when I got off that train."

I sighed. I'd heard this story before. "Wanda, in another year, if we hadn't come today, you'd be on your back in some brothel, meeting at least ten new friends every night. Your pal there," I gestured to the boy beside her, "would be working a pickaxe in somebody's silver mine until he got so worn out he wasn't any good for them anymore. Some of these others, like this guy here," I ruffled the hair of the hair of the smiling towheaded kid with cornflower blue eyes sitting in front of me, "would be a toy for someone with no good intention and games he wouldn't like to play. That is what these people do. Correct me if I've got it wrong and you get letters from your friends about how wonderful their lives are. I'd bet my life you don't."

Her face reddened and she looked down, mumbling something.

"What?"

"I said, you're right." Murmurs of what sounded like agreement wafted through the gathered children but we had more work to do. Colin stood up and held out his hands. The afternoon sun was low on the mountains beside us.

"Listen. We all got decisions to make and people to take care of. Let's get some food going and we'll talk more. You're safe, from us and from anyone outside of here. Come on."

We spread out, Isabella, Colin and Francisco organizing the kids inside and out and I headed to the kitchen with Wanda and three of the other older girls. Unlike Angel's Refuge, there were no outside workers at the Sanctuary. The older girls were in charge of the kitchen and food supplies, which were much better than the diet we'd been fed at the Refuge, or at least we certainly made sure this meal was. An hour later, we all sat down at two long tables to chicken stew, biscuits and vegetables from the garden. They even had two milk cows and made cheese.

One of the girls, Marianne, had made four apple pies from the orchard, another thing we'd never had at Angel's Refuge, and they were delicious. We all felt better, sitting back in our chairs, while the younger children went outside to play before full dark fell. Wanda and the older boys and girls watched us carefully but stayed in their chairs.

Colin and I talked privately for a few minutes and came back into the dining room. He'd looked through the office and discovered the money which now wasn't going to MacNeil or anybody else. We didn't need it, but these kids did. I could tell they were apprehensive and it made me sad. Hopefully, a new day was coming.

"Here's the plan, if you want it. Some of you may want to move on and see the world, which of course, you can. No one will stop you."

Glances were exchanged.

"However, here's another plan. This place has no overseers now, and no one will show up to tell you what to do or rule you anymore. Now, it's yours. It's got resources – ample gardens, livestock, an orchard, water, everything for a successful farm just as it sits and is self-sustaining. You're already doing all the work, from what I can see and from what I've heard today. Prescott's not that far, and you've got horses and a wagon to get whatever you need. Those kids out there," I pointed to the windows where we could see the kids playing hide and seek outside, "have nowhere to go, same as you. They need a home, a place to grow up without fear and with people who care. People like you. It's all yours if you want it, for as long as you want it. It's an opportunity most people are never going to have but a big responsibility, too. We're going to take a walk outside now. You talk it over and decide what you want to do."

We left and went to sit on the front porch. Isabella and Francisco lit thin cigars, their favorite, the fragrant smoke making patterns against the pale lilac light. Colin passed the whiskey bottle around. God knows we'd earned it.

"Good speech there, Josie," Isabella said, blowing smoke into the dusk. "I mean it. I couldn't have done it. I don't give a damn about anybody anymore but I like that you do, honey. Maybe you learned something from all those goddamned bible lessons after all."

I hadn't. What I did learn is not to leave people without a chance at a future if I could help it. It made me feel a little better about killing people who didn't want them to have one. Billy would have liked it, I knew.

I smiled in the darkness.

"Hey, Isabella, you got any more of those cigars?"

CHAPTER 21

We left the next morning at sunrise. Nearly all the children waved goodbye as we rode out and we waved back. Most of the older kids had decided to stick it out and take care of the little ones, or so they'd said, and I believed them. They were nice kids, despite the place they'd grown up in. From what they'd told us, it wasn't as bad as Angel's Refuge had been in most respects: no bible lessons, no beatings and better food. On the other hand, Mr. Wiggins had been free with his hands and Mrs. Wiggins had turned a blind eye and been quick with a strap. But all that was over now. I felt good about this, like this time we'd done some good along with the bad.

"So where's Globe?" Colin said as we reached the end of the drive.

"Hell if I know," I said. "Southeast and we'll figure it out as we go. I got a map back in Prescott, so we'll take a closer look tonight. For now, turn left."

It was rugged country, going down off the Rim, as they called it. We decided to bypass Phoenix and any law complications. We didn't run into anyone but a few wagons and an occasional stagecoach and four days later, we were east of most towns and only ran across a ranch or two. We were running short of supplies but we could see lights in the valley below, rimmed with high hills when we made camp that night. If that was Globe, we'd find out in the morning and we were in no hurry.

I missed Billy. The days without him left me feeling like there was a hole inside me. He understood me like nobody ever had and I was pretty sure it was the same for him, but different. He'd been at this on your own thing longer than me but had dealt with it earlier. I hadn't realized how angry I'd been until I'd had the occasion to put it into practice and I'd scarcely taken a breath since, except for the time at Hiram's horse ranch, which had only taught me how to refine it, much to Hiram's regret, I knew. Not that Hiram hadn't done much the same in his past, but still. I always was a quick learner. Even Joanie Higgins had known that. Now I needed to refine it further. No more impulse and much more contemplating. No more reacting, and much more planning. That's how it had to be, because it wasn't just me. It was Colin, Isabella and Francisco and a lot of children that were depending on us.

Sometimes at night when I looked at the stars in the midnight blue sky above me before my eyes closed I wondered how I'd become the leader of this pack of wolves, maybe heading them into perdition. *I'm sixteen years old,* I silently screamed at those stars and they shone down with icy unforgiving glares. *"You're Josie Fallon,"* they said, *"you wanted this. Figure it out."*

They were right. I would.

"Shit," Isabella said. "We're out of coffee. Everybody only gets one cup and that's it." She looked across the valley. "That better be Globe, or at least someplace with a store." She glared at the coffeepot like it could magically produce more. She did like her coffee. Probably those years at Stella's, I thought, and couldn't begrudge her. You'd probably need a lot of coffee to get your morning going in a whorehouse. We'd had a few conversations about what our lives had been like since we'd been apart but she wasn't the Isabella I'd known. She was harder, angrier than even I was, and as I'd come to see, impetuous and merciless. Francisco had tried to rein her in sometimes but that didn't always go well, but Francisco was a gentle guy and Isabella had come to depend on him, so I had hopes there. Sometimes their relationship reminded me of Billy and me, and I was trying as I hoped Isabella was, too.

"It'll be fine," I said. I sat down beside her. The boys were still asleep. I poured some coffee. "We got any breakfast fixings?"

She shrugged. "Some tortillas and beans, a can of peaches. That's about it, Josie. We can't keep dodging towns any longer and it looks like there's one ahead. Hope it's the one we want."

"Me, too." I sipped my coffee. It was weak but that was all right. We'd ride in soon.

"Listen, Isabella. I need to get something off my chest."

She tossed her head back and glanced at me suspiciously. "What?"

I'd been dreading this. I put my hand on her arm. "I know you're angry. You've a right to be, just like me and Colin, probably more so. Maybe we need to be a little more careful about just shooting people right off. Sometimes maybe they got something to say that we could use, or if we had a minute, we could think of an alternative. You know?"

Her eyes flashed and she shook off my arm. "That's a good one, coming from you, Josie. Do you hear yourself?"

I winced. "I know," I said. "You're right, I've done my share. Sometimes it wasn't well thought out, but that's what I'm saying right now. Maybe there's another way. MacNeil is dead, their network is over even if they don't know it before we show up."

She smiled and flicked her tongue at an eyetooth, staring at me. I sat my coffee cup down and stretched, feeling the muscles in my spine contract. "You like it, don't you, Isabella?"

"Yes, very much. Every time it feels like payback for every

minute I spent on a mattress with some smelly bastard on top of me. I could do it a hundred times and it wouldn't be enough." She looked at me. "So do you. It's not because of mattresses. I know it's not that."

"No," I said. "It's something else. It makes me feel like I'm setting things right, somehow. Taking out people who don't deserve to breathe the same air as us, people who are evil, who take advantage of others and don't care who they hurt, whether it's because they get pleasure out of other's pain, or stand to make money from it."

Isabella shrugged. "See? We're the same, really."

"Yes. But follow my lead." I stared at her. " 'Cause like it or not, I've somehow become the leader of this outfit or whatever they're calling us now, and I'm taking that seriously. If I'm going to hang for it or keep running, I want it to be because of my decisions, not somebody else's whims. I don't want to just keep killing people before we've even had a chance to talk to them. Somehow that doesn't seem right. Can you do that for me?"

Isabella stared at the fire for a long time and finally back at me. "Yes, Josie, I can do that. You found me, just like you always promised you would, the day I left. I owe you."

She flung her arm around me. "Even if none of that was true, it's damn clear you make the decisions around here and you haven't failed us once. I always said you were the smartest girl at Angel's Refuge and I wasn't wrong."

She kissed my cheek and buried her face in my hair. "I love you, my little wild girl. I'm here for you, every minute from now on. Or at least I'll try my best."

Colin and Francisco stumbled towards the fire, clearly half awake. "Is there any coffee?"

"Yes, one cup each. Globe or whatever town that is down there awaits, boys," Isabella said. "If you want more coffee or anything else, say retribution, it awaits in that valley." She glanced at me and winked. "I'm pretty sure we're going to find one thing or another."

Oh, how right she was about that.

We rode slowly into Globe, the horses still sending clouds of puffy dirt as they stepped. It had the beginnings of a nice little town, hastily built. There were some two-story buildings, and a couple of stone ones nearly completed, a bank and a couple of churches. Stores and houses lined the main street, and others were built up on the hills. People were making their mark here in this mining town, for surely that's what it was, given the ravaged earth we'd passed on the way here. It might do very well, as western towns could do, but it was a far cry from Prescott or Tucson. Then again, my experience with towns of any size was limited. We tied our horses up outside a saloon on the main street and entered through the door, brushing off the dust before we did. *Not that anybody'd notice*, I thought, once inside the door. A more exhausted collection of humanity I'd never seen. Men in workclothes covered in dirt sat at tables around the room, one bunch playing cards, and they all looked a little done in. The floor was an inch deep in the same brown grit they wore themselves.

"Howdy," Colin said to the bartender. He looked up and smiled, a good sign. "We'll have four whiskies."

The bartender looked us over. Isabella and I had both tucked our hair up under our hats and put on jackets but there was no disguising the fact we were smaller than our two companions, and whiskerless, even though we'd rubbed a little dirt on our faces.

"Sure those tadpoles you got there can handle that? They look like a good wind would blow them out of here, much less a shot of whisky."

Colin laughed and Francisco grinned. "They're fine, those two, meaner than they look, believe me. We been working over on the Bar T, on our way down to Tombstone."

"Well then, all you boys deserve a drink or two," he chuckled, filling the glasses.

"These boys in here look like they been hard at it, too," Colin said, draining his glass.

"Yeah. Night shift on the mines," the bartender said, his voice low. "It's a rough go, that one. They'll be leaving soon, home to bed." He shook his head. "You lucky you don't want to get on with that. At least cowboys got the fresh air every day even if you don't make much."

Colin nodded. "I hear that. Set 'em up again, will you?"

"Sure."

We drank our whiskies and waited. Sure enough, before long, the crowd cleared out and nobody was left in the place but us.

"Say, friend," Colin said. "Any hotels you'd recommend we can get a bath and room for a night? We sure could use a little comfort."

"Sure." The bartender eyed us again. He knew there something a bit off, but he hadn't worked it out quite yet. I figured we needed to get out of here before he did. "On down the block, there's Logan's. It's clean enough and there's a restaurant next door. That should do."

"Thanks, mister. Appreciate it."

We strolled out the door of the saloon like we didn't have a care in the world. Once outside we were silent, making our way down the street until Isabella put her hand on my arm.

"Christ, if that bastard stared at me one more time I was about ready to shoot him. As it is, he might be re-thinking his fucking choices...girl, boy, sheep...so confusing now...hmmm."

I couldn't help but laugh and I don't know if it was the whiskey for breakfast or just the craziness of it all, but then all four of us doubled up right there on the street. People passed by and smiled indulgently, shaking their heads. Just young cowboys letting off a little steam after being out on the ranch too long.

We had no intention of taking a hotel room, bath or no, but the restaurant sounded good and we found it, sitting down at an empty table. A rather grumpy heavyset girl no older than we were took our orders but the food was good when it arrived.

Eggs, biscuits and gravy and potatoes and lots more coffee than we'd had earlier. Our waitress was happy with the large tip we left and finally smiled. I thought it was worth a try.

I put my hand gently on her arm before she left our table. "Say, you ever heard of a place around here called St. Mary's Hope, an orphanage?"

She jumped a little, jerking her arm away from me. "Maybe. What you want at that place?"

"I'm looking for my little brother," I said. "Heard he might be there, if he's still alive. We got jumped by Apaches. Our parents got killed and I ain't seen him since. I got away but I heard they traded captives and he might have been one." I allowed a tear to leak down my cheek and truthfully it wasn't too hard, since that's what happened to me, minus the imaginary little brother. "I'd give anything to find him again."

She softened. "I know about St. Mary's." She glanced fearfully behind her. "I can't talk about this here, I'll get in trouble. Meet me behind the hotel in an hour when I get a break."

I nodded and we left the restaurant, heading to the general store across the street to stock up before we left town. We bought coffee, bacon, sugar, flour and whiskey, and led the horses with the full saddlebags around to the back of Logan's, to meet up with our waitress. After a while, she peeked out of the back door and ran up to us. She was clearly frightened, not of us, but whoever may have been inside the hotel. She was worn down, this girl, her hair lank and skin grey.

"What's your name?" I said.

"Sally. Sally Jensen," she said, her eyes apprehensive. "Listen, they'll punish me if they find me out here with you, whoever you are. It's just...I was at St. Mary's for five years. They sold me to the Logans and now I do whatever they tell me. It's an evil place and if your brother is there, you need to get him out. I just come out here to tell you that."

Isabella took off her hat and fluffed out her hair. She stepped up and gathered Sally up in her arms. "Honey," she said in the softest voice I'd ever heard from her since we were at Angel's Refuge, "they did the same to me, only I was a whore instead of a waitress. You never want to go back in that door, we can make sure that happens. Tell us about St. Mary's."

Sally burst into tears while Isabella patted her on the back. Sally looked up at Isabella like she was the baby Jesus come to life. "Who are you people?"

I took off my hat too, my pale hair tumbling down. Sally gaped at me.

"You're Josie Fallon."

"Guilty," I smiled. "How'd you know that?"

"The Logans were talking about you," she said, "and there's a wanted poster up for you at the sheriff's office. I saw it yesterday. For murder, it said." Her eyes were huge.

I shrugged. "Well, some people deserve killing, Sally, but I never set out to do that to anyone who hadn't done me harm first. You don't need to be scared of me or any of us. We aren't here to hurt you, only help if you need it. Tell us how to find St. Mary's."

So she did. Afterwards, we gave Sally two hundred dollars and put her on a stage for Prescott, right after Colin and Francisco paid a visit to the Logans. They wouldn't be buying orphans or anybody else ever again. Sometimes you have to make people see the error of their ways. They may have been reluctant but Colin was quite certain once they recovered they'd see he was right. At least they were breathing to do so.

I was pretty happy we hadn't killed anybody in Globe yet. 'Course we hadn't been to St. Mary's but it had been a busy day and we decided to wait until tomorrow morning for our visit there, after stopping for some beefsteaks. Between that and the whiskey, we'd have a good night, one we deserved. Besides, a little planning couldn't hurt. We'd had too little of that before.

We rode out of Globe and headed southeast as Sally had directed. These people never set up in towns but in the country-side because it was too risky that others could see what they did.

We made camp under a grove of cottonwoods and Francisco got the fire going in no time.

I watched the flames rising in the twilight sky and missed Billy with a pang I could feel in my chest like a tether that bound him to me. He'd be proud of me today. Josie, with restraint. I smiled when I thought of him and I hoped things were turning out all right. He'd been vague but from what he told me he couldn't trust a lot of people in New Mexico and I worried he was walking into a trap or worse. Still, there was nothing I could do about it and Billy sure was one to make his own decisions. Sort of like me.

"This time," Francisco said as we sat around the fire, our bellies full of meat and whiskey, "we try to avoid just killing people first and dealing with the *ninos* later. *Verdad?*"

"Yes," I said and Isabella and Colin muttered their assents as well. "It's dangerous for one thing, and shortsighted for another. For all we know, they don't want to be doing what they're doing either." I doubted that last very much but as trigger-happy as we all tended to be, it wouldn't hurt to try.

When we bedded down by the fire, Colin reached out his hand and touched my fingertips. "Josie."

I glanced over at him and took his hand in mine. "Yes?"

"I think we're doing the right thing, aren't we? I mean, all those kids just like us, they need a better chance than what they've been given, you know?"

I squeezed his hand in encouragement.

"So we're not just vengeance killers, if it's for a good purpose. I guess what I'm trying to say is sometimes I feel good about this and other times I wonder just where in hell this is taking us, maybe to get hung in one of these half-assed towns. That scares me. What scares me even more is that I don't feel bad about gunning down these people. I don't remember much about religion, but I don't think God would like that."

I'd been thinking about this. Long time back I figured God turned his back on us, if he even existed at all. Those bible stories we'd learned didn't seem any more likely than the fairy tales I'd read. Dragons and walking on water both seemed as unlikely one way or another.

I sat up on my elbows and stared into Colin's eyes. "Listen. If there is a god, which I doubt, if he permitted people to turn kids into slaves and whores, he's no god I want to have at my side. I think we're doing the righteous thing, shutting down these places and if god doesn't like it, he can make his will known. So far, he's been pretty damn quiet, seems to me."

I could see Colin smile in the dim light of the coals. He squeezed my hand. "I think you're right, Josie. We make our own way with our own justice. Goodnight, girl."

"Goodnight, Irish boy. Sweet dreams." We feel asleep holding hands and it felt good to renew that connection we'd always had.

CHAPTER 22

We came upon St. Mary's mid-morning, on another bright sunny day. You ask me, it was a day for clouds and a storm but those were rare around here. It wasn't a big two-story house like the others, but a compound of low-lying whitewashed adobe houses built in a half circle, barns and fields off to the sides, just as Sally had described. Francisco was quick to point out the corrals, which held at least half a dozen horses.

We pulled our horses up at the end of the turnoff and dismounted. We'd decided this morning we'd try a different plan. Isabella ruffled her short hair while I hid mine under my hat. As far as we knew, there were still no wanted posters for her or Francisco, unlike me and Colin.

"If you hear two quick gunshots, come running," I said. "Otherwise, wait for just one and that'll be the signal that all is well and come in slow."

Colin and Francisco nodded, neither of them happy with this plan but Isabella and I figured it just might work and we convinced them to hold back. I hoped we were right.

The two of us rode up to the compound. We saw some children in the fields, weeding and a couple of them shoveling horse dung at the corrals. They looked up briefly and went back to their tasks as we slung our reins over the hitching post beside the largest adobe house and knocked at the door.

"Who are you?" The careworn woman at the door was about thirty, her hair pinned up haphazardly and her apron dirty. She didn't look happy to have visitors. The odor wafting out of the place smelled of piss and old cabbage.

"Good morning," Isabella said and gave her a dazzling smile. "I'm Maria Jones, here with my friend Mr. Thompson. We are looking for a place for his young cousin and people mentioned you. May we come in?"

The woman seemed mollified and she opened the door wider. We stepped into an entry hall of sorts, doors leading off into other areas.

"I'm Alice Johnson. Me and my brother run this place, according to the teachings of Jesus and St. Mary. You know, like the name. If you ain't Christians, you might want to look elsewhere, just to git that out of the way." She snuffled and crossed herself.

I guess she was exorcising the devil, but it was my turn now.

"Oh, ma'am," I said, kneeling on the floor and grabbing hold of her skirts, "I feel like we've come to the very place that would welcome poor Joshua, isn't that right, Maria?"

"Oh yes," Isabella said, throwing out her arms, looking like a beautiful saint herself. "It's like the lord led us to you, Miz Johnson. Do you have a place for our little lamb?"

Maybe we overdid it a little because Alice Johnson eyed us like the liars we were for a minute and I reached my hand towards the pistol I'd stuffed in my britches just in case.

She closed her eyes and breathed deeply. "Truly you have been blessed to have found us. We always need another boy." She opened her eyes. "I mean, we always have a place for a child within St. Mary's arms."

Heavy footsteps followed a door crashing open to the right. "Hell's bells, woman. What's going on out here?" A heavyset bearded man strode up to us, pulling up his suspenders. A little boy, maybe five, followed behind him, his thin face pale and frightened, and after a frantic look at the man, he dashed away through another doorway like a rat freed from a trap.

I glanced at Isabella and she shook her head. So far, we weren't very impressed with the managerial instincts of Alice Johnson and her brother. I'd been hoping for better this time and I sighed inwardly as I stood up, dropping Alice's skirts. Were all these people just rotten? Where had MacNeil found such a crew of horrid people, I wondered. I guess if you're going to exploit and enslave children there was no better way than using religion to do so but not a one of them had been a good person and most of them he must've scraped off the barroom floor to pretend to be so.

Alice put her hand on the man's shoulders, apprehension on her face. "Abraham, we're real sorry if we disturbed you at prayer. This nice lady and her friend are looking to place a boy with us. Ain't that wonderful?"

Abraham finished tucking his undershirt back in his trousers and looked us over. "Could be, Alice. How old you say this boy is? Got to make certain he ain't been tainted and turned by this wicked world."

I already knew what Abraham was and he was no man of the Bible. At least at Angel's Refuge they weren't interested in anything much beyond hypocrisy and money. We hadn't known how lucky we'd been. "He's thirteen and quite a handful, but I'm sure a good Christian home would do him fine," I said.

Abraham frowned. "Too old. We ain't got no room."

"Well sure we do, brother," Alice said, her face pleading. "I just been telling these folks we'd take this boy in. Especially after James and Seth, bless their souls. We got room and I got love to spare and then some."

He glared at her. "No, Alice, we don't. And that's my final word on this." He stomped off through the same door the boy had run through and I judged it led to the kitchen or something like that, as I could smell chicken broth before the door closed.

Alice swallowed hard. "I'm so sorry," she said. "I didn't mean to mislead you, Miss Jones. I miscalculated." She turned to me. "Mr. Jones, I guess you'll have to find another place for your cousin." She opened the door.

"MacNeil's dead," I said and slammed it shut with my boot. "Time for a reckoning, Alice."

Her already sallow complexion turned dead white and she dashed for the door her brother had gone through. Isabella stuck out her foot and tripped her and Alice fell in a tangle of dirty skirts. Isabella stuck her gun in her face.

"Just so we keep this civil," Isabella smiled, "if you yell at that ape, I'll shoot you. Take us to the office and the money."

"What? There's no money, we already sent it to Prescott," she said. I knew she was lying but it didn't matter anyway. We marched her down another hallway and of course there it was, an open safe. I tied her to a chair and tore off pieces of her apron to gag her. I'd never done this before and I was quite proud of my handiwork. Isabella ignored me and was busily stuffing a carpetbag full of money until I stopped her.

"Listen, we need to get the boys in here now," I said. "We have to take care of Abraham wherever he went and figure out what to do with these kids. We don't even know how many of them we have to deal with."

"All right, Josie," she said, clearly annoyed. "Get them in, then. Sometimes I swear you only care about the kids while I know we have to get rid of the managers or whatever they are. And we do need money. Who knows what we'll find in California?"

"Maybe," I said. "Remember what I said the other day, Isabella? I'm calling this. What we need right now is food and packhorses, girl, and to take charge of this place. Between us and those things is Abraham. You want to take him on alone?"

She grinned. "Why not? Didn't look like a problem to me, fatass pervert."

I sighed. Sometimes she had a point. Maybe it'd be nice for once if we didn't need to call on men to help us out.

I grinned back. "So, let's get this done."

We went back down to the entry hall and through the door the boy and Abraham had used. As I suspected, it led to the kitchen. Two women, maybe Mexican or Apache, were busy stirring pots and chopping vegetables when we entered and they looked up at us with startled eyes.

I held up my hand, my voice consoling. "It's all fine, ladies, all fine. Where's Abraham?"

One pointed towards the open outside door, and I could see the barn beyond it.

"Stay here and say nothing," I said and they nodded. I wasn't sure they understood what I'd said, but I knew they understood the meaning. They probably weren't friends with Abraham either.

I pulled my gun from my pants, wishing I'd worn my gunbelt and hoping I didn't need any more bullets. Abraham was big but Isabella was likely meaner so I wasn't that worried. I should've been.

He came out of that barn before we'd taken ten steps, his head down like a charging bull, butting Isabella in the stomach and knocking her flat, her pistol flying out of her hand. He turned to me and laughed.

"You little shit," he bellowed. "You think I didn't see you were just here to cause trouble? You're dying today."

He ran towards me, the Colt in his hand, and a bullet tore my hat off. Damn, I hoped there wasn't another hole in that hat brim. I really liked that hat. There wasn't a lot of choice now.

I shot Abraham between the eyes, just like Billy'd taught me. He would've been proud. The fat bastard fell on his back and the only mark on him was my bullet on his forehead. Isabella rolled over, groaning and holding her gut, staggering towards me.

"Christ, Josie, I hoped you killed that bastard," she said, brightening up considerably when she saw that I had indeed fulfilled her wish. She still looked a little green.

Colin and Francisco pulled up in a cloud of dust, jumping off their horses like they were going to save us girls from our dire fates. To be fair, neither one of them expected to have to do that.

"Well hell, Josie, you scared me a little," Colin said. "You said one, all right, two come running. So we did, but it looks like you got things under control here." He nudged Abraham with his boot, scanning the houses and yards. "Anybody else to worry about?"

I grimaced. "Well, yeah. There's the fat guy's sister we got tied up inside. I'm not sure if she's good or bad. She's likely the latter, if not crazy, and then there's the kids. Don't even know how many. We didn't have time to find out."

"Josie, it's all right. Francisco's got a plan. There's a mission he knows down the road, going south. It's run by Franciscan friars, and one of them's his uncle. Francisco tells me they are good people who will take care of children, doesn't matter who they are."

He looked at me for a second and then unexpectedly pulled me into an awkward hug. "We're not doing this stupid split up thing again."

I clung to him and for a minute the world stopped and I just felt comforted and safe, something that had been rare in my life. Also something that right now, none of us could afford to get used to. We had an agenda.

I pulled away. "As I always say, we'll figure it out, *amigo*."

THIS TIME, THANKS TO FRANCISCO, WE WERE MORE organized. He and Isabella went to the kitchen and got to know the women there, along with two others who handled the housekeeping. They looked at us like saviors, rather than marauders, which was nice for once.

There were eighteen children here, from four years old to fourteen, all of them scared. Colin and I rounded them up, from the fields and the barn and then on to the house, where some of the older girls were looking after the younger ones. St. Mary's was the poorest run of the orphanages so far, the children dirty and wearing worn clothing, some of them barefoot. Apparently Alice Johnson did nothing but prayer and church services. Any education seemed to have gone by the wayside, between her religious obsession and her brother's predilection for young boys, which she conveniently ignored.

We told them things were going to be different from now on and I winced inwardly at the skeptical glances from the older kids and the blank stares from most of the younger ones. They didn't even know what "different" was. Only with time would they learn that. The fact that a few of them saw me kill a man was a hurdle they'd need to overcome, although nobody seemed to grieve for Abraham. I saw a frail little boy smile as he passed the body when we took them into the house and that smile nearly stopped my heart.

Francisco sent Juana, one of the women, off to the mission on one of the horses with a message for his uncle. In the meanwhile, we became the caretakers of a bunch of children and the new managers of St. Mary's, at least for a time, not something we'd planned on but we should have and I felt as though this time, fate had caught up with our headlong journey into justice.

While Francisco and Colin dragged Abraham behind the barn and dug a grave, I checked on Alice Johnson and found she'd fallen asleep, likely saying her prayers, slumped in the chair we'd left her in. I closed the door softly. We had more pressing matters to attend to. Isabella and I rifled through the sparsely furnished bedrooms in the adobe casitas, finding some clean clothing and organizing the older girls into giving everyone baths, sorely needed. We ripped the filthy sheets from the beds and took them to the washing tubs near the barn, Isabella's nose crinkling at the smell.

"Stella's was heaven compared to this," she snarled. "These poor kids have been living in filth and piss." She threw the sheets into the tubs of water, along with the heaps of ragged clothing we'd gathered, throwing in soap. "These people deserve whatever's coming."

"Well, one's dead already," I said. "Our friend Alice isn't looking at a bright future."

"Good thing." Isabella grabbed a pole and shoved the washing down into the soapy depths. "She's your call, Josie. I know what I'd do with her."

Watching her stab those sheets, I didn't have much doubt either. "I'm going to the kitchen. We'll have some decent food tonight."

"Send out one or two of those kids to hang this stuff out so it'll be dry by tonight," she said. "I'm only going so far with this crap." She grinned at me. "Never did get the hang of domesticity. One of the few things whores don't need to bother with."

I assured her I would and couldn't help smiling as I left her stirring the laundry. Isabella surprised me constantly. Then again, I was about to become a cook, or at least supervise it. After my tortilla disasters, I hadn't planned on that either. Mateo would've loved this.

With my limited Spanish and the women's limited English, we managed to figure out we were having chicken enchiladas with every trimming we could find and they gleefully set to work, two of them going to the chicken coop and then the garden, while the other two set about beans and tortillas. We'd lost two greedy adults but added four hungry pistoleros and a lot of kids and cooks who hadn't eaten well in some time, so everyone was enthusiastic.

I sent two of the older boys out to help Isabella and found bath time done, with clean clothes, what we could find at least, distributed to most of the rest. I was faced with a pack of damp haired clean children staring at me as though I was their mother. It was a bit unnerving and I wasn't quite sure what to do with any of them at this point. One of the older girls spoke up.

"Miss?"

I'd taken off my shot up hat a while back. "Yes?"

"What do you want us to do now? Go back to work?"

"What's your name?" I didn't really care but I was scrambling for time."

"Carol." She was maybe thirteen, red-haired and sharp-featured and she reminded me a bit of Amy, which came with a pang.

"Carol, good," I said. "You know, to tell you the truth, I don't know. I only know nobody's going back to work, not here and not now."

They stared at me. "Help me out. Is there a room big enough for everyone, like a school or something?"

Carol shrugged. "The chapel, maybe, that's all."

Of course, I thought. No school, just church. "All right then, let's go there. Show me."

Carol led us all down to the last adobe casita, the one with a cross on top. I hadn't even noticed it before. We filed into the cool dimness. Wooden pews were lined up in the good-sized space. A wooden altar sat on a raised dais, a bible open upon it. Sunlight filtered in through the small arched windows set in niches on both sides of the building, patterns of brightness among the dark wood of the pews. The children stood motion-less, not sure what to do. They stared at me, eyes apprehensive.

I strode up to the dais. "Sit," I said, waving my arms, "any-where you like."

They filed slowly down the aisle, and perched on the pews, clearly not sure what was coming next. I sat down on the raised step, the stone cool beneath me.

"Once upon a time," I said, "in a land far away, there was a kingdom ruled by an evil king and queen..."

For the next three hours I told fairy tales, all the ones I knew and then resorting to ones I made up about children who perse-vered through the worst of happenings and had a happy ending each time. At first suspicious, by the end they were laughing each time the ogre or the dragon or the evil fairy or king met their fate, clapping their hands and moving closer to me to catch every word. I was just as caught up in my stories as they were, and finally glanced up to find Colin, Isabella and Francisco and some of the women who did all the work in this dismal place sitting in the pews behind the children, along with a new arrival, a black-robed friar who sat beside Francisco, smiling as well.

The light had dimmed with the sun, going down on this long day. Delicious smells wafted in through the open door and I stood up, stiff from sitting all this time. I rubbed my backside.

"That's all for now," I said, smiling at the protests from the disappointed faces in front of me. "More tomorrow, I promise."

We slowly left, heading for the kitchen and the tables inside. A little girl, her blonde hair the same color as mine, wiggled her fingers into my palm.

"Are you a princess, too?" she said, her blue eyes wide.

"Maybe I am," I said. "Princesses come in all shapes and sizes, you know. We don't always have crowns or beautiful dresses."

She thought about that for a minute as we walked along. "I think you are." She gave me a dazzling smile. "Maybe I am too."

I leaned down and whispered in her ear. "I'm sure you are. For now, it's our secret."

She nodded. "I've been taught how to keep secrets."

My heart nearly broke. I'll bet she had.

❧

WE STAYED FOR TWO MORE DAYS AND IT WAS A GOOD TWO days. I was constantly apprehensive that some lawman in Prescott or somewhere had begun to figure out our agenda but it was two days we put to good use and two days all of us badly needed. From time to time, I wondered how Billy was doing, but there was little time for that.

Francisco's uncle wasn't just a friar, he was the abbott and head of the monastery. Just after supper, two more friars arrived and within an hour, after they appraised the situation, he met with us. We sat at the table in the kitchen with them, coffee and sopapillas on the table. The children had been put to bed, clean and fed and the women from the kitchen were in their quarters in the back. The long black habits the monks wore put me off a little, but my friends had seen it before and seemed fine with it.

"Miss Fallon," Father Juan said. "My nephew has told me of what happened here, and what happened before you came."

I started to interrupt but he held up a hand. "Please, let me finish," he said, his voice firm but gentle as his manner. His dark eyes were kind and I had taken an instant liking to him but still he was just another person in authority who had relied on religious teachings that as far as I could see had only done harm to the children I now had to find a safe haven for.

"I do not condemn you. Only God can do that." My hackles went up but he looked down as though he could tell and then stared back intently at me. "Instead, I must laud you for defending these helpless children. We have discussed this and decided to take them to the monastery, if you agree. This is not something we had ever planned to do, but God has his reasons for all things. We have ample room and while they will have to help in the gardens just as we ourselves do every day, they will not be slaves. We will ensure they receive a good education, something I been informed has been sadly lacking here, and they will not be subjected to any injurious behavior. Upon reaching age, they will make their decisions to enter the larger world, equipped with the best teachings and tools we can bestow. We are not a rich parish but we will petition the Church for funds to help with this new endeavor. Even if none are forthcoming, we are determined to do our best."

"Why?"

He smiled, a bit taken aback. "Because it is what God would want, Miss Fallon. And, because it is what I want. We were placed on this earth to take care of one another but many times we do not. These children have no other future and some have been abused. If I can right this wrong, and it is within my power to do so, I will."

I glanced at the other three. "What do you think?"

I was looking at Colin, because I knew Isabella and Francisco had been raised with the Catholic church but Colin had forgotten what little Catholic religion he had started with, aside from growing up on the streets.

He stared at me and then Father Juan. "I don't believe in God anymore, Father, but I'm willling to take a chance and believe in you because you look like an honest man under that habit." Isabella and Francisco both nodded. All three looked back at me.

I didn't believe in a benevolent God or even a vengeful one myself, but I needed a solution here and this looked like one I could live with.

"All right, it's a deal, Father." I stood up. "Thank you. We need to get this done quickly. Anyone objecting to what we've done here and other places could show up. That wouldn't be good, if you understand what I'm saying."

Father Juan gave me a bleak smile. "I understand completely, Miss Fallon. We can accomplish moving the children and settling them in little time."

The women had arranged accommodations for them at the house and I was sure they were as ready for their beds as we were.

We said our goodnights and headed upstairs to our own beds, nobody saying much. Isabella and I were sharing a room, as were Colin and Francisco. Any bed would be welcome after sleeping on the ground.

Colin took my hand before he continued down the hallway, the only light now from the moon outside.

"It'll be fine, Josie. They're good men. We've done a good thing today." He kissed me on the cheek. "Sleep well. See you in the morning."

I closed the door. Isabella flung herself down on one of the little beds and pulled the blanket over herself.

"Quit fretting, Josie. I wish Francisco was here with me, but we're being proper with monks in the house and all," she chuckled. "It's fine, I could stand a night off. He's pretty intimidated with his uncle anyway."

"You are truly something," I said, smiling in the dark and laying down too. I couldn't condemn her. I missed Billy laying beside me and hoped he was in a soft bed too. Alone. Even with that thought, I slept well. It had certainly been a day.

CHAPTER 23

We waved goodbye as the last wagonload of children rumbled down the drive, on their way to the monastery. Father Juan had been as good as his word and Colin and Francisco had been back and forth, ferrying children, horses and supplies.

"*Es bueno*," Francisco said, watching them leave. "My uncle has plenty of space there for them. It's one of the old missions, built by the Jesuits when my people first came here." He glanced over at me and smiled. "They will be happy there, Josie. School, and not too much church, because I know you don't care much for that."

"No," I said. "I do not. Then again, there's church and there's church. Benevolence versus oppression, *comprende?* Your uncle is a kind man. Believe me, I know the difference."

"And well, I think," he said, his glance sharp. He never did miss much, our Francisco.

Back at the house, Colin and Isabella were stuffing sacks with food for the road in the kitchen and I left Francisco to help them. The house was quiet and bleak, full of the ghostly memories of life, a little laughter but a great deal more pain, the floors echoing beneath my feet.

I unlocked the door to the study where we'd been keeping Alice Johnson. I'd asked Father Juan to take her but he'd said no after talking with her for a few minutes.

"Josie, this lady is beyond my help. I need to focus on the children she and her brother have damaged, and she needs to be somewhere they care for the *insana. Lo siento.*"

I couldn't blame him, but I didn't know what the hell to do with her, either. I wasn't about to drag her to some asylum, if there even was one anywhere in Arizona. Isabella suggested we just bury her with her brother and truth to tell, she was probably right, but I didn't want one more needless death on my conscience. We'd just have to take with her us and find some kindly soul to take her in. She could likely help around a ranch, or even a church. I wasn't very worried she'd give us away to the authorities because she didn't even seem to know one day from the next, or where she was.

Alice sat at the desk. I'd untied her the day before and just locked the door. She didn't seem to have any desire to go anywhere anyway. She'd used the bucket I'd left and eaten the food we'd brought. The smell was horrific, a combination of unwashed Alice and waste and I breathed through my mouth after a good whiff.

"Oh, there you are, Mary." She beamed at me. "I've been talking to your son and he told me to seek atonement with you."

I coughed, trying to breathe through my mouth but it wasn't working out well. "Yeah, Jesus always was a bright kid. What did you have in mind?"

She stood up, still smiling, and drove a brass letter opener into her throat, blood spurting onto the desk and the bookcase behind her. She fell onto the floor and before I could even raise her up to a sitting position, she took a last breath. I lowered her onto the floor, her blood still pumping. I stood up, wiping my hands on her dress.

Holy shit. I backed out of the room, shut the door and

headed to the kitchen. I washed my hands at the sink, scrubbing furiously at the blood while my friends watched silently.

"How's Alice?" Colin said.

"Dead."

In the end, we all agreed to set fire to the house before we left, and it burned quickly, the old dry wood the perfect kindling, a bonfire of cleansing retribution, a fitting pyre for poor Alice. Between the flames of the fire and the setting sun behind us, we rode silently southward towards our next destination.

⁂

"LAMBS OF THE LORD? WHAT KIND OF FUCKED UP NAME IS that?" Isabella scooped more beans from the pot, chewing contentedly. "These people are crazy."

"Who knows?" I said. "And yes, they are crazy. That's why we're doing this."

"True," she said, reaching into the pan for a biscuit. "And I like it, just as much as you do, Josie. Only difference between us is you like to plan, and I don't see the need for that." She smiled at me, lips glistening in the firelight. "But when it comes to the killing, we all know you're the one to count on, if I didn't get them first." She bit into the biscuit. "I don't make apologies to them or anybody else. Neither do you."

Well, that was true. Even Colin nodded and Francisco shrugged, as usual. We girls were the driving force here when it came to vengeance and everybody knew it, which was fine with me. I'd tried to harness this thing and make myself feel like I should be at least accountable for the body count but the truth was I didn't care about the awful people we'd killed, from the very beginning until this very moment. My name had been on a wanted poster for murder from the start and a higher or lesser body count didn't matter a whit to me or the law. Might as well be hung for a sheep as a lamb.

We'd been riding for three days now and hadn't seen much of

anything. We were following a road that looked well-traveled, or at least near it. We'd seen a couple of stagecoaches go by in both directions but we kept our distance. No point in seeing people that could recognize us and start trouble either here or further on down the road.

"So where is this place?" Colin said. "All we got is "near Tombstone" to go on and that's not enough. Lot of country out there that I don't feel like riding through for nothing."

He was right about that. Neither did I. Next ranch we came on, or anything close to a settlement, we'd have to start asking questions, always a risky business but there was nothing for it.

They came up on us before we knew it and Colin and Francisco both jumped up and pulled their guns, holding them at their sides while Isabella and I stuffed our hats on. Girls were not only identifiable in my case, but easy prey for anyone looking for easy pickings.

"Hello, the camp," someone called and three riders emerged into the firelight. "We're friendly, no harm."

Well, that was to be seen. For now, we watched them dismount and leading their horses, walk towards us. The spokesman was a tall cowboy, not much older than we were, while his two companions were older. They all looked like they knew what was what, spurs jingling and clothes dusty.

"Saw your fire and thought we'd stop by and say hello," the younger one said. "Jeb McLaurie. Got a ranch south of here, been out rounding up some strays. We got some beef to share if you're interested, specially if you got some biscuits and beans to go with it." He laughed and I relaxed a little, shooting a glance at Colin.

"Sure," Colin said. "Fire's up. Steaks wouldn't go amiss." He holstered his gun but mine was within easy reach and he knew it. "Sharing is a good thing with folks. Come on in."

I couldn't blame him. I was heartily sick of scrawny chicken myself. The newcomers set about cooking steaks and before long, we were all properly stuffed, and cigars and whiskey had come out, making the rounds.

"So where y'all headed?" Jeb said, leaning back on his haunches, picking bits of steak from his teeth.

"Tombstone," I said before anyone else could answer. I was taking a chance but damn, I was sick and tired of wandering around. "And, looking for my little sister on the way. Heard she's in some orphanage type of thing, a place called Lambs of the Lord. Thought we'd gather her up and take our chances on some mining."

McLaurie exchanged glances with his two wranglers. "Hey Mack, Bob. You ever hear of a place like that? Little lost lambs?"

They both smirked. "Naw, the only lost lambs I know are the girls down at Betty Ann's," Mack said. "You get to Tombstone, you look her up. Tell her Mack Sidbury said to give you the good rate." He nudged my boot. "You and your pal there," he nodded at Isabella, should get half off, you two shrimps make up about one real man."

They thought this witticism hilarious and Colin and Francisco laughed along with them. I wasn't worried. We were all just a pack of good old boys, weren't we? Shootin' the shit and talking about whores. No need to make them think anything different. The talk got coarser and finally I stood up, along with Isabella.

"We're turning in, been a long day," I said, "besides, we don't got no stories to tell since we ain't been to Betty Ann's nor anyplace else yet. Next time we meet up we shrimps will be real men and we can talk about who's best, the skinny ones or the fat ones, right Mack?"

We rolled out our blankets behind some mesquite trees a little further off. It wasn't very cold and besides we couldn't take another minute of their bullshit. I'm sure Colin and Francisco weren't very interested either but they'd have to make do. We were stuck with these men the minute they rode up, not to mention the steaks, unless we wanted to raise their suspicions. I was hoping those steaks didn't eventually come with a bigger price tag than some beans and biscuits. Their voices drifted over to where we lay, the words mostly unintelligible but the tone and the bursts of laughter clear as day.

"Stupid bastards," Isabella muttered. "Had to put up with their kind for two years. Also," she propped herself up on an elbow and leaned towards me. "Be careful. I'm not entirely sure that Jeb thinks we're boys, Josie."

I agreed with her. We decided to sleep in shifts, me staying up first, her second. Within minutes, I heard her soft snores and it was a struggle to keep my eyes open for the next four hours. Colin came to check on us around midnight and wasn't surprised to see me awake.

"Good call, Josie. I don't trust these guys either but so far I haven't seen anything that worries me too much. They're sound asleep from what I can tell." His eyes gleamed in the moonlight and I was glad he'd come over. I reached towards him but before my hand touched his shoulder, he stood up.

"See you in the morning, girl." He patted me on the head. "Take care."

Just as well. I get sentimental when I'm feeling lonely.

Then again, neither Colin nor anyone else saw me in the morning because by dawn I was tied up like a Christmas goose riding in front of Jeb McLaurie without so much as a cup of coffee or a hello. I despise meanness like that. No call for it, in my mind, which of course was one of the reasons I was riding hatless and damn near on top of that saddlehorn. Another was Jeb Henderson, whispering in my ear, his warm breath blowing my hair as sweetly as the morning breeze and equal in its empty eloquence. This was a man who thought a great deal of himself.

So far, in my admittedly limited experience, those were the easier ones. I sure hoped so.

CHAPTER 24

According to my backside, it seemed like we'd been riding for days but it was only just past noon to my reckoning, when Jeb called a halt. He hauled me down off his horse, my hands tied and sat me down against a mesquite tree, while his pals went to fill the canteens. He handed me a stale biscuit and some jerky, watching me as I ate. I was a firm believer in food, having been deprived of much of it for years. A girl had to keep her strength up. All the better to fight you with was my amended fairy tale line and one I heartily believed in.

He smiled at me. "Josie Fallon."

I chewed my jerky. I'd figured the bastard knew that and it wasn't just my fascinating face that had ended me atop his saddle.

"I thought you'd be, I don't know, bigger or meaner maybe," Jeb said, fingering his short beard, "not that I'm disappointed. In fact, you're just cute as a button, as my mama used to say. Them big green eyes and that pale hair, uh-huh. I'm tempted to just keep you for myself, but five hundred dollars is a lot of money and there's a lot of girls out there I can find for free."

"You got any water to go with that hot air coming out of your mouth?" I said, swallowing the last mouthful of jerky. "I could use some. And you? I might have something for you, too, I wasn't so damn thirsty."

In short order, I had a cup of water which I gulped down quickly and was awarded seconds. It made me nervous that Jeb hadn't moved much and his two riders had moved off a ways but there wasn't much I could do about either of those things at the moment.

"Put your hands over your head." Jeb loomed over me, pushing me down on my back. "Goddamn, girl, you got me stirred up some. Let's just git this over with before I turn you in."

He pulled my britches down far enough for access, unfastening his own. My breath was coming in short hitches and all I wanted was to kill him but the ropes around my wrists held fast. He flipped me over onto my stomach which made it impossible to get my hands around his neck and went to work.

No, no, you godamn bastard, you will not do this, kept running through my head as my body bucked and my wrists, frantic from trying to escape their bonds, bled slowly down my arms as he went at me and it didn't take long before he gave a satisfied sigh. I was hoping for an act two so I could get to the knife I'd stuck in my boot but he'd been too eager to wait for my other charms.

When a rifle shot rang out Jeb jerked forward and collapsed upon me and I wasn't sure what had happened for a minute or so. When more shots rang out, I knew. Jeb's warm blood trickled onto my back and it felt good, like the retribution it was meant to be. I hadn't needed that knife after all.

"CHRIST JOSIE, YOU GAVE US A SCARE."

Colin handed me the whiskey bottle and I took it without hesitation. That he didn't baby me, nor did Isabella and Francisco, made me feel stronger and not like a fool that had been taken like some helpless idiot.

"Guess we need to be a little more careful who we ask about orphanages around here." I took a long drink before passing it to Isabella. "And a little better about staying awake on watch." I held the bottle a second or two and she winced. "The real problem is that Jeb knew who I was. Which tells me that he'd been to Tombstone and seen a wanted poster, or that he'd been to the orphanage and they already know we're coming. We have to be really careful."

There wasn't any argument about that. We took some time to bury the bodies, not because they deserved it but to cover our own tracks. We still didn't have the slightest idea where we could find Lambs of the Lord. It was like looking for that needle in the haystack. There was a lot of open country and not many towns. Still, somebody must know something, or at least we hoped so. This was the last job we had to do, and we didn't want to leave Arizona before we'd accomplished it. It might seem foolish and like we were really pressing our luck, but we'd all agreed.

We rode out in the morning, full of eggs and bacon from good old Jeb's saddlebags. It was a nice morning, the breeze wafting in our faces, smelling of mesquite and sage. The sky was blue as a robin's egg but there was a faint hint of spice in the air and I turned to Colin.

"Remember that smell?"

He nodded. "I do. I'd say storm's coming by afternoon, up from Mexico. I love that smell. It's early, this year."

I smiled. "I love it too. It always made Higgins nervous but it was wonderful far as I was concerned. I always wished those big storms would wash Angel's Refuge away and we'd be like Noah's Ark or something, paddling away on some raft to another place. A good place."

Colin's hand brushed my shoulder. "We're going to a good place, Josie. It looks far away now, but that storm's going to help us get there." He grinned. "We need to find somewhere to hole up before it hits, though. You know well as I do how bad they can be. We don't have much but we need all we got."

We passed a couple of big ranches but they looked forbidding, with adobe walls and cowboys patrolling and Francisco would shake his head and we'd ride on into the empty desert. We didn't need questions or worse. I guess I was looking for something like Hiram's but as the day wore on, the wind picked up, the skies darkened and we were running out of options.

We stopped and gave the horses a rest while we chewed on jerky, looking at the sky like it was going to explode on us at any minute, which it truly could.

"Anybody know where the hell we are?" I said. It was a feeble question because the only one who could possibly have any idea was Francisco, and I doubted that even he did. "Or got a guess or suggestion?"

Silence. No surprise.

"Well, after you and Isabella left the other night," Colin said, swallowing some jerky, "Jeb and his friends were talking and they said they went often to Tombstone, that mining town that's booming. From what they said, it's south and east from where we were. We been heading sort of that way and it can't be that far. 'Course, this damn country is so hilly it could be right beside us and we'd miss it if we were two miles away. We need to find a high spot and look around for lights at night."

Well, that was true. None of us knew anything about finding places without guidance and I was surprised we'd gotten this far on luck, stars, old stage roads and a compass. We were like the nursery rhyme about blind mice except on horseback instead of a clock. Maybe that's one of the reasons we were so damn quick to lash out. I shrugged off that thought. It didn't matter. We were doing what we had to do.

"You're right," I said. "We been riding around like dumb rabbits and not thinking." I looked up at the sky and stood up, brushing off my backside. "Although we don't get out of here and find someplace right now we aren't going to see anything but water pretty damn quick."

We rode on while the light faded and it began to resemble

twilight although it couldn't be past three o'clock. The wind picked up and the horses didn't like it all, prancing around and crowhopping, their tails high and unless you kept a firm hand, you'd find yourself in a cactus. Animals always know.

Raindrops the size of silver dollars spattered us now and then, stopping and starting as though teasing us into thinking it would be just fine. You could practically hear the rain laughing as they began again, each time a little harder and longer.

A few minutes later, the raindrops didn't stop and nobody was laughing. We were drenched in seconds, with rain like I'd never seen, or at least not from the wrong side of four snug walls.

We literally were those blind mice now, the curtains of rain drawn closed against our progress. We plodded on in sheer misery for a time until Francisco shouted.

"Lights! Over there!" He wheeled his horse to the west and we instantly followed. We rode towards the lights barely visible through the rain, going as fast as we dared. As we got closer, I could see it was another large two-story house that was again strikingly familiar to Angel's Refuge, with some shadowy buildings behind it. The lights came from a couple of windows, flickering, while another, more steady, burned at a building which looked to be a barn behind the house. We followed that one like it was the light of the fabled Christmas star.

We rode clear to the barn and since the door was open, right on inside, the horses blowing, and quickly dismounted. An oil lamp was hung on a hook outside the barn. There was no one inside, just some horses and with the noise of the rain and wind, I doubted anyone anyone had heard us arrive, or even seen us, the storm so intense. The barn smelled good, of horse, hay and leather, scents I always loved.

I wrung my hair out as did Isabella but there was little help for our clothes at this point. We needed to get somewhere warmer than the barn and get dry.

"What do you want to do?" Colin said. "We could just hang

out here but I don't think that'll last long, since somebody's going to check on the horses sooner or later. I got no idea what kind of people own this place, but they may not recognize any of us and we'll just leave after the storm blows itself out."

"Let's just go introduce ourselves," Isabella said. "Josie can stick her hair up so nobody recognizes her. Besides, I can't believe word travels so fast to a place as out of the way as this. I'm thinking they'll be happy to chat with some travelers." She grinned. "Specially some as charming as us. Besides I want dry clothes and I sure as hell ain't getting them in this goddamn barn."

Francisco threw out some hay for our horses and checked the water. He started to take off his horse's saddle when I put my hand on his arm and shook my head. "Leave it, they'll be fine for now and we can do more later. If we have a later."

He understood quickly and checked his guns, watching me as I pulled my gunbelt out of the saddlebag and checked my Colt, buckling it on as Colin watched, his face paling.

I twisted my hair atop my head and slapping my soggy hat back on. "We sure were lucky to stumble onto this nice ranch. I bet these folks are just friendly and chatty as can be. Maybe we can even convince them to give us some hot stew. Yep, those bastards always did have stew of some kind."

I put my hands on my hips. "Place looks a little familiar to me, but maybe that's just my imagination. Then again, can't hurt to be careful. What do you think, Colin?"

He'd figured it out too.

"Let's go, Josie," Colin grinned and patted his holster. "Shit, I could use some hot stew. Reminds me of when I was a kid, back at the home place. Good times, you know?"

I was certain we'd stumbled across the very place we were searching for.

CHAPTER 25

We couldn't have gotten any wetter in our dash for the nearest door visible. We burst in and startled the three women in the kitchen, their shouts of *"dios mios"* echoing in our ears. We calmed them down with Francisco's help and they went back to stirring the proverbial stew pots or whatever else steamed on the stoves, somewhat nervous but no longer terrified. It did smell delicious. Whatever they were cooking here, it was a long way from the slop they made at Angel's Refuge.

Before we left the kitchen, I put my hand on the arm of the plump young woman who looked to me like the boss and pulled Francisco over.

"How do you say "lambs of the lord"? I said. "Let's be sure." This whole thing could just be wishful thinking on my part.

So handsome, was Francisco. He smiled gently and leaned close. *"Senora, es esto Corderos del Senor orfanato, por favor?"*

She looked up at him, blushing. *"Si, guapo, es Corderos del Senor."* Then, surprisingly, she spat on the floor. *"Salvar a los ninos, vaya con Dios."* She waved us towards another door and put her finger to her lips.

Francisco grinned and blew her a kiss as we headed for the

door. The stew smelled good but it wasn't going anywhere and we were.

Looked like somebody was going a lot further. We emerged into a hall where trunks and suitcases were stacked near the front door. A wide staircase led to the second floor, empty for now. The sound of raised voices filtered down a hallway and we stopped to listen.

"We can't just leave them all here with no food or resources, Roy," a woman's voice said. "Those lazy bitches in the kitchen will just help themselves and run off. You know how they are."

A man, Roy apparently, laughed. "Caroline, you are the most hypocritical bitch on the planet. Those women in the kitchen take more interest in those kids and care more about them than you ever did. You don't give a shit about any of these kids. I mean, even I thought after a while you might develop some maternal instincts, or whatever passes for it with bitches like you, but that didn't happen, which was good. So, don't pretend you care now. Course that one kid, Diego or whatever, he definitely caught your eye, didn't he? He should've been out of here last year but you liked keeping him around."

There was some banging about, perhaps things being loaded or perhaps Caroline's temper exploding. We exchanged amused glances and Isabella shook her head. No matter how much we hoped every time for decent human beings, these people were always the same, in one way or another.

"Fuck you, Roy. We wouldn't be in this mess except for your stupid brother in Prescott who thought this was such a grand plan and look what happened to him. Sometimes the worm turns, you know? I always tried to warn both of you MacNeils but you never listen to anybody."

More banging and a shriek.

"Get your head straight, Caroline, or I'll leave you here for Josie Fallon and her pals to take care of, just like they did my brother. Cullen warned us. I don't care about these damn kids and I don't care if it's raining, we need to get the hell out of here, because I don't think Fallon and her motley crew give a shit about weather."

I sighed. How insulting to call us a motley crew. I cared quite a lot about weather too, but I'd heard enough, and a quick glance at my companions told me they had too. Waiting until they emerged or following the voices and confronting them now was the only question.

"I'm wet, cold and tired of listening to this bullshit. I'm not seeing anything different here than we've seen before. Josie?" Colin held back a sneeze.

I nodded. "Let's go, before my shivering disturbs my aim. That wouldn't be good." I grinned at Colin and he grinned back. Sometimes I just didn't give a damn and I knew right now he and Francisco didn't either. Isabella never had.

We walked down the hall towards the room the voices were coming from. I entered first, gun drawn, and the others flanked me as we spread out in the small office. A man, maybe forty years old, brown-haired, well-fed and well-dressed, stood beside a desk while a pretty red-haired woman, blood trickling from her mouth, looked at us in astonishment from her chair behind it. Both seemed paralyzed in place, staring at us as though we were monsters. I thought it only kind to put them out of their misery.

"Hi," I smiled. "I'm Josie Fallon, just in case you were wondering." I glanced over at Roy. "I knew your brother. Nice family."

He howled and lunged for the pistol on the desk. I shot him and he fell backwards into the wall behind the desk while Caroline screamed in an annoying high-pitched vocal until Isabella shot her twice and she landed damn near on top of her partner on the floor. It might've been the Diego comment, but it didn't matter. Isabella had issues and Caroline likely deserved it.

We'd deal with them later. We closed the door. Now it was about the children. The killing was easy. This was the hard part. We had learned as we went, but it was always different. We headed to the kitchen and our allies, hoping they still were our allies. We could use some.

FRANCISCO'S FRIEND SMILED AS WE CAME BACK TO THE kitchen, redolent with the mouth-watering aroma of whatever was in those pots. He softly spoke to her and her friends, and they seemed unperturbed by the news. The gunshots hadn't been muffled by the pouring rain but the women were far from traumatized. Maybe it was because two of us were women but I think it was more than that. They offered us coffee and gestured to one of the long tables. We gratefully accepted and peeled off our coats, hanging them on the back of the chairs to dry. We were still wet, but at least warmer and getting dryer. Francisco kept chatting with them and after a few minutes, he joined us at the table and the women set bowls of steaming stew in front of us, smiling. A platter of tortillas followed.

"So. That is Marta." He gestured to his friend. "They have been like slaves here, these ladies, and try to take care of the children that need care. They are happy the bad people are dead. There's only twelve kids here, is all. They just took a bunch of them away last week so we're too late for them. Right now, they're upstairs in their bedrooms but she thinks they should go get them and bring them down here for supper soon and tell them they are safe now. That is what I know."

He finished his coffee and Marta poured him another cup before he could ask. She did the same for us. I sure liked her on such a brief acquaintance. I grinned at her and she laughed.

Francisco smiled. "She said they have heard of you, Josie, the *rubio* girl who would rescue them."

Well, from the conversation between Roy and Caroline, they clearly knew about us but I hadn't expected the whole household would. I took a spoonful of stew, blowing on it to cool as I was starving. It was delicious, spicy and hot, full of chiles and chicken. I felt the warmth seep through my whole body as I spooned it in as fast as I could.

"Ask her who else besides the children and the couple live here or come and go, if anybody," Colin said, clearly agitated. He fiddled with his empty cup and peered around the room. The rain pounded against the small windows and there was no sign of a letup. Isabella had been silent as the grave as she ate her stew, likely just hungry and cold.

Francisco spoke to Marta again and I sure wish I spoke better Spanish, because they were having a lively conversation. I wished I'd ask him to see if she had any ideas about what to do with these kids, but I guess we'd get to that. Maybe leave them here with them. They had supplies and horses. Without Roy and Caroline, they'd likely do just fine. I finished the stew.

"*No, dos,*" Francisco said, surprise in his voice.

"*No, tres,*" Marta said, smiling. "*Tres balazos, tres hombres, si?*"

One of the other women shook her head. "*No, Marta. Senor Cullen fui a Tombstone esta manana. Estabas arriba.*"

Who the fuck was Senor Cullen? Roy MacNeil had mentioned that name too. The look of dismay on Marta's face might as well have been a warning shriek. I shoved back my chair at the same time as Colin did, the alarm on his face likely a mirror of mine. The chicken stew felt like lead shot in my stomach. I knew two from three, no matter what language it was in and so did everyone else.

Isabella put down her spoon and looked at me, her face pale, bright spots of angry red on her cheeks. "Goddamn it. I knew there was something not right about this place the minute we got here." She shoved her bowl away, food spattering everywhere. "We need to get the hell out of here, Josie. Right now. I don't give a damn about kids or storms. Whoever Cullen is, he knows about us and we didn't know about him. Which is bad."

Marta started to cry, and so did the other two. She and Francisco had a rapid fire conversation while we gathered ourselves and headed for the door. Isabella pulled her gun but Francisco held his hand out, still talking to Marta and I put my hand on Isabella's arm.

"Put the gun away, they don't know anything and it's not their fault," I said. "We just need to get out of here before this Cullen or anybody else shows up. Sounds like he went for reinforcements even if our friends here didn't know it. So get your ass to the barn, all right?"

She glared at me but put the gun away and went out the door. Colin and I followed quickly. The horses had a brief respite and some food and looked at us balefully when we ran in and grabbed their reins. I'm sure they were hoping for a longer rest than this but I had been too and my sympathy levels were pretty low.

I slung myself into the saddle and the others did the same. We rode out of the barn and away from the Lambs of the Lord into the rain. We didn't get far before we ran into the avenging angels, a posse headed by the illustrious Senor Cullen, who was clearly a dedicated servant of the Lord.

CHAPTER 26

"There's somebody out there," Colin said, swiping his hand over his eyes to get rid of the rain, a fruitless endeavor. "They're headed right for us, Josie."

"Shit," I said. I could see something ahead but I couldn't make out exactly what. It was moving so it likely wasn't a mesquite bush. Whatever it was, it couldn't be good. "Head right."

He did and we followed right behind him, horse to horse. We weren't riding fast, the rain was too hard to see through unless we wanted to ride off a cliff. When some big rocks loomed up, Colin pulled up and the rest of us did the same. We got off the horses and holding onto the reins, leaned into the rocks for some shelter.

"What the hell," I said to Colin, "you think whoever's out there is this Cullen guy or some law?"

"I don't know," he said. "Just as soon not find out."

We huddled into the rocks, rain running down our heads and trickling down our backs. We crushed together, the four of us, like a pack of rabbits huddled down taking strength and shelter from each other. I didn't mind and I don't think anyone else did either. We liked it.

It was the last solace we had.

The rain lessened then stopped altogether, the way it did in Arizona. We decided Colin and Francisco should head for the back side of the rocks and continue to scramble up to get better shots at our pursuers, while Isabella and I kept them occupied below. They did, taking two of the horses. It wasn't that late, a late-breaking feeble sun trying to get through the low hanging clouds, some of them right at ground level. It was misty, the moisture off the plants and desert floor rising, wisps and tendrils of fog swirling about.

We waited and it was eerily quiet. The rifle shot hit the rock an inch from my eye, bouncing tiny flecks of stone into my cheek.

"Hey, Fallon, you murdering bitch. Come on out. Dead or alive, it says, and I don't give a shit either way."

Christ. We scrambled like mice, dropping to the ground and releasing the horses, smacking them on their rears. They didn't deserve to get shot any more than we did. I crawled around one side of the rocks, Isabella beside me. I leaned back against the rocks and checked my gun. Loaded and I had a pocketful of bullets. Isabella did the same and nodded.

"How many are there?"

"I have no idea," I said. "Doesn't seem to be a lot. Easy enough. Although I'd prefer to take care of this myself. You go around to Francisco and Colin and get the hell out of here while I hold them off. After all, I'm a better shot and we all know that."

She snorted. "Fuck that, Josie. We're in this together and better shot, my ass." She kissed me on the cheek. "I'm getting better every day."

We waited. I couldn't see them but I could hear them, creeping closer. There were at least six of them, maybe more. I didn't want to die and even more, I didn't want Isabella to die, or the boys. I kept thinking if Billy was here, he'd know what to do, even if that wasn't true. He might've. The unexpected was his forte, but it was sort of mine, too. However, nothing came to mind before a tall man in a duster loomed up right in front of me. I pulled the trigger at the same time he backhanded me. I heard him yell as I went down, and I kept shooting until I ran out of bullets. Mine weren't the only shots, though.

Isabella made a muffled sound when she fell next to me, her face contorted in pain, her Colt falling out of her hand. I grabbed her arm and pulled her under me, her blood warm in the icy air, and scrambled for her gun. My hand closed on the grip but before I had a chance to aim it, stars exploded in front of my eyes and darkness enveloped me. I remember the toe of a large boot slamming into my head, the gun falling from my hand, Isabella moaning and then nothing at all.

❧

"She's a cute little thing. Can't quite credit her with killing all those folks. Looks to me like she oughta be playing with dolls and going to church socials."

"Ha. You always was soft on women, Frank. You heard about her, same as the rest of us. She's a nasty little piece, that one."

Frank still didn't sound convinced. The clink of a bottle on a glass echoed against the bare walls. "Burl, you look for the worst in everybody, especially women. 'Course if I had your face, my luck would've been shit with the ladies, too."

Chair legs hit the floor. "Fuck you, Frank. I don't have to listen to this. You can run your mouth and handle things just fine your own self tonight."

A door slammed and Frank chuckled. "Bye, asshole."

I couldn't see although my eyes were open. My head felt like it'd been hit with a shovel. I closed my eyelids since there was no point to keeping them open.

. . .

THE NEXT TIME I OPENED MY EYES, I COULD SEE EVEN though it was blurry, but there wasn't all that much to see. Iron bars between the hard surface where I lay on my back and beyond that, a room sparsely furnished with a desk, two chairs, a woodstove and a small window where a bright shaft of early sunshine shot through, right into my face. It smelled like old cigars and burnt coffee.

A man sat in a chair, a hat pushed over his face and his feet propped up on the desk. His snores weren't loud, but they were consistent.

I shifted my weight and propped myself up on an elbow. Which hurt, a lot, and everywhere. My head spun and I lay back down. I ran my hands over my arms, legs and body but everything seemed to be intact with no bandages. Except for my head which hurt worse than anything else. It was bandaged. I pulled a strip loose and peered at the bloody gauze. Ah. Yes. I remembered the kick. Then I remembered everything and sat up quickly, not caring about the pain.

Isabella.

I swung my legs over the side of the cot and took a deep breath. Shrieks needed preparation.

"Where is she?"

The man in the chair jerked, feet flying off the desk and he fell onto the wooden floor, blinking rapidly like an owl in the morning light.

"What the hell?"

He brushed himself off and glared at me.

"Where is she?"

"Jesus, girl, you got a set of lungs on you. Who you talking about, that girl that was with you?"

"Hell yes, who you think I'm talking about, the Virgin Mary? What'd you assholes do to her?"

He held out his hands. "Calm down, all right? She's over to the doc's place. She got shot and all, so it's hard to say how things are going. I can check later."

He walked up to the bars, like he was enchanted or something. I grabbed two of them with my hands, my face pressed onto the cold iron. "Fuck that, check now."

He stared back for a few seconds and blinked. "All right. I will." He held out a small brown bottle maybe two thirds empty. "Doc left this for you. Said you'd need to take just a sip or two when you woke up."

I snatched it from his hand, jerking it through the bars. Laudanum, from the look of it. I'd wait until I had some news before taking that so my head, what was left of it anyway, stayed clear. I had to make plans.

He walked unsteadily towards the door and turned back. "Your eyes are really green."

The door shut and I collapsed back onto the iron cot. This wasn't how it was supposed to go. And where were Colin and Francisco? I didn't dare ask, in case they'd gotten away. I hoped they had.

I must've dozed off, even without the laudanum. The door slammed and roused me from my troubled sleep. The dreams didn't begin to prepare me for the reality.

A man I hadn't seen before entered my cell. His suit was rumpled, but his eyes were kind if bloodshot. His moustache was a pale brown and it twitched as he sat down on my cot, and I inched my body over to accommodate him.

"Miss Fallon," he said, "I'm Dr. Edward Finch. Let us take a look at your wound. If you haven't taken any of that laudanum yet, now might be a good time to do so." I took his advice and nearly spit it out, nasty as it was. He gently proceeded to unwrap the gauze that encircled my head, wincing a little as he came to the end, throwing the bandages to the floor and waving his hand to a boy that looked about the same age as me. "I need warm water and carbolic, now." He gestured to the bloody gauze strips.

"And get these things out of here."

The young man reacted immediately, gathering up the debris,

his eyes flicking to me now and then which I ignored. He scurried out and the doctor sighed and turned to me.

"Ugly wound you have there, miss. Someone didn't like you much, although it could've been worse, I suppose."

"Yes," I said, smiling mindlessly the way people do when they've taken laudanum. "I could be dead, that's true. Does it say Dead or Alive on the poster?"

"No, it does not."

"Well, there you are then, Dr. Finch. Someone had an eye to their financial future."

"Indeed." He gave a dry chuckle. "You are very cynical for one so young, Miss Fallon."

"Ah. I come by it through experience, sir. Hard-won and all."

His assistant returned with a pail of warm water, carbolic acid and more bandages and I was cleansed and re-wrapped in no time. My laudanum haze was beginning to wear off by the time Finch finished and he took another small brown bottle from his bag and stood up.

"You'll need this in a while. I'll check on you tomorrow."

"Wait," I said, blinking myself into consciousness. "My friend. How is she? I want to see her."

He looked down and didn't meet my eyes. "I'm sorry, my dear. She...passed. I did everything I could, but she left us early this morning."

I felt as though all the air had left my lungs and would never return. I couldn't process the words he went on to say, more about sorry and he'd taken good care of her and some other platitudes that meant nothing to me. I finally managed to take a breath, then another and then I screamed my anguish, my grief and my relentless anger as loud as I possibly could, never wanting to stop. All I ever wanted was love and justice. Seems I wasn't getting either one today. I could only hope that Isabella finally experienced some of both.

I took a healthy swig of the laudanum and fell back onto the narrow bed.

CHAPTER 27

The food wasn't bad, I'll say that. No chocolate cake, but I wasn't going anywhere just yet so I held out hope. Frank, my main jailer, wasn't too bad either, unlike Burl, the other one. Seems I was in the Cochise County Jail, Tombstone, Arizona, under the tender care of one John Behan, Sheriff. I hadn't seen much of him, only one time.

Quite a dandy, he was. I wasn't too conversant with men's clothing styles, but Behan sure was, from his hat to his spats. I'd have to tell Colin about this if I ever saw him again. Behan came over and peered at me like I was a creature from myth, holding his handkerchief to his nose. Hell, I didn't smell that bad. I'd only been in here a week then.

I approached the bars with a sweet smile to give him a better look and when he took another step forward, I spit in his face. He jerked back like it was rattlesnake venom, swiping his handkerchief wildly at his face.

"Christ, Frank, the little bitch spit on me," he said. "That judge can't get here too soon."

The door slammed and Frank looked at me, not able to hide his smile. "You didn't make a friend there, Josie."

"I don't need friends like that idiot," I said, and went back to my cot, turning my back on him. I could use a couple of others though, and I didn't dare inquire about them. So far I hadn't heard a word about two men who might have been with Isabella and me that day. I had a small window that I could see out of in my cell, if I stood on the cot, but it didn't show me anything but an alley. The window in the front was bigger, fronting on a main street, but neither one had given me a glimpse of Colin or Francisco. I kept watch from both windows constantly but I'd never seen anyone who looked like them pass by. The thought that they'd just abandoned me not only hurt but made me angry, although I was trying not to be. Saving Colin had been the start of the road to this stinking cell and I couldn't believe he'd just leave me. Although, for all I knew, they could both be dead. It made my head hurt.

It was also my heart that hurt every time I thought of Isabella, and I thought of her a lot. I'd tried my best but in the end I'd failed her. I didn't want to have failed Colin or Francisco as well. We tried to save orphans but we were in search of a better life too and we'd lost sight of that. You can't save anybody if you don't save yourself first.

This epiphany may have come a little late, Fallon, I thought. *Neither the judge or Sheriff Behan gives a damn about any of us anyway. Justice has an entirely different meaning to them. For them, it means you swinging from a rope for your sins.*

Then I met my lawyer.

"Miss Fallon?" A nervous cough. I regretfully woke from my nap and turned over. Sleeping at any time was my only escape from this place.

Jonathan Casey was the most awkward young man I'd ever seen. A bad haircut topped an equally ill-shaven face plastered with a nervous smile. A brown suit that looked a size too small for him had pants that ended two inches above his ankles, showing sagging socks and a well-worn pair of shoes. I sat up to get a better look at him. The view didn't improve. Nor did my confidence level with every word that came out of his mouth. If he was what stood between me and a rope, I was doomed.

Truthfully I was surprised that I had a lawyer at all, but I guess John Behan followed the letter of the law. Jonathan Casey was from Pittsburgh, seeking legal fame and experience by defending dangerous outlaws in the west. I wasn't his first client, but close to it. I didn't think he was going to have a stellar career. Then again, I hadn't ever met a lawyer before but even so, he didn't seem particularly accomplished or confident.

Frank brought him a chair and he sat down awkwardly outside the bars of my cell. He cleared his throat nervously.

"Miss Fallon," he said. "I'm Jonathan Casey, here to defend you against the charges of murder. It is my understanding that you killed one Robert Maloney while escaping from your home, Angel's Refuge, leaving in the company of one Colin Donnelly, current whereabouts unknown. It is further charged that you and your colleagues have been on a crime spree across the state, culminating here at the orphanage Lambs of the Lord where you killed the proprietors there, a Mrs. Caroline Pearson and Mr. Roy MacNeil before being apprehended and brought here to stand trial and account for your crimes."

"None of that is true."

I stared at him. He stared back, I'll give him that.

"You may not be aware of this, Miss Fallon, young as you are, but as your attorney, anything you tell me is in complete confidence and between you and me only. It is to your advantage that you are honest with me, and in that way, I can defend you better when I know the truth. I will defend you even if you tell me you did kill these people and I cannot divulge that information. It is my job to try and make you a free woman, if I can."

I took him at his word, since I had nothing to lose. Truthfully, I was pretty skeptical about Mr. Jonathan Casey and his abilities but he was the first avenue I'd seen out of this mess. In the next hour, in whispered conversation, I told him all of it, only leaving out Billy, Francisco and of course, Hiram and Sally. I didn't think Mule Gulch was going to be on the table and I was right. He'd brought along a pad of paper but once I got to the part about Stella's, he capped his pen and just listened.

His face paled a few times here and there, but he stayed the course. It was actually good to let someone know what really happened and why we did the things we did. In my mind, it was justified. I knew, however, it wouldn't be in the eyes of the law.

"Just to be clear. In every single incident you've described, except with Robert Maloney, there was never a witness, not counting of course, young children who would likely never be called upon to testify, due to their age and circumstances. Is that correct? Even at Stella's?"

"Correct. Even at Stella's, I was disguised as a boy and no one else intervened or saw us."

He thought for a while and then nodded. "From what you have told me regarding Maloney, I think we can call that one self-defense, and for the others, since there are no witnesses, even for Maloney's death, since the girls that were with you have disappeared, it would be against the law to find you guilty of any of them, even at the Lambs of the Lord. None of the workers there have had anything to say about you or your companions. It's as though you were never there. That seems to be case with all the other ones as well."

I smiled at him and before he could stop himself, he smiled back and then coughed, staring down at his notepad.

"Are you shocked?"

He looked up at me. "Frankly, yes."

"So you think I'm a depraved killer, Jonathan Casey?"

He didn't meet my eyes for a minute or so and then when he did, his gaze was intense. "No, Miss Fallon. I think you found yourself in circumstances beyond your control and you had to make choices. Unfortunately, they weren't good ones."

He coughed again. "Especially when you could have stopped at any time. That is what bothers me some. However,

I am not your judge, only God and perhaps Judge McIntyre tomorrow have that privilege. It's not the issue, legally. Since there are no witnesses, as I said, we might have a chance to have you found not guilty and defending yourself in the first instance.

"So, Jonathan Casey, will I walk away from here a free woman?"

He stood up. "I'd like to say yes, Miss Fallon, but that is based upon the case the judge will make. We'll use the self-defense for Maloney, but in point of fact, there are no witnesses to any of the crimes they say you've committed, or even those of your colleagues, the late Isabella St. James and the two men who rode with you, one Colin Donnelly and an unnamed gentleman of Mexican ancestry, both of whom seem to have disappeared from the face of the earth."

That said, there are a lot of powerful people, and not just here, who want to see you hang. What lies they may concoct to make that happen, we cannot foresee. Nor what the judge will do. Judges in the territory are not always, shall we say, equitable in their verdicts, depending on many factors. They've only given me two days to prepare a defense for you and this is day two. The trial is set for tomorrow."

I reached through the bars and took his hand. It surprised him but not unpleasantly so apparently, since he didn't pull away and moved a trifle closer.

"I'm counting on you, Jonathan Casey. Don't let me down."

He squeezed my hand. He had sincere brown eyes and he blushed, just a little. "I'll do my best, Miss Fallon."

"Josie," I said. "We know each other much better now."

After he left, for a little while I felt hopeful. Since I hadn't had a bath in some time and I likely looked like I'd been left out in the sun too long, I had no illusions it was my feminine charms that had enticed him to plead my case. Still, it had been good to get all that off my chest. What Jonathan Casey didn't know, appalled as he was at what he did, is that I didn't regret a damn thing I'd done and I'd do it all again, given the choice, most of it anyway.

Dinner was for once, pretty good, the tortillas had chicken and tomatoes to go with the usual beans and I ate every bite. I stood at my usual vigil at the tiny window, looking out at the alley. Tonight there was an old Mexican man in a serape and sombrero, his head down on his knees, sleeping in the stony dirt. He didn't look as though he was in much better circumstances than mine. I wished him well. Life wasn't easy for anybody.

Just as I was about to turn away, he lifted his head and tilted the sombrero away from his eyes. Francisco smiled and raised his hand before getting to his feet and walking away.

It seems I wasn't alone after all.

❧

I COULD HARDLY SLEEP AFTER THAT, BETWEEN TALKING TO Jonathan Casey and seeing Francisco. I'd been sitting in this jail and never talked to anybody but the deputies and then today it was like the whole world remembered I existed. I lay on the hard cot and tried to sleep anyway, my skin itching. I hadn't seen any lice so it was likely just nerves and dirt, but it still felt as though something was crawling on me.

They're here, I kept saying to myself, they're here. If I got convicted, maybe somehow they'd get me out of Tombstone before they hung me. I looked over at Burl, sleeping with his feet on the desk, his snores echoing through the small building. How hard could it be to shoot that guy and break me out? I knew Isabella wouldn't have had a problem, but then neither did Colin. My mind was reeling with the thought that maybe, if things went in a righteous way for me, one way or another, I could say goodbye to Arizona forever.

Something woke me just before dawn. I pulled the thin blanket over my head when a pebble hit me on the head. I jerked up, nervous as a ringtailed cat, and peered between the bars on the tiny open window. Billy stood in the alley close under the window, the familiar grin I loved on his face.

"Hey princess," he whispered. "You want to get out of this place?"

I stifled a laugh, my heart thudding with joy. "Hey prince. This is no tower. I missed you. What the hell you doing here?"

He shrugged in that Billy way. "Colin came to get me and here I am."

So that's why I hadn't seen Colin. God, I loved these boys. "Thing is, prince, I have a trial today. Now I got a lawyer who thinks maybe he can get me off, so maybe we should wait before you guys get in even more trouble on my account."

He cocked his head. "Think so?" He pushed his hat back and scratched his head. "I don't see no percentage in that, Josie. Lawyers are snakes and none of these people can be trusted. I know that better than anybody."

"But if he's telling the truth, I'd be a free woman, Billy. It's worth a try," I said. "If it goes bad, then..."

He sighed. "All right, I'll tell Colin and Francisco. I have to tell you something, though, and you ain't gonna like it."

"What's that?"

"They built a gallows down the street here. It's all set to go. I think it's ready for you, Josie."

My stomach lurched. "What?"

"Telling you true, girl. Anybody else in that damn jail?"

"No," I whispered, scarcely believing what he was saying. I pushed my hair from my forehead, sweaty now. "That can't be. I've not even had a trial yet."

"Trials don't matter a damn to them. We killed too many important people who been giving money to the law to ignore their shit, Josie. They can't have that. Not when they can find somebody to blame it on. Hell, I learned that in Lincoln County the hardest way you can."

I tried to breathe. It wasn't coming easy.

"Still, I want to try. Just as easy in two days as one, wouldn't you say?"

He shook his head. "No. You're wrong, Josie, but if it's what you want we'll wait. Then, we'll only have one night so be ready."

He melted away into the dark and I sat back down on my bed. I hope I hadn't just sealed my own death warrant. My stomach twisted again and I threw up in the slop pail in the corner. I had a horrible feeling Billy might be right.

CHAPTER 28

I sat at a table in the courtroom, Frank standing by as though I'd make a break for freedom at any minute, watching the seats fill up with eager townspeople and god knows who else, all of us waiting for the judge to enter and take his seat at the raised bench at the back of the room and the proceedings to begin. It wasn't a very impressive place to have my fate decided. A relatively small room, perhaps the town meeting place or a schoolroom, doing double duty as an arena of justice, bare wooden floors and what looked like hastily arranged tables and chairs. As we waited, more people filed in, until the room was very crowded, most of them standing around the room, murmuring to themselves. I tried not to listen to the comments I overheard since none of them were good. My stomach was churning, threatening to launch the bacon and eggs I'd eaten early that morning. It wasn't every day you got to be on trial for your life, after all.

Jonathan Casey entered and took the empty chair beside me, thumping his leather briefcase on the floor between us, taking out a sheaf of papers he placed on the table. He gave me a quick smile and squeezed my hand before leafing through his notes.

"It'll be all right, Josie," he whispered but he looked as nervous as I was.

We waited, the minutes ticking by, and then Judge McIntyre entered and took a seat at the raised bench. He was an older bearded man, gray-haired and rangy and he didn't look happy about being where he was this day. He banged a small wooden hammer on his table and stared out at the assembled people in front of him, then focusing his gaze on me.

"We're assembled here today to hear the case against one Josie Fallon, accused murderess. We already know the charges against her and they are attested and well documented, and in my possession at this time, so we are prepared to move forward with no further testimony and witnesses needed for the prosecution. Mr. Casey, I understand you are here to defend Miss Fallon against the charges, so please state your case for this court."

Jonathan Casey stood up, cleared his throat and took a deep breath. "Thank you, your honor. Miss Fallon is innocent of these charges, a young girl who only defended herself against imminent danger. If your honor allows, I will expound further. I further request that she be granted a trial by jury, as is her right."

Judge McIntyre straightened in his chair and scowled at Jonathan Casey for a long minute. "In the interests of time and justice, Mr. Casey, we are dispensing with the jury option in this instance. I am the adjudicator here and well familiar with Miss Fallon's alleged offenses. Please go ahead and state your case. I am all ears."

Jonathan Casey launched into an articulate and in my opinion, heartfelt defense and Judge McIntyre allowed it, for all of ten minutes. Then he held up his hand and banged his hammer once again.

"Mr. Casey. Allow me to interrupt and there is no need to expound further on her behalf. The court finds your arguments to be spurious. We do not need to hear more. Do you need to see a tornado to know what damage it has wrought in its path?

No, Mr. Casey, you do not. So it is with the death and destruction that has been dealt in this case."

Miss Fallon is clearly a menace to society, a vicious and misguided young woman who has taken out her wrath upon innocent and devoted members of communities across the territory, those who have only sought to provide solace and benevolence to the unfortunate. She has enticed others to her evil cause and has committed havoc and murder. This cannot and will not be tolerated. We are a territory of the United States government. These sorts of horrifying crimes and vigilante style justice cannot go unpunished. In a civilized country of people who observe the laws of the land, true justice must prevail."

"Miss Fallon. It is my judgement that you are guilty of the crimes of murder, as accused. Furthermore, it is my judgement that you shall be punished for these crimes by hanging by the neck until dead, under the jurisdiction of this court and this county." He banged the hammer once again emphatically on the table, rose and left the room.

Cheers and applause erupted from the crowd assembled in the room as Jonathan Casey and I sat at our small table, stunned and looking at each other in shock. He took my cold hand in his.

"God, Josie," he stammered, "I never thought it would go this bad, or so fast." He looked around like he was looking for salvation, but there was none to be had. "Shit, how could he do this? It's not even legal. It's not supposed to be like this."

I took my hand away. "Shut up, Jonathan Casey. Too many people lost money because of the people we killed. There's bigger forces at work here and neither one of us can do anything about it."

He stared at me. "I'm sorry, I'm so sorry, I didn't know."

"Maybe now you do. This one wasn't really your fault, except for giving me hope you had no right to give. Go back to Boston or wherever you came from, because this isn't the place for you."

Frank grabbed my elbow and jerked me out of my seat. I

shook him off and he had the sense to let go. "I'll go with you, Frank. You don't have to make it hard."

Rather shamefacedly, he walked beside me out of the courtroom and down the street to the jail.

"Sorry, Josie," he said. "I was kinda hopin' it wouldn't go this way."

I snorted. "Gee, thanks, Frank. But you all knew it would, didn't you?"

He nodded and looked down the street. I followed his gaze and found Billy was right. The gallows looked new and well made, the crossbar on top sporting a noose. Wouldn't be any cheating that. I swallowed hard.

"You might've told me," I said.

"Sorry," he said again. "I didn't want to make you feel bad."

I started to laugh then, so hard it turned to tears and I was gasping for breath by the time he put me back in my cell. That goddamn Billy. He was always right.

My fate had been decided so fast it wasn't even noon. As soon as Frank turned the key and left I curled into a ball on my cot, my back to the outer room. No more tears. I needed every ounce of energy to put towards getting out of here before they led me out and down that street to put a rope around my neck. I heard Frank leave as usual for his noonday meal, locking the street door behind him. I stood up and went to the window but the alley was empty. I wasn't surprised, really, it was too risky in broad daylight but still, disappointed. It was going to be very long afternoon.

Just as I started to turn away, movement caught my eye and a man wearing a serape and a sombrero ambled into the alley, carrying a bottle of whiskey. He tipped the sombrero with the top of the bottle and I saw it was Francisco. He came up right under the window.

"*Hola*, Josie."

"*Hola*."

"We will come back tonight when the fat one is on his shift.

He sleeps a lot, we have seen. This girl brings his dinner from the hotel every night. We have seen this too. Billy has some powder to put in his food to make sure he sleeps very well. Be ready, *amiga*. As Billy says, we have only this one chance. *Comprende?*"

"Yes," I said. "Oh hell, yes."

Francisco smiled and ambled away, stumbling as he reached the end of the alley and saw two men standing on the wooden sidewalk. I watched as he took a swig from his bottle. One of the men shoved him a little.

"*Perdon, senor*," Francisco mumbled and staggered away as they watched him go, shaking their heads.

"Goddamn worthless drunks, too many of 'em around here lately. Most of them Mexicans and they need to just go back over the border."

"I'll say. Oughta just shoot 'em, you ask me. Course then I might end up at the end of a rope like that gal in there."

"True. You gonna be here tomorrow for the hanging?"

"Hell, wouldn't miss it. She's got it coming, what I hear. Too bad, she's a cute little piece."

They wandered off and I sat back down on the cot, wishing once again I had my gun. Like Billy said, some people just deserved killing. Those two were no exception. Not to my rules, anyway.

❧

JUST BEFORE DARK, FRANK SLID A TIN PLATE UNDER THE BARS.

"Didn't know what you wanted, Josie, so I took a wild guess. Since it's going to be your last meal and all, I made sure they put in a treat. Enjoy."

Frank was a jerk, but he wasn't mean, not like Burl, who was. Burl enjoyed taunting me and saying filthy things whenever he got the chance, which was pretty much all night, until the fat fool fell asleep. I ignored him but it did always get to me, just a little.

I took the plate. Fried chicken, potatoes and biscuits. And there it was: a slice of chocolate cake. Memories surfaced and tears prickled behind my eyelids which I blinked desperately away. We'd still have chocolate cake together again, the four of us with just a little luck. Maybe not in Prescott, but somewhere.

Burl came in and Frank left, the same every night. Burl came up to the bars and stared at me, smirking.

"Looks like this is your last night, girl. Ol' Burl here's got just what you need before you see them Pearly Gates, you know?" He cupped his hands around his privates and shoved himself towards me.

I stared at him from my cot, silent as the grave.

"Just say the word and I can slip in there and make you happy."

"I'd sooner fuck a pig covered in shit before you, Burl."

He stepped back. "We'll just see about that in a little while, missy. Ain't like you're goin' anywhere and I got the keys."

The girl from the hotel came in with his supper as always. She was young, her brown hair lanky around her thin face. I wondered what he paid her but it didn't matter. I stood at the bars and her eyes flicked towards me as though if she looked too long I'd infect her with something, her usual routine. Sometimes she stayed and I could hear Burl's grunts before he tackled his food. Tonight though, she left pretty quickly. Maybe he had something else planned.

Well, good, I thought. So did I.

Burl finished his food in no time like he always did and broke out the whiskey. This could go on for some time, as it did every night, him talking nasty to me until he passed out. Occasionally somebody would stop by to ask a question, or rarely Behan would come by, to make sure things were up to his standards at the Cochise County Jail. Tonight it was quiet. I waited for Burl's usual conversation, but tonight it was limited to his usual suggestions and died off fairly soon. Then I heard the snores, earlier than usual. It seemed Billy had done his work well.

I stood up, my nerves strung to the breaking point. I didn't know when they'd come. When the door opened, Colin and Billy stood there, bandannas over their faces, guns drawn and my heart leaped. They shut the door behind them, glancing over at Burl, who hadn't moved a muscle. Billy rustled around in the desk drawers and brought out my gunbelt, the Colt still in its holster. Colin reached for the keys hanging on the wall behind him and came over to my cell.

"Hey Josie. You ready to go for a ride, girl?"

"Real funny, Irish. Open the damn door. I'd ride to hell to get out of here."

He fumbled with the keys and door swung wide. He hugged me, and then Billy joined him, clutching me to his chest, his face buried in my hair.

"Goddamn. You all right?"

I smiled at both of them. "Now I am."

Billy handed me my gunbelt and I buckled it on. Colin left the keys in the cell door and we walked past Burl, who was making snuffling noises that turned my stomach. He blinked and looked blearily up at me.

I pulled out my gun and pointed it at Burl.

"No, Josie," Billy said, his voice rising. "We can't afford this."

"Oh, yes we can," I said. "I can't afford not to. Like you told me, some people just deserve killing. I've had to listen to this bastard every night."

"No," Billy said, and pushed my hand down, pointing the gun at the floor. "For one thing, it'll bring 'em runnin' and we need to get away clean. We've got a long way to go tonight. Think, Josie."

He was right, I was being stupid. I flipped the gun around and brought in down on Burl's head instead. He'd be out from the drugs anyway, but it was satisfying.

We ran around to the alley, where Francisco waited with three more horses. We rode south into the desert night, the moon as full as my hopes. I took a deep breath of fresh and free air.

CHAPTER 29

We stopped just before dawn to rest the horses. The sky had a yellowish cast, then some darker patches of clouds scudding by as the darkness began to pale. We sat in the sand and watched the pale streams of pink, lavender and gold light up the sky, passing around the whiskey bottle as usual. None of us had said much since we left Tombstone, we rode hard with just terse directions and hand gestures. So far, there didn't seem to any sign of pursuers. I guess Burl had stayed undisturbed a long time. When they come to hang Josie Fallon this morning, they're going to be disappointed.

I stood up and paced around, feeling awkward and stupid, because I'd managed to get us all into this mess, and so grateful to all of them that I had a hard time getting the words out.

"I'm sorry it went like this. I'm sorry about Isabella. I'm sorry you had to hide out and get my very sorry ass out of that jail. I thought I was going to die today. Because of you, I'm here and not hanging from a rope. Saving me from that --"

My throat closed up like that rope really was getting tight around my neck. I gulped for air and Billy was there, his arms around me. Good thing because my whole body began to convulse, tears rolling down my cheeks. I hadn't cried since the day Isabella left Angel's Refuge, the first and until now, the last time. Josie Fallon never cried.

But Josie Fallon did. It was messy and ugly and what I needed more than anything. It all poured out, grief, resentment, anger, Isabella's death, the pain of never being good enough and unable to help those who couldn't help themselves except in the only bloody way I knew would work. Impetuous and violent decisions that most of which I wouldn't change and didn't regret, because from the first one, the results now sat around me. I smiled blearily at Colin, patting Billy's damp shirt.

"Where we headed?"

"Mexico."

"What?" I croaked the word out. "Why are we going to Mexico?"

Billy kissed me on the temple and hugged me, a little too tightly. "Josie girl. You and Colin ain't safe anywhere else right now. You been up to some shenanigans since I been gone, not that I wasn't expectin' it. You stay anywhere on the north side of this border, it's only a matter of time before they arrest you again and hang you without a thought. Believe me, I know how that works. You got some serious law after you, especially after that piece of shit trial. Mexico is the only place, and it's a pretty good place."

I didn't have the slightest idea, but every Mexican I'd ever known had been a good friend so their country likely was too. Lawmen from the territory couldn't follow us there, I knew that much and that was good enough for me.

Francisco laughed. "We could be there already. The border is tricky around here, *amigos*. Although, we may be some time from a cantina or any of my esteemed *familia. Sin embargo,* we ride on."

We did find a cantina, a few hours further on. We passed fields of green, likely corn and other things and came upon a small village, with adobe houses and a church with a bell tower, with people going about their business in an open air market. We tied up our horses at the rail outside a low building across from the church. Francisco was in charge now, since everyone else's Spanish was terrible. I practically fell off my horse at this point, and Colin righted me, leading me inside into the cool depths of the saloon. It wasn't fancy, but it had a long bar across the back wall and some scattered chairs and tables. Francisco talked with the bartender, a friendly fellow, and we sat down at a table. A bottle of tequila and glasses followed quickly, along with water and we took full advantage of both.

An older woman bustled in, bringing plates of tortillas and beans and we fell upon the food like ravenous wolves. I'll remember that food forever. It wasn't just good, it was reviving. We all had seconds and sat back in our chairs. We were safe. We were in Mexico. We could all breathe.

"Now what?" I said, setting my glass down. "We going anywhere special or just going?"

Francisco nodded. "*Tio Raul's*. My uncle, *amigos*. From there, we will make plans."

"So he lives around here?" I said. "Where are we anyway?"

"Sonora," Francisco smiled. "We will be there tonight, Josie. I sent him a letter. Have no fear. We are welcome."

Apparently they'd already discussed this and that was fine with me. These little villages looked friendly and right now I'd be happy to stay on, herd some goats and plant corn. We got back on our horses and rode west.

The countryside was similar to that of Arizona, but with more cactus and more rolling hills. We passed a few more villages and planted fields and just as the dusk was falling, came upon a tall adobe archway. It was wide enough to drive two wagons through side by side, festooned with burning torches in sconces, lighting up the letters painted on tiles that curved in a semi-circle across the top, "Rancho del Valle Dorado". Low adobe walls led off in both directions, as far as I could see. This was a big ranch.

Beyond the archway, a road led toward more lights and structures in the distance, along with half a dozen mounted men.

Francisco waved at them, grinned and we silently rode on with our escort.

We passed corrals, barns and smaller houses before the road ended at an adobe house which seemed to stretch out forever on both sides, ablaze with torches on patios and courtyards and lining a brick entryway. Francisco vaulted off his horse and embraced a tall man who stood at the end of the walkway.

They had quite a conversation. I looked at Billy and Colin and they shrugged, waiting just as I was. Finally Francisco turned towards us. The older man stepped forward. He was very handsome, dressed in a snowy white shirt and black pants, his boots decorated with crimson swirls. A man clearly in charge of his world, one in which we had arrived uninvited.

"Come. You are my guests here, for as long as there is need." He smiled and opened his arms. "You are *compadres* of my nephew, that is all that matters. It is good he has come home. You are all welcome here."

THIS COULD BE HEAVEN, I THOUGHT, LEANING BACK AGAINST the edge of the tin bathtub prettily painted with flowers and vines. The water smelled of lemons and orange blossoms as did the soap the smiling maid had handed to me. I had thought being clean again was a dream gone with my freedom but I was wrong about that, clearly, likely with a host of other things.

I wasn't sure how long it'd been since I nodded off but it was the chilly bathwater that finally woke me. I rinsed my hair a second time and stepped out of the tub, wrapping myself in a fluffy white towel. Earlier, while I had been soaking, the young maid had come in and left some clothes on the bed, taking away the ones I'd worn on arrival. A white blouse and a full skirt, both embroidered with multi-colored flowers fit perfectly and I wrapped the red sash around my waist, similar to the outfit I'd seen on the girl. I'd never worn clothes like this before, so soft and pretty. They felt wonderful against my skin. I wasn't quite sure the image I saw in the mirror was even me. The dressing table held some toiletries, including a brush and comb, so I set to work on my wet tangled hair.

The bedroom was large, furnished with a four-poster bed, the dressing table and a nightstand with a candlestick, and two chairs in front of a beehive fireplace. Colorful rugs softened the tile floors, and the breeze wafting in through the window open to the night carried the scent of flowers and spices.

Billy, Colin and Francisco were somewhere in the house, but I'd had no objection to being whisked off immediately by a pretty older woman that Francisco introduced as his aunt Evangelina, her eyes kind, and deposited in this lovely sanctuary. I needed to go find them and thank Francisco's family for their hospitality, but all I really wanted to do was throw myself on that bed and sleep for days.

Still, there was nothing for it. I opened the door and peered into the hallway. I could hear guitar music and murmured conversation as well as the aroma of food that made my mouth water. I stepped out, closing the door behind me. All the rooms seemed to empty out into a pathway that led towards the center of the complex and I followed the sounds through gardens lush with greenery and flowers, the tiles smooth under my bare feet, until I came to open double doors.

Sitting around a long table were Francisco, his aunt and uncle, a couple of other older men I'd never seen before, along with Colin and Billy. A chandelier blazed overhead, lit with dozens of candles. Silver serving dishes, some still covered, as well as china and crystal glittered in the candlelight. They seemed to be having a grand time.

"Hello."

"Ah, Senorita Fallon, please," Raul said, pulling out a chair beside him. "We were hoping you would join us."

Billy shoved his chair back and took my hand, leading me to the proffered chair. "You look beautiful," he whispered. Colin smiled, as did everyone. My hair was still damp but at least it was clean, and the clothes really did help me feel pretty.

"Feel better?" Evangelina said. "I hope you like your room."

"Oh yes," I said. "Thank you so much. For everything." I looked down and smoothed my skirts. "I love these."

"*De nada*," she said, waving her hand. "We will get you more if you like them. They suit you. Now, you must eat, *mija*."

A maid brought me a plate and silverware and I filled my plate from the delectable offerings. Francisco introduced the two handsome men I'd not met before as his uncles Vitorio and Paulo. These Montoyas were a large family. While I concentrated mainly on my fork, conversation resumed and flowed around me, discussing food, music, cattle, land, banditos, human nature and eventually, centered on law and those who would corrupt it as well as those who had broken it, both on this side of the border and on the other. It became clear that Francisco had shared everything with his uncle, from Hiram's ranch until Tombstone, perhaps before.

I sat back in my chair, thinking I wanted to give these kind people some sort of explanation, even though it might not be needed. I cleared my throat.

"Please, I don't want to ruin the evening, but I have something to say. I've done things that I'm not proud of, but things that I felt had to be done. These young men have joined me in those pursuits. Sometimes to save others, sometimes for justice and it is true, sometimes because there was no other way, at least not a way I knew. Perhaps it not good to say this, but I think would do most of those things again in the same circumstances."

I looked up at Raul and then Evangelina. "I haven't had time to become older and wiser." I gestured at Francisco, Colin and Billy. "None of us have. That doesn't mean we don't wish to. For now, all I can do is thank you for giving us sanctuary. I hope we can prove worthy of your trust."

I meant it all too, at least most of it. No point in going into bloody details or that I had a really terrible temper. Nobody offering you solace wants to know those things. Maybe if I actually made it to older and wiser I could curb my baser instincts. I'd work on that. I looked down at my hands, afraid to make eye contact with anybody in the room. It was dead silent.

Evangelina came over to me, putting her arms around my shoulders. She smelled of roses and aside from Isabella, no woman had ever shown me the kindness and sympathy she did at that moment.

"*Mija*. You are a child who has suffered and done things you should have never had to do. You are safe here with us. It is now time to find peace. *Verdad*."

Tears prickled behind my eyelids once again but I swallowed and pushed them away. I did my crying this morning. Instead, I stood up and turned into her embrace.

"*Gracias*," I said, employing one of my few words of Spanish. "I am in your debt forever as are my friends, *tia* Evangelina, if you allow me to call you that."

"Of course, Josie," she smiled at me. "I was hoping you would."

Raul laughed and clapped his hands. "*Amigos*. To the terrace and some tequila, eh?"

God, these were lovely people, I thought, gathering my borrowed skirts around me. They do exist in this world. I smiled at Francisco and took his hand and brought it to my lips as we walked outside to a patio

"God, Francisco. You have been riding with us all this time and never said a word about this place or your family here. It's like a kingdom and you a prince."

He smiled ruefully. "I know, but I am the youngest and perhaps foolishly wanted to make my own way and to see more of the world, but I am glad to be home."

"I wish more than anything Isabella was here with us."

He grasped my hand tighter and closed his eyes for a second. "As do I, Josie. She would've loved it here. She is at peace now and I must believe that."

Outside in the courtyard, a fire burned in a pit, the smell of mesquite mingling with the scent of the jasmine all around us, the firelight making flickering shadows on the trees, flowers and cactus around us. Upholstered chairs and sofas were scattered around the fire while trays of tequila and glasses sat on the tables where Raul and Vitorio were pouring enthusiastically.

Billy and Colin came up behind us. "Josie, you are special," Colin grinned. He was on the road to being very drunk and who could blame him? It had been a very long day in a series of them.

Billy took my other hand and pulled me away from Francisco, who went to take a seat beside his uncle. "It's been a busy couple of days," he said. "I love you, Josie Fallon." He kissed my cheek and smiled that lazy Billy smile, those blue eyes bright even in the firelight.

I wanted to throw my arms around him and go back to that beautiful bedroom more than anything else right then, but we'd have to wait a bit on that. I pulled him back into the shadow of a looming cactus. "No more than I love you. You came for me."

"I always will."

I hugged him and kissed him so long they probably thought we got lost on the way.

"Let's have some tequila," I said. "I bet Raul has the best you've ever tasted."

Billy laughed. "I kinda like the taste of you better, but tequila does have its charms, too."

That tequila went down like liquid silver and we savored every last drop.

CHAPTER 30

I rolled over on my side and found my face resting on Billy's chest. I stuck out my tongue and licked a rib. Salty. That boy was a hard worker. He snored softly and I smiled and rolled onto my back. It was still dark but as I lay there, I could hear birds chattering and the aroma of coffee somewhere close by.

Maybe I should get up, I thought, because there was a whole world to be explored on this *hacienda* we'd been lucky enough to land in. Then again, there was a very nice world to be explored right in this bed. The *hacienda* could wait. I fell back asleep, smiling.

"Josie."

"Mmmmh."

Billy's arm came around me, pulling me into him as close as he could. He kissed the back of my neck at the same time as his hand slid seamlessly between my legs. My eyes flew open and then closed again with pleasure. A soft bed, the man you loved with his body next to you was the ultimate way to begin the day.

A soft knock on the door came a while later. Startled, we looked at each other but there was no time for him to sneak back to his room or any other subterfuge. The same maid from last night's bath time opened the door and deposited a tray on the table, giggling softly as she glanced over at the bed. I put my finger to my lips and she nodded, giggling again, shutting the door silently behind her.

It was full daylight now and Billy padded over to the table, lifting the silver lids. Hot chocolate and cinnamon buns revealed themselves and the smell of both drew me over like a lariat around my waist. We sat on the chairs, naked as the day we were born, and wordlessly devoured every crumb, draining the pot of chocolate.

"Well, hell. That's the way people should start a day, I swear."

I couldn't disagree, my tongue running over my upper lip, getting that last bit of chocolate. We'd eaten, drank and made love but the one thing we hadn't done yet was talk about Tombstone: how I got there, how I got out, where he'd been and what was next. For now, we were in a safe paradise here and somehow all that was best left alone for a bit.

We dressed, me in my riding skirt and shirt, which I'd discovered laundered and folded neatly in my room last night, along with my boots which had been polished and looked like new. Billy pulled on his clothes from last night. They'd all had a bath, but I doubted it was as lovely as mine had been, and had put on clean clothes from their saddlebags. I was a little short on much more but I had a feeling Tia Evangelina would help me out. We were resplendent compared to what we looked like when we arrived. We grinned at each other, opened the door and entered into the world of Golden Valley Ranch.

Colin was sitting on the patio where we'd been the evening before, drinking coffee, the sun bright. Water glittered in cascades from a tiered fountain I'd not noticed the night before and the sound was soothing.

"Ah, there you are," he said. "Not exactly up with the chickens, eh?"

"That jail cell wasn't exactly conducive to rest," I said, daring him to say another word on that subject. He chuckled and went back to his coffee.

"Where is everyone?" Billy said. "It's pretty quiet around here for such a big place."

"Francisco and his uncles rode out early this morning," Colin said. "Ranch business. I thought I'd relax a bit and wait for you two. Besides, I could use some time out of the saddle. Evangelina said something about a picnic later on, meeting up with them."

"This is quite a place," Billy said. "Francisco sure kept this under his hat, didn't he?"

"I'll say. This morning Raul was saying they're running 30,000 head out there, and they've got room for more. Close to half a million acres. They've got 200 some people on the payroll. Seems unbelievable."

Billy whistled. "Christ, those Texas boys could learn a lot from our Mexican friends. Makes the States' cattle operations look penny-ante. The Montoyas sure know how to do it."

Colin nodded. "'Course they been at it for close on a hundred years here, according to Raul. They came over from Spain." He laughed. "The Irish could learn something there, too."

For a while, we sat in the sunshine and for the first time in what seemed like forever, my muscles began to still. I leaned my head back in the chair and closed my eyes, listening to the tinkling of the water until I felt Billy begin to twitch. He did that.

I'd thought to wait a bit, but it seemed a good time to talk.

"So, tell me. How did you get together to break me out?"

"That Colin. I swear that boy could track a hawk in the sky," Billy said. "All's I said when I left was something about Lordsburg and he rode in there hell for leather tellin' me you were in jail, Isabella was dead and I didn't need to hear anythin' else. I was just about to head north too, so his timin' was good."

"That's about it. People know Billy and they like him, so he wasn't that hard to find if they think you're a friend," Colin grinned and nudged Billy with his boot. "God knows why. Must be the way he plays croquet or something."

Billy laughed. "Aw, come on Colin. It's just that I'm so handsome and charmin' they can't resist. Besides, I buy them a lot of drinks."

"Hmm," I said, winding my hair around my finger, a bad habit I have. "So you thought you needed help and didn't want to try it on your own, Colin?"

He stood up, shoving the chair back. "Come on, Josie. Did you ever think for one fucking minute that Billy wouldn't want to know you were about to hang? Even though he was fighting to try and clear his name? Sure, Francisco and I could've done it but I sort of thought Billy just might give a damn, so I went to find him. Thanks for nothing."

He stomped off down the brick pathway.

Billy stared at me for a minute, shook his head and followed him. This day wasn't going well at all. Sometimes I'm not nearly as smart as I think I am. I followed them down the same path. I had some apologies to make and I hoped it wasn't too late.

I found them sitting on a corral fence not far from the house, smoking Billy's hand-rolled cigarettes.

"Hi."

They ignored me. They weren't going to make this easy and I couldn't blame them.

"I'm sorry. I know that's not enough. It's always been hard for me to think anybody gives a damn about me even when they do. When Isabella died, it was like a part of me died too. I didn't care anymore. I didn't care what they did to me. I didn't even care enough to try and get out of there on my own. I didn't know where Colin and Francisco were, or even if they were still alive until I saw Francisco in the alley. I never thought I'd see Billy again he was so far away."

I climbed up onto the corral fence between the two of them and shoved on each of them so they'd give me room. They both stared off at the horses, smoke curling around their heads.

"I love you so much." I put an arm around each of them. "Can you forgive me?"

Silence. *God, I was so stupid sometimes*, I thought. I was close to giving in to tears which I hated more than anything.

Colin leaned forward. "Billy, should we give her another chance?"

"Aw hell, I guess she's worth it," Billy said, tamping out his cigarette on the railing. They both grinned and I let out a breath I didn't know I'd been holding.

They jumped down and pulled me off the fence, putting their arms around me. The three of us were still standing clasped together when Evangelina pulled the buggy up beside us, two magnificent black horses stamping their feet. A wagon was close behind her, driven by two men in white.

"Ah, there you are," she smiled. "Get in, we are already running late."

⚜

BEFORE ME WAS THE MOST BEAUTIFUL PLACE I'D EVER SEEN. We came over the last hill and down a gentle slope to a grassy plain that surrounded a turquoise blue lake, fed by a waterfall that cascaded over white rocks. Poppies, lupine and other wildflowers created a rainbow of color everywhere. Cottonwoods and other trees provided shade where the two men in the wagon behind us quickly spread blankets, unpacking baskets of food.

"*Hermosa no es?*" Evangelina said, touching my arm as we walked towards the lake.

I needed no translator. It was very beautiful. "*Si*, I said, leaning into her. "*Verdad.*"

She laughed. "*Muy buena*, Josie."

Francisco and his uncles were there before us, along with a host of vaqueros, their horses grazing contentedly nearby.

"*Hola*," Raul waved. "Come. Sit."

What followed was the most wonderful afternoon I'd ever

had in my life. True, there wasn't much competition, but the incomparable surroundings, the delectable food, the warmth and friendliness on display here were all relatively unknown to me and I soaked it up, basking in the sunshine and the hospitality of the Montoyas. I envied Francisco.

We learned his father, Hector, had died in a fall from a horse when Francisco was a child and he'd been raised by his uncles, one of whom was dear Mateo, who had gone north to partner with Hiram, and Francisco had left the ranch against Raul's wishes, wanting some independence and to see the country beyond the border, where two of his uncles had gone. Now I fully understood why Francisco had come with us on our vengeance ride.

"Mateo was beside me when he died," I said. "Tucking tortillas into my saddlebag, because as hard as he tried to teach me, I was hopeless at making them. He was so patient, so kind, like an uncle I've never had. I killed the two men closest to us, but I couldn't be sure either of them were the ones." Tears prickled just like they had for two days now and I blinked frantically, staring down at the empty plate on my lap. This maudlin whimpering wasn't who I was.

"Josie, *querida*." Raul stood over me and held out his hand, pulling me awkwardly up from the grass.

"You have another uncle now," he said, "if you will have me." He put his arm around me. "And these *malos hombres* here, as well." He gestured at Vitorio and Paulo, who nodded. We would be proud."

Francisco smiled as well. That was all I needed. I threw my arms around Raul.

"Oh yes," I whispered. "*Gracias*, sir. I have no other words."

"So." Raul patted my back and sat back down.

"I promise to work on those tortillas," I said. Everyone laughed. It wasn't that funny but we all needed relief from the past. I sank back down on the blanket.

"You'll have to work on a lot more than tortillas," Colin whispered, cutting his eyes towards me. "Like not killing peop –"

I jabbed my elbow in his stomach, pleasantly surprised at his pained exhale. "Shut up, Colin. Maybe after I master tortillas, all my frustrations will be gone. Ever thought of that?"

Only Billy tried to hide his smile. "Ain't no tortillas gonna redeem your ass, Donnelly. You could use another profession yourself. Better have another taco."

The perfect afternoon ended when everyone climbed on their horses and went back to business. We rode back in the buggy with Evangelina and at the main house, everyone dispersed to their various rooms for the traditional afternoon siesta, a custom I could get used to, especially after a meal like the one we'd enjoyed.

I had just sat down on my bed when Billy poked his head in the door. "Want some company, *senorita*?"

I patted the comforter. "Get your skinny butt over here."

He stretched out on the bed, his arms behind his head. "The Montoyas have sure figured out the good life, haven't they?"

"It didn't happen overnight, Billy. They've been at this for a long time and looks to me like they've worked hard for it."

"Whoa, don't think I don't see that. They're fine people all right. I guess I've never seen any place quite like this before. There's cattle ranches and I've seen quite a few, but this place is something special, you know, Josie?"

"I do." I ran my fingers under his shirt, tickling his tummy. "We don't belong here, though."

He smiled lazily. "I think you could fit right in. Unless I miss my guess, Uncle Raul pretty much gave you approval this afternoon. You might even learn to embroider along with that tortilla-makin'."

"What about you?" I smoothed his hair from his face. His forehead was pale where the sun hadn't touched it under his hair and hat. "Think you'd like to live in Mexico? That would solve your problems just as well as mine, after all."

He put his hand over mine. "Yes, but listen to me now. There's a lot you don't know about me, Josie, but there's one thing I need to tell you. I did things to help my friends, just like you have and things haven't turned out well. There's another reason I went to New Mexico when I did. I had a friend who was like a brother to me who got killed just for trying to help me. His son is six, and he's been staying with some people first in Lordsburg, and now up near Fort Sumner with my friend Pete Maxwell. I'm all he's got, and maybe I ain't much, but I made a promise and I keep my promises, you of all people know that. We been saving orphans, and now we've got one more."

I knew something had been bothering him. "What's his name?"

"Charlie."

"Where's his mama?"

"Dead. She got pneumonia when he was two." He sat up. "He's a good kid, Josie. You'll see. And here's another promise: I'll be back in no time and we'll start over. This life we been leadin' can't go on much longer without at least one of us endin' up dead. Time to start over."

Well. He had a point there. "I'm done with killing, Billy. I did what I set out to do and I'd never planned to do any of it. I'm like you, I have an anger inside me to make those who hurt others pay for what they've done. We did that. For me, the slate is clean, debts paid and no matter what anybody says, I don't think I need any damn redemption, not for them. What I need is to have a normal life, maybe a small ranch, a family, or even teach school. I'd be good at it too."

"You would." He nodded. "I'm right there with you, Josie, except for that school part. I'm better with horses. You practice up on your Spanish. By the time I get back you may even be making tortillas."

There was no talking sense into him, even though I knew in my heart this was a dangerous decision but he was stubborn as a mule and I couldn't fault his promise to take care of this child. I took his face in my hands. "Billy, I love you. You're going to do what you have to do, just like you came to Tombstone for me. You better be damn sure you get yourself and Charlie back here in one piece so we can get on with our lives. You got a restlessness in you but you're going to have to think about Charlie and me. We need you with us and we got a lot of life ahead of us."

He smiled that crooked Billy smile and put his arms around me. "Don't worry about me, Josie Fallon, I'm right where I want to be. We'll all be seeing that ocean in no time. Whales, too."

I snuggled into him and wished this afternoon could go on forever, but I knew we'd have many more afternoons to spend just like this after he got back. We fell asleep in each other's arms, dreaming of our future.

CHAPTER 31

"You sure about this, Cullen? I can't see no rhyme or reason why they'd go thisaway." Harley wiped his forehead with the back of his hand.

Dell Cullen spat some tobacco juice into the nearest cactus. "Goddamn, Harley, I told you, there was a Mex ridin' with 'em the day we caught her up by the orphanage. He got away, with the big blonde one, but I just got a hunch, is all. Ain't like they showed up anywhere else. Had to be them that broke her out. The little bitch is smart, too smart to stay around Tombstone for sure."

"Maybe," Harley Gorman said. Cullen thought he was smart too, but Harley was beginning to think this whole thing had been a mistake. True, there was a $1,000 reward for Josie Fallon now, dead or alive, after she'd escaped from jail. That was pretty good incentive, but Harley figured after they found her, Cullen was thinking to kill him before they got back to Cochise County. He didn't look like a sharing kind of man. Harley knew there was only going to be one thing to do but he was a patient man and knew he was a better gun hand than Dell Cullen. People thought he was slow in a lot of ways but they'd always found they were wrong, although there weren't many of them alive to tell anyone. Harley'd been in the bounty business a long time, which was why Cullen had propositioned him in the first place. He'd been planning on a rest but this sounded like an easy deal even if he had to ride with Cullen.

Even so, he wasn't at all sure that going to Mexico was the right choice, and he'd never been comfortable down there. So far, even though he was a decent tracker, there hadn't been the least sign of Josie Fallon or anybody else going this way. True, it'd been a while, but there was nothing but desert, wind, mesquite, cactus and sun. A lot of sun.

It was late afternoon by the time they rode into the village. It was small, boasting only the usual church with a bell tower, with space for market stalls, now mostly empty at the end of the day, along with a stable and the usual cantina. Only a few people were on the dusty street, farmers loading wagons and a few women herding children, hustling them along as they saw the Anglo riders coming in.

They tied their horses up outside the cantina and went inside, the dim interior and cooler temperature a welcome respite from the bright sun. Cullen went to the bar, fashioned from adobe but nicely done, Harley thought. The room was empty except for a few tables and chairs. Cullen strode up and pounded on the bar.

"*Rapido, rapido.*"

A short moustached man in the usual white pants and shirt came through the doorway into the backroom, waving his hands.

"*Si, si senor.*" He smiled somewhat nervously. "What can I do?"

"Tequila," Cullen said. "Two." He glanced at Harley, who nodded. "And two more."

The man poured the tequila into two glasses. "Would you like any food or?" His English was quite good.

"Hell, yes, *amigo,*" Cullen said, slapping money down onto the bar. "Whatever you got cooking back there that smells so good, for starters."

They sat at one of the tables, the bottle of tequila now between them, as well as two full plates of beans and tortillas with what Harley figured was beef, but he didn't really care. By the time they finished the food and the tequila bottle was half full, Cullen went back to the bar.

"So, *amigo*. You got anyplace a man could spend the night with some companionship?"

Harley had no objection to the tequila, food or companionship, only to Cullen's way of asking for it. He'd never liked the way of men like Cullen. Harley had done his share and more of things he wasn't proud of, although he didn't have any problem sleeping at night. It was just that there was no point in being an asshole, which Cullen surely was. The man was an embarrassment to ride with, Harley thought. Loudmouths had never been Harley's first choice for a partner but he was in it now, with this Fallon thing. Not that he hadn't wanted to go after her anyway, but when Cullen had propositioned him in the saloon the night before, the whiskey had kept him from making a better decision. He'd have to see it through.

The bartender delivered. As the night descended and candles lit the little cantina, two girls showed up, smiling and sashaying around them, and taking a new tequila bottle with them, they'd been led to a small house behind the cantina. The place had two beds and they were tired and drunk enough now they fell into them with their eager-seeming ladies, but not before taking off their gunbelts and putting the guns themselves under the pillow. It was a pretty good end to the day, Harley thought, before he passed out.

The sun struck his eyes like a knife. Harley blinked and sat up, coughing, dislodging the naked girl asleep under his arm. She grunted and rolled over, curling up on the side of the bed. He looked over at Cullen, still asleep beside the other girl. Their guns and saddlebags were right where they'd left them. Those were some sweet honest girls, Harley thought. That wasn't always true, as he'd learned to his regret.

He thought back over the night before and smiled. He didn't think the girls had been in this life for long. A year or two from now would tell a different story, but that wasn't his concern. People did what they had to do and he was no judge. That wasn't to say the place didn't stink of unwashed sheets and sex but he'd been too drunk to notice last night.

He dressed and woke Cullen, who thrashed around and peered at him owlishly. "What the hell?"

"Get up," Harley said. "I didn't come down here to drink tequila and fuck whores. I could do that anywhere. We got things to do, you want to make some money." He left some extra money on the pillow beside the sleeping girl.

They went back to the cantina, where they got some coffee and damn good sweet rolls, still warm from the oven. The proprietor was standing behind the bar, watching them. Harley went up to the bar.

"So, I was wondering. You seen anybody lately, like a girl with yellow hair with a couple of men, riding through here?"

The man looked at him blankly. Harley put some money on the bar and slid it towards him. "Maybe?"

The man smiled. "There was a girl, *rubio*, with three men. Not long ago." He shrugged.

Harley poured himself another cup of coffee from the pot on the bar. "Three? Was one of them Mexican?"

The man waited. Harley put some more money down which disappeared as quickly as the last had. He smiled.

"*Si*, I think perhaps a Montoya. I overheard them talking. They didn't stay long."

"What's a Montoya?"

The bartender smiled. "A ranch, southwest of here. Old family."

"How far?" Harley said. "Big place?"

"Oh yes, big enough. Some miles away, though."

Cullen joined him. "What's big?"

Harley sighed. "The ranch our friends might be headed to. Let's go."

The Mexican smiled to himself, looking down at the bar. Harley had a bad feeling, but he'd had a bad feeling since they'd ridden out of Tombstone. Best to see it through.

They'd only ridden an hour or so before Cullen had to stop. Apparently the tequila or something hadn't agreed with him. Harley waited, not bothering to get off his horse.

He came back, buttoning up his pants. "Christ, this Mex food is going to kill me. These people don't know how to cook."

Harley rolled his eyes. There was no point in answering. So far, hadn't been any kind of food agreed with Cullen. Harley thought the man likely needed to see a doctor. They moved off down the dusty road once again. Cullen glanced over at him.

"You're pretty quiet."

Harley shrugged. "Nothing much to say."

"Well, I got something to say," Cullen said. "You don't seem too invested in this, but I can tell you something, friend. We're going to find Josie Fallon and I hope I get to be the one to shoot her. She killed my friends back in Arizona and I owe her for that. The rest of her pals can lay over a saddle with her, far as I'm concerned."

"You are surmising she killed your friends," Harley said. "You don't know that for sure, nobody does. I'd just as soon bring her back to get hung. I'm a bounty hunter, not an executioner, not if I can help it."

"What the fuck is surmising?" Cullen snarled. "Sometimes you talk funny, Harley and I have to tell you it's gettin' on my nerves."

"Deal with it," Harley said and snapped the end of the reins on his horse's rump. Cullen was as ignorant as he was mean. He hoped this ranch wasn't far. Harley was getting very tired of Dell Cullen and this whole hastily planned idea.

Late afternoon sun slanted off the sand-colored adobe arch

that held the letters "Rancho del Valle Dorado". The same low adobe walls stretched into the distance on each side of the arch as far as the eye could see over the rolling hills. Cullen whistled.

"This is a very big ranch, Harley," he said. "I'll bet this is it."

Harley agreed. "Biggest place I've ever seen. Still, we need to know more before we ride in there." He glanced over at Cullen. "Josie Fallon could see us coming for a long time and put a bullet in us both before we even got to the house."

He didn't think that was necessarily true, but it was approaching dusk and he was reluctant to ride blindly down the entrance road under that arch before he knew more. They sat on their horses for a few minutes and when the saw the four riders coming towards them, he knew it was a few minutes too long.

The riders pulled up in front of them in a cloud of dust, their horses chuffing. They were all vaqueros, all armed and grinning, which was a bit disconcerting.

"*Hola, senores*," the man in front said, eyeing them disdainfully from head to toe. "Do you have business with this place?"

Cullen opened his mouth and Harley clapped him on the shoulder, which startled him enough to give Harley a chance to speak first.

"*Si, senor*," he said. "*Perdoname*, my Spanish is not so good. We are looking for work. We are experienced cowhands and have heard this is the place to go."

"Hmm." The leader said. He looked at his friends and turned back to Harley. "Maybe? My English is not so good either. However, not tonight. Come back in the morning and ask for Senor Paulo."

Harley nodded. "*Si, gracias. Senor* Paulo Montoya?"

The man laughed. "*Definitivamente, senor*. Did you not know where you were?"

They rode away, laughing at the stupidity of the gringos. Harley didn't mind and Cullen, for all his posturing, turned his horse around and set off down the road to find the nearest camp-site. So this was the Montoya ranch. They'd be back in the morning, perhaps not too early, get into Valle Dorado and hopefully see if Josie Fallon was even there. Harley had a hunch she was. All that would have to wait. He didn't look forward to another night with Cullen but at least there was bacon, eggs and whiskey to dull the pain.

They'd find her. Harley had never had the slightest doubt.

CHAPTER 32

Billy had been gone for two weeks now and every morning I woke up trying not to worry. I missed him even more than I had the last time but at least I was making progress on positive pursuits for a change, rather than shooting people. That life was behind me. Joanie Higgins would have been proud, a thought I didn't want to entertain for long.

Every morning, I showed up in the kitchens, put on an apron and set to work. This was a very big operation, many burners, many cooks and many pots, some of them big enough to bathe a colt in, it seemed to me. There were a lot of people to feed at this place and everyone ate well. The family's meals were a bit fancier with more trimmings, as I'd come to learn, but the quality never varied in the least. At first the cooks were dubious and sometimes downright unhelpful, even after Evangelina has assured them of my desire to learn, and it didn't make it easier that in order to help me with my Spanish, no English was to be spoken. I could blame no one else for that one, as it was my idea. The best way to learn, I'd discovered the hard way, was when you had no choice.

The first week, I did nothing but haul buckets of flour, masa, beans, rice, bushels of avocados, tomatoes and limes, store and measure and follow shouted instructions, punctuated with plenty of exasperated sighs and Spanish words. I didn't have any problem understanding *estupido* or *imbecil*, because to them, at this point, I surely fit them both. I wasn't angry, only more determined.

Every morning when I stepped foot in that kitchen and tied on an apron, it was like a new world full of colorful vegetables, silky flour, sharp spices and sizzling meats. I loved it. By the second week, I was elevated to chopping vegetables, tomatoes and limes. Consuela, the head cook, looked at my knife skills and shook her head, snatching the knife from my hand.

"Por aqui," she said, swiftly cutting a tomato into tiny cubes, then looking at me. I nodded but she took my hand anyway, fitting it onto the knife handle properly and then demonstrating, her hand on mine, the right way to cut. It truly was a revelation. My only knife skills until then had been used on people. Vegetables were a better choice and took much more precision. I even learned about peppers and how to put your hands in milk to take out the sting and to never, ever touch your eyes or face before scrubbing well. By the end of that afternoon, I had red eyes and sore hands but I was elated. I loved the food here, maybe because it woke me up to how wonderful food could taste, rather than the bland stuff I'd had to eat for so long.

On the way back to my room, I ran into Colin on the pathway. He'd been working with the horses, out every day with Francisco, his face darkened from the sun, his hair, now even lighter and reaching to his collar. His green eyes blazed in the late afternoon shadows.

"How's the kitchen, Josie?"

"Wonderful," I said. "I'm learning so much. I chopped so many vegetables today and I know how to do it right, Colin. Can you believe that?"

He laughed and twirled me around. "You're going to be a great cook, Josie. I'm happy that girl I used to weed the vegetable gardens with is now destined to be a chef."

I laughed too and he set me down. "Not hardly. What have you been doing?"

"Just like you," he said. "Learning. Everything I ever wanted to know and master about horses, from birth to training to even how to bury the poor things when they die."

His face took on a more somber cast. "It's given me a new perspective, I guess you could say." He gazed intently at me. "It's not just about horses or cooking, is it, Josie? It's about making a life when you've never really had one. Doing the everyday things people do when they aren't slaves. Doing the things that can lead you to an everyday future where you can forget you had to kill to find it. Or try to."

I didn't want to hear anymore about the past. I grabbed him around the waist and buried my face in his shirt, holding him tightly. He smelled of horses and sweat, not unpleasantly so. My head was still far beneath his, but somehow he managed to put his chin atop my skull and hold me. I didn't cry. Somehow it was a comfort for both of us.

We stood that way for a long time, or so it seemed to me. Maybe only a few minutes, but to me it felt like many more, so comfortable it was to simply hold Colin in a way I'd never experienced except that day in the barn at Angel's Refuge when I'd warned him about our fates and chances. Such an innocent time and how far we'd traveled down the road of no redemption based upon evil people's designs and our own need for vengeance. I finally pulled away, stepping back awkwardly. I didn't want Colin to get the wrong idea, whatever that was.

"I'll see you at dinner," I said and slipped into my room.

The days passed. Quite a few evenings brought music and dancing on the many patios around the main house, torches aflame even in the summer heat, which had come on full strong. The women's colorful skirts would flare out as they twirled, looking so pretty with their hair flying and their golden earrings twinkling, and the men's tight pants and short jackets they wore for dancing made every man lithe and handsome. In the evenings after the sun set, a breeze made it not just tolerable, but pleasant to be outside. Inside, the thick adobe walls kept the heat away very well and every morning I woke to the curtains fluttering in the dawn wind, the smell of jasmine and honeysuckle perfuming the room.

I loved it here. I didn't know all that much about the country I'd fled, but I did know the one I'd found here was the one I wanted. I'd only heard about snow, but it didn't sound like something I'd care for and if the rest of that country was as pitiless as Arizona, I didn't want to live anywhere in it. Colin's descriptions of New York and the places he'd passed through on the train reinforced my mindset.

I thought about Billy every night, imagining his journey and traveling with a six-year-old child, a child who had probably learned to keep silent and cater to the adults who cared for him. I imagined what that would be like and thought back to my former life and the other children in the orphanages, especially the little boy who'd held my hand so tightly. I couldn't wait to make his life one filled with love instead of violence, something Billy, Colin, Isabella and I had never had. Six weeks had passed now and as much as I tried to keep occupied, the worry crept in, although there was nothing I could do. I dreamed of whales and sand beaches instead.

I woke up early the next morning before most of the family was awake. I tiptoed into the kitchen and a smiling Consuela handed me a mug of chocolate without a word. I took it outside to watch the sunrise. Once again a man stood outside the boundaries of the patio, staring at me in a way that made me uncomfortable. He didn't look like the vaqueros I was used to seeing and after a few minutes he turned away. This was the second time I'd seen him out there but it was probably just some curious ranch hand. No one could know where I was and I was probably just being overly cautious, one more trait I'd have to leave behind.

I spent the day making a special dinner for the family, under

Consuela's tutelage. We planned an albondigas soup, chicken with mole sauce, a host of tangy salsas, and a salad bursting with avocados, ripe tomatoes, new lettuce, cilantro and peppers, along with of course, my tortillas. I had finally learned the secrets of tortilla making. I kept thinking of Mateo and how proud of me he would be.

When we sat down at the dinner table that evening, Evangelina spoke up as the soup was served. "Josie has made this entire meal herself. I am very proud of her."

I grinned like a Cheshire cat and Colin nudged me with his foot. "Thanks to Consuela. I hope you find it delicious."

They did, too, heaping compliments on me. As I watched them eat the food I'd made, I was delighted, proud and somewhat embarrassed to tell the truth. These people had been so kind and welcoming to us strangers at their gate I was happy to repay them in this little way. By the end of the meal, I ventured another way.

"Your family has been so kind to us, I'd like to not just repay you with the food your hospitality has allowed me to create. We would be happy to contribute for our costs."

Raul put down his wineglass. "Senorita Fallon, you insult my family with your offer, no matter how well intentioned you may be."

"*Lo siento*," I stammered. "Please forgive me, I never thought to do that."

I'd made a mistake. These were not people who needed my money, as though Colin and I were hotel guests. I didn't dare look at Francisco.

Evangelina looked at Raul and then me. "Josephina, you have brightened our days. We have been so happy to have you here with us. Please say no more about this. We are happy to have you as long as you wish to stay."

I couldn't help it. Maybe it was the strain of worrying about Billy, or maybe just the fact that no one had ever been so generous as these people were. Francisco looked at me, his eyes sympathetic. I burst into tears, burying my face in my napkin.

"*Lo siento mucho*," I said, coming up for air. "I've never known people to be so kind, especially with the things I have done. I'm a fool. *Perdoname.*"

"It is done," Raul said, picking up his glass. "We will say no more about it."

The king had spoken. My indiscretion would be considered no more, at least I hoped not. Consuela's assistants brought in my *tres leches* cake with strawberries and festivity returned. Sometimes sugar in your mouth makes for sweetness in the mind too.

We sat outside on the patio, as we did most evenings and everything seemed back to normal. I looked out at the velvety dark night, the stars just coming out, and remembered the man I'd seen.

"You know, twice now I've seen a man outside the patio just before sunrise. He was staring at me," I said. "He was nobody I'd seen before, looked *norte americano* to me. Forgive me, I am always suspicious."

Paulo sat up straighter in his chair. "We hired a few new men on a while ago. We've been short-handed with the roundup. What did he look like?"

"Anglo, had a little beard, wore a brown hat. I wouldn't have noticed him but he kept staring at me and it made me uncomfortable. Then he left."

The Montoyas looked at each other. Oh no, I thought, I've done it again. Another Josie mistake in an otherwise perfect evening. Colin stared at me.

"Why didn't you say anything about this to me, Josie?"

"I didn't have a chance before now and besides, it's likely my overactive imagination."

Paulo disagreed. "I hired on two more *norte americanos* a couple of weeks ago." He shrugged. "They aren't very good, *comprende*? But I thought I would give them a try. They seemed hungry for work." He frowned. "They are always asking questions about us which no one answers, now that I think about it."

"Maybe they are hungry for something else," Raul said, glancing at me. "Get rid of them in the morning, Paulo. Just in case."

The shot shattered the glass in Raul's hand before embedding itself in the chair an inch from my head. I dove for the bricks, as did most of us except for Vitorio, who had just risen from his chair to pour more tequila. The second shot hit him in the shoulder and he collapsed at my feet without a sound.

Horrified, I grabbed a napkin from the table to staunch the blood and pulled him into my lap. Raul knelt beside us, his face pale. "We must get him inside, now."

Raul and Colin carried Vitorio inside to the dining room, the table thankfully devoid of dishes, and laid him upon it. Raul issued terse instructions and Francisco ran out of the room, Colin beside him. I could hear shouting and more gunshots outside as I gripped Vitorio's hand. He opened his eyes, tried to smile and closed them again, groaning.

"We need a doctor," I said helplessly.

"He's on his way," Raul said. Consuela came in with a steaming bowl of water and clean napkins, and just as she put them down on the table, a tall man in a black suit entered, carrying a medical bag, accompanied by a woman with another satchel. They took charge, shifting me and Raul out of the way, and began cutting away at Vitorio's shirt, exposing the wound. They were extremely efficient. I was no longer needed here. My very presence had done damage enough. I ran back to my room. It seems my killing days weren't over after all. That another member of the Montoya family had nearly died beside me was all the reason I needed.

Colt in my hand, I stepped into the patio, empty now. I stepped cautiously into the dark towards the flares of gunshots, my boots crunching on broken glass. The moon was full as I headed into the desert. Before too long I made out Colin's broad back in his white shirt, and headed towards him at a run.

"Who are they?"

He wheeled around at the sound of my voice. "I don't know. Maybe the guys Paulo hired, likely bounty hunters looking for us. Far as we can tell, there's two of them and I'm pretty sure I hit one of them, if we can find the bastard out here. He can't have gotten far."

"Oh, we'll find him." I touched his shoulder. "What about the second one?"

"Paulo and Francisco took off, with some of the vaqueros, riding him down."

"They both on foot?"

"This one is, because he fell off his horse when I shot him."

We walked out into the moonlit desert, the lights of the hacienda behind us. The sharp scents of sage and mesquite drifted on the night wind, and I nearly shot a rabbit that bounded out in front of me.

"Easy, Josie. I don't think this guy will be moving that fast. Just listen."

After another hundred yards or so, we stopped beside a big sahuaro and Colin put his finger to his lips. Silence reigned, as it had forever, in this pristine place. I could hear the soft patterings of the small creatures on the desert floor, the hoot of a nightbird hunting his prey and Colin breathing beside me. Then, a groan. Colin put his hand on my arm.

Another groan, closer now. "Shit, that godamn Harley left me out here to die. Should've known better."

We came upon him twenty feet later, just as he was struggling to his feet. He was hatless, holding his side and I could see the dark patch on his side where the blood had soaked through. He was holding a rifle, pointing at the ground.

"What's your name?" I said and he jerked, pulling up the rifle. Colin knocked it out of his hand and it spun away into the sand.

The man lost his balance and sat down hard on the ground. He stared at us, a sneer on his face.

"Well, well, if it ain't Josie Fallon. I been looking for you."

"Mission accomplished," I said. "Like I said, name?"

"Dell Cullen, the man whose friends you killed," he snarled. "I was looking forward to watching you hang, but at least I got that bitch you rode with."

I remembered the name from that day in the kitchen at Lambs of the Lord, the missing man. Isabella's death was something I'd never forget.

Colin smiled at me, the moonlight shadowing his face. He held out his arm in a welcoming gesture towards the man in front of us. "Ladies' choice."

Pretty clothes, soft music, mole sauce and serenity warred with the rage singing in my blood, but not for long. Cullen began to scrabble backwards, his heels making little puffs of dirt.

"For Isabella." I shot Dell Cullen three times and watched him die, his blood black on the moonlit sand.

"Leave him for the buzzards."

As we stepped through the French doors, we heard more gunshots not far away. Hopefully Paulo had been as successful as we'd been. The dining table was empty, polished and gleaming in the candlelight, and the doctor was gathering up his things, speaking softly to Raul. He nodded at us and left with his silent assistant.

"How is he?"

"In his soft bed with two lovely nurses beside him." Raul rolled his eyes. "Vitorio is quite the *lotario*." Well, that was certainly true, women followed that man around like a flock of lusting chickens. "Couple of weeks in a sling and he'll be good as new, as you say."

He smiled wearily and to my relief, put his arm around me. "Tequila? Inside, I think."

Evangelina joined us after a few minutes eyeing the gunbelt

at my hips. Paulo and Francisco had still not returned. For a few minutes, no one spoke, processing the evening's events.

"*Lo siento mucho*. I have brought this trouble to you. We killed one of them."

Raul raised an eyebrow. "*Excellente.*" He refilled our glasses. "Soon we shall hear the fate of the other. This is far from the first time we have defended ourselves and those we care for from evil. We would do no less for you, Josie Fallon. One can never be certain what life will bring from one day to the next."

Evangelina pulled me to her. "You have become dear to me, Josie. Do not blame yourself for the actions of others, and never for what you do to protect yourself. *Esta bien*. Nor you, my Colin. You are both *familia* now, and we Montoyas take care of our own."

We heard horses outside and Francisco and Paulo came in, flushed and dusty. Raul poured two more tequilas. It was as though he'd never had the slightest doubt to the outcome of this night and I was just beginning to realize the power this family had.

"How is my brother?" Paulo demanded. "The ladies would be keening for months if anything happened to him."

"He will be fine," Evangelina said. "Senor Fernandez was here and Vitorio has good nurses."

"What about you? Good hunting?" Raul gestured at me and Colin. "They were successful."

"*Si*. We'll bury him in the morning if the coyotes don't get to him first," Paulo said. "He said his name was Harley, a bounty hunter out of Arizona. My *sobrino* Francisco sent him to his Jesus. The young one here is a very good shot." He drained his glass and poured another. "These vermin should not venture into a civilized country. I will be more careful with my hiring."

"Ours was the man who killed Isabella," Colin said. "Jesus will not be looking for him and besides, he would not recognize him without a face."

Francisco raised his glass. "*Gracias*, my friends. I wish I'd had that one. But it is over now."

I had little to say. Let them think Colin had killed Cullen. Francisco likely knew better, but there was no point in telling the Montoyas. A bottle or two of tequila later, we wandered to our respective beds. For an evening that began so well, then tumbled into disaster, it ended well enough. Except for Vitorio. And me.

I had brought peril to this family I had come to love, a family that had taken me in with no questions and cared for me. I would not allow this to happen again, and it could. Who knew how many bounty hunters might be looking for Josie Fallon as long as that reward was posted? Cullen and this Harley had figured out where we went and they were clearly not that smart, since their bones would rot in this desert. Billy had told me of Pat Garrett, the man who was determined to find him no matter what. For all I knew, someone like that could make the journey south to find me.

More than that, I was disturbed at how easy it had been for me to kill again. There was no question he deserved it, as Billy always said, but there was also no question how much I'd liked pulling that trigger either. I thought that life was behind me and I was determined to keep it that way.

I dreamed of Joanie Higgins that night. "Josephina Fallon could be dragged to hell for her wayward ways," she always said. I sat up in bed, shaking the dream out of my mind. I didn't believe in hell, but if there was one, it was sure Joanie was roasting in its flames. I drank a glass of water, breathed deeply of the night air and fell back onto my pillows. Too much tequila and too much blood. I dreamed again and this time it was of Isabella and me running through a field of flowers, free and happy. Somewhere I lost hold of her hand, but I kept running, the flowers as high as my knees, the perfume of freedom and love still in the air.

CHAPTER 33

Tequila aside, I got up early and went to the kitchens. With Consuela's help, I made breakfast for Vitorio and took it to his room. A pretty girl opened the door and motioned me inside with the tray I carried, along with a vase of roses, putting it down on the table beside the fireplace. Vitorio was propped up on half a dozen pillows, his arm resting on a few more. I tiptoed towards the bed, placing a cup of fragrant chocolate on the nightstand, with a barely perceptible sound. His eyes flew open anyway and after a second, he smiled.

"Josie." He sniffed. "*Gracias, mija.*"

"*De nada*, Vitorio," I said. "*Como estas?*"

"*No es nada,*" he said, as the girl lifted the cup to his lips. "I have had much worse."

"Not to me, Vitorio," I said. I kissed him on the cheek and left them to enjoy breakfast together. A girl as pretty as that one would do much more for him than I could. Outside the door I took a deep breath, hoping my stomach would settle. Seeing the damage to someone innocent I cared about made me only more certain that I needed to make an important decision.

The rest of the day went pretty much as usual. If there was a burial detail for bounty killers, I didn't hear of it and I didn't ask.

It seemed a waste of time to do those men that favor when there were plenty of coyotes and buzzards that could do the work.

When I saw Colin later that afternoon, I stopped him and led him into my room.

"I need to talk to you," I said. "Have a seat."

He took off his hat and sat back in the chair, eyebrows raised. I plopped down in the one beside him.

"I can't speak for you," I said, "but I need to leave here. What happened last night is likely to happen again. Maybe not soon, but it will, and we both know it. Just because those two are done, doesn't mean there won't be more. I can't put this family at risk."

"Josie, listen a minute," Colin said. "You might be right, but I have to say, this family is the least likely group to be at risk I've ever seen. They are not lambs, but wolves. They have made the choice to take us in, knowing full well who we are."

"I know that, Colin, but Vitorio could have been killed last night, so now we know that can happen, no matter what precautions are taken. There is another issue. We can't just stay here forever. We are not of this family, generous as they have been. We need to make our own way, Colin. At least I do and I don't have the slightest idea how to go about that."

He smiled ruefully. "Neither do I, but I'm learning, right now. So are you, at least you know how to cook."

I threw a pillow at his head and he caught it, laughing.

"Seriously, Josie, we are safe here and so are they. This morning Paulo rounded up the men and there isn't anybody going to set foot on this place he doesn't know everything about them. They've always been on alert. Tranquility isn't something that's easily won and they've had their share of trouble, believe me."

That was true. We'd heard many stories about the ranch since we'd been here and the Montoyas were no strangers to violence and defending what was theirs.

"Yes," I said, "but the fact remains we are not Montoyas.

Unless you plan to wait until Raul and Evangelina's daughters are old enough to wed, you never will be."

Colin chuckled. "You've discovered my secret plot, you clever girl. And you should forget Billy and just marry Francisco, then we'd be fine."

"Well. Looks to me our futures are settled then." I looked up at him under my lashes and we both burst into laughter. It felt good and it had been too long since we'd done this. We caught our breath and sat back.

He sighed. "You're right, Josie. We have to decide what to do with our lives. The Montoyas have been wonderful, but this can't last forever. I've never had much of a choice before, nor have you. When Billy gets back with the kid, do you have any plans?"

"Not really," I admitted. "We haven't had time to make any, except for running from the law. Then he told me about the boy." I smiled. "Good thing I like telling stories to children, since I'm going to have one, ready-made."

"You'll be fine," Colin said. "You're like Scheherazade or whatever her name was. I remember that day when you told stories for hours to those kids. We were all in a trance. You ever thought about teaching school?"

Actually, I had. I loved learning, and that was the one thing I'd been able to do at Angel's Refuge that kept me sane. As much as the rest of the place was hateful, Joanie made sure we got a good education, for some bizarre reason. Perhaps she'd been a teacher in her early life, before turning into a monster or she was determined to produce educated whores.

"Maybe," I mused. "What about you? Anything you'd like to do? We've still got bags full of money that have come with a heavy price. Buy a farm, start a general store, breed horses now that you're becoming such an expert? Hop on a boat and go back to New York?"

He was quiet for a moment. "I like horses. I like them a lot, Josie." He stared at me. "Billy does, too. He and I been thinking lately we could do that, sort of like Hiram does. Raul might sell me some breeding stock, if we had a place. Not here, but still in Mexico, maybe near the coast. When Billy gets back, we'll put it together, the three of us."

He looked at me and smiled. I felt much better. We'd figure it out. We always did.

That afternoon, I was in the kitchen, chopping tomatoes and peppers for salsa when Raul appeared in the doorway.

"Josie." He beckoned to me and he waited patiently while I hastily washed my hands and took off my apron, following him down the hall.

"What is it, Raul?"

"In time," he said, his face solemn. He took my elbow and steered me into the great room, where Evangelina sat on the couch. Francisco and another man, clearly a vaquero but one I didn't recognize, stood near the fireplace. Raul deposited me carefully beside Evangelina, who took my hand.

What the hell had happened, I thought. *More bounty hunters that killed someone dear to us? Colin trampled by a horse?*

There was a silver tray on the table, with whiskey and tequila, the crystal glasses empty. Raul glanced at the man beside Francisco and then at me. I had the urge to bolt from the room at that moment, but Evangelina gripped my hand tightly, as though she could read my mind.

Raul cleared his throat. "There is no easy way to say this, Josie. Billy will not be coming back to us. He was killed by Pat Garrett two weeks ago in New Mexico. I am so sorry, *mi querido*."

I stared at him. "What?" The words he spoke made no sense to me.

"Josie," Raul said, "I sent Julio to New Mexico to find him because he was gone too long and I worried." He looked at the man beside Francisco. "There is no question."

Evangelina turned to me. "Josie. I know how much you loved him. He was a charming young man." She dropped my hand and pulled me into her arms. I felt as though I had turned to stone.

This could not be. Not my laughing boy who taught me so much, even how to love.

"No, no, no, no." I pulled away from Evangelina. "There must be a mistake. He's tricky, that one. Of course he got away. It was someone else, not Billy."

They all just stared at me.

"No, there is no mistake," said Julio, his eyes sad. "I saw his grave. *Lo siento, senorita.*"

I don't remember much after that, just running to my room. I lay down on the bed and stared at the ceiling. No one knocked and no one came which was exactly what I needed and they seemed to know it.

It was dark when my door opened and Colin sat down on the bed beside me. He smoothed my hair away from my face.

"Billy's dead, Colin."

"I know."

"He wanted it to be different. One of the last things he said to me was we couldn't go on the way we'd been or at least one of us was going to end up dead. He sure was right about that." My voice broke on the last word and I couldn't talk over the lump in my throat. Colin lay down beside me and gathered me into his arms. I cried for a long time, until I couldn't cry anymore.

I wandered around the house and grounds like a ghost for the next four days, scarcely talking to anyone and they kindly left me to myself. That's how I measured time now, as in days since I knew Billy was dead. On the fifth morning, just after sunrise I went to the stables, saddled a sweet-looking mare and rode out. The boy in the stables looked worried for a minute, until I pointed to my gunbelt.

It was still relatively cool with a breeze that carried the tang of mesquite, fresh and clean against my skin as I rode through the desert, the only sound the morning birds and the call of a hawk high above. I wasn't sure exactly where I was going, but after a while I passed through the arroyos and came to the lake and the waterfall where we'd all picnicked that day that now seemed so long ago. I let the mare graze for a bit and sat on the bank. It was just as beautiful here as it had been before.

In my heart, I knew when Billy left that he wasn't coming back. I didn't want him to go but I couldn't stop him. I also knew he was far from perfect and given to violent impulses and poor judgement, much like me. We'd been attracted to each other like iron to a magnet because we were so much alike. Hiram had been right, but no matter how much it hurt, I didn't regret one single minute of my time with Billy and I never would. I'd carry the memory of that quirky smile and those blue eyes and every second we spent together with me forever.

I wasn't a mourner. I was a rememberer. I thought back to all those that had helped me for the last year, Hiram, Sally, Mateo, Amy, Isabella, all the cowboys on the ranch, and Billy, who had taught me how to believe in myself. I think he'd want me to live my life to the fullest in a way that I think he knew he never would. I wasn't going to waste another day of it and I knew he wouldn't want me to do so.

Colin was sitting on the corral fence when I rode back in. When I came out of the barn, he was still there.

"Waiting for me?"

"Yep." He shoved his hat brim up a little and peered at me. "You look better."

"I am."

He swung down and we walked towards the house. "Good, because it's my turn to say we need to talk. Let's go inside where it's a little cooler. When Francisco gets back, we'll talk about it."

I hated when I had to wait to find things out, and Colin knew that but he wouldn't budge. Well, at least it gave me something else to think about. Besides, I was hungry for the first time in days and we headed into the kitchen to see what we could find. Consuela gave me a big grin and fixed both of us a plate of roast chicken and rice. We sat down at the kitchen table and the food was gone in no time. Fresh air and food helped but I knew an empty ache would be with me a long time.

Francisco stuck his head in the door.

"Ah, there you are," he said. "Raul is waiting for us in the study."

Why would Raul be waiting for us in the study? I glanced over at Colin but his face was decidedly blank.

Raul smiled as we entered and gestured us towards chairs. Paulo was there as well. *What in the world had Colin been up to?* I thought. It didn't take long to find out.

"Josie," Raul said. "Colin and Billy had come to me weeks ago about their wish to have a horse breeding facility. Now, it is different, of course but Colin still thinks it can be done. We had discussed some land, near the coast of the Sea of Cortez, not so very far."

I stared at Colin. "We talked about this a little, but nothing definite. Besides, Billy...won't be here. We can't run a ranch by ourselves, Colin."

"You won't be," Francisco said. "I will be there, and as we grow, some of the vaqueros from Valle Dorado. Still, this will be our operation, helped just a little by the family."

We'd talked about leaving but I guess it was the suddenness of it all that surprised me.

"Well." I took a deep breath. "Have you a piece of land in mind? And," I gazed at Raul, the Montoya himself who held all the cards, "what exactly does "helped by the family" mean?"

"*Madre de dios*, Raul," Paulo laughed. "This one gets down to business, *si?*"

"I would expect nothing less," Raul said. "I hear *Senorita* Fallon has run things for some time, and my nephew respects her greatly."

I felt alive today and my usual pragmatism was beginning to surface through the murk of grief. Francisco and Colin exchanged amused glances and I snorted. "Well, if you're leaving this decision up to me, gentlemen, I need a lot more information. Also, there better be whales in the Sea of Cortez or the deal's off."

"Hell, Josie, I already checked on that," said Colin. "First requirement."

In the next few days, we got down to business, as Paulo said. The Montoyas already owned some land near the coast, and there was another piece that met the sea right next to it. There was nothing but small fishing villages on that stretch, and the nearest town of any size was Hermosillo, not that far to go for supplies.

It was decided that Colin, Francisco and I would buy the land near the sea and adjoin it to the Montoya land. The three of us would buy horses and breeding stock from Raul. If the ranch was successful, we had the option to buy their land at any time for expansion. Paulo did not think it would take more than five years for that to happen. As for houses, stables, fencing and outbuildings, they would supply workers to accomplish all that right away, for a cost, of course.

"Do we have enough money to do all that?" I said to Colin and Francisco. I'd never paid much attention to the money we'd stolen, whether from Stella's or the orphanages. I only remembered Isabella stuffing cash into carpetbags.

"There is more than enough, Josie," Colin smiled and then then his smile faded as he gazed at me. "It came with a cost, though, didn't it?"

I sat back. "A big one. Maybe the best thing we can do to honor that is to use the money well."

"As we will." Francisco took my hand. "I think we should name our ranch *Verdadero Casa de Isabella y Porra.*"

My Spanish was still elementary. "*Por favor*, Francisco?"

He smiled at me, gripping my hand. "The true home of Isabella and Billy."

Colin took hold of my other hand. "And be damned to anyone that ever comes to us unbidden who knows how much those names mean. Those two will be with us forever no matter where they lie."

It took weeks to organize it all, but we were all pretty good at that and it gave me especially a lot to do besides making salsa. I fell into bed at night exhausted with making plans, organizing supplies and talking endlessly with Raul, Paulo, Francisco and Colin.

Things stayed quiet, and no more bounty hunters surfaced, luckily for them as the whole ranch was on high alert, and from the nightly table talk, most of Sonora.

One morning, at last we were ready to go. We had a small wagon train, full of supplies, building materials and people, along with a small herd of horses. I was not good at goodbyes but once Evangelina put her arms around me, I wept as though I was leaving my own mother, and truly she felt like one to me. I think she shared the same feeling, and when Raul put his arms around both of us, I knew I had found a true family at last, as had Colin. Reckless, impetuous and murderous as we had been, there were people who forgave, understood and cared for us. I knew full well how lucky we were.

"We will see you when the weather cools," Raul said, "once I hear you have a roof over your heads. We do not camp. My bones are no longer those of a younger man and Evangelina likes a featherbed and a room to put it in."

She laughed and nudged him playfully. "*Si, verdad*, Raul is correct." She kissed my cheek. "Take care, Josephina. I will be there when your time comes."

"*Excellente*," Raul said. "*Vaya con dios, mis queridos.*"

And go with god we did, god and the Montoyas. For some time now and I suspect forever, it would be hard to tell the difference.

And along with god, there were guns, of course. I am Josie Fallon, after all.

He came running down the beach, holding the starfish like it was a precious jewel.

"Look, mama!"

I dropped the book I was holding before he jumped into my lap, sandy feet, starfish and all.

"It's beautiful, Billy," I said, pushing his blonde hair off his forehead. "You're so lucky to have found it."

He smiled, his blue eyes bright, snuggling close. "Now I have found two."

"Indeed." I only hoped we could keep this one on the patio before its smell pervaded the house like the last one.

It was nice to hold him for a time. This was a child rarely calm, just like his father. He twitched. He peered up the beach and squirmed out of my arms and started running on those sturdy four-year-old legs, his hair like a haystack flying in the breeze, clutching his treasure to his heart.

"Papa, look!"

Colin strode across the sand, and scooped Billy up. "That's a big one."

He bent down and kissed my cheek. "Hello, my love." He

deposited Billy on the sand, who plopped happily down, talking to his starfish.

I smiled up at him. "Hello you. How's the horse sale going?"

"Perfect. Francisco has become a master at this. I'm much better off just staying in the stables. Paulo was right. We'll be the owners of the entire ranch next month. But right now, there's something you have to see."

I'd never had a doubt. Our deal with the Montoyas had been a godsend but Colin, Francisco and even my limited hard work had assured our success. There had been ups and unwelcome downs, but we managed them, one way or another. We had a good life, a life we'd been determined we would have.

I patted my stomach as the baby moved. It wouldn't be long now. I was hoping for an Irish lass this time. I held out my hand and Colin pulled me up.

"What's that?"

"Quit asking questions, you are the most contrary woman sometimes. Head's always buried in a book or a class lesson."

"You knew that when you married me," I said. "That's why the school has twenty students now and now even you can recite sonnets to me in the evenings."

Colin smiled. "Look," he said, putting his arm around me as we walked closer to the cerulean sea. The dark shiny backs surfaced just above the waves, and a spout of water shot into the blue sky.

The whales had returned. How Billy would love this.

Todo esta bien.

ABOUT THE AUTHOR

Kathleen Morris is an award-winning writer, an aficionado of American and Western history, is a graduate of Prescott College in Arizona and lives and writes in the desert Southwest. She loves being able to immerse herself in the lives of her characters, especially bringing to life the charismatic and capable women of the West, both real and imaginary. Her debut novel, The Lily of the West, the story of "Big Nose Kate" Haroney, was published in 2019 to critical acclaim and was awarded "Best First Western Novel" from Western Fictioneers. Her second novel, The Wind at Her Back was published in November 2020, and The Transformation of Chastity James in 2021. Visit her website www.Kath leenMorrisauthor.com for more and to see what she's currently working on.

www.ingramcontent.com/pod-product-compliance
Lightning Source LLC
Chambersburg PA
CBHW071422200726

48294CB00002B/482